A Flock of Innocents

The Third Book in the Superintendent Lorrie Sullivan Series

by

Angela Hossack

This book is a work of fiction and any resemblance to individuals, either alive or dead, or any resemblance to past or current events are purely coincidental.

Copyright Angela Hossack 2019

The right of Angela Hossack to be identified as author of this work has been asserted in accordance with the Copyright, Designs and Patents Act 1988

ISBN: 9781092279345
Imprint: Independently published

Also by Angela Hossack

Maelstrom of White – the first book in the Superintendent Lorrie Sullivan series

A Murder of Clowns – the second book in the Superintendent Lorrie Sullivan series

Dedicated to the men I love – my dad, my husband and my two sons

PROLOGUE

God was not in church that day – the devil was.

Abandoned, the congregation had reluctantly succumbed to the inevitable. Few of them had even a moment to consider where their saviour was before the pain came and before the life sighed from their bodies and evaporated to nothing.

They had collapsed – one by one, and sometimes two or three at a time – and there was no stopping it and no escape. There was no one to observe their agony and neither God nor his angels intervened to prevent the abomination of their deaths. They were in His house, had been worshipping Him, but He had deserted them to the devil and to their fate.

A baby screamed. Perhaps it was the smell and sense of death that caused his little lungs to screech out such an excruciating sound? Perhaps it was the fact that his mother failed to reach over to comfort him, or that he was cold and hungry?

Whatever the reason, the baby couldn't and wouldn't stop crying.

At twelve weeks old, all he knew was what was familiar to him - the soothing smell of his mother, the reassuring touch of her lips on his cheek, her breast in his mouth. He was not familiar with the agony of total silence nor the absence of warmth. He was not used to his cries being ignored. He was a much-loved child and, despite him barely being born to the world, his little body knew it was in trouble.

Dead bodies could provide him no comfort. The silence could provide him no succour and, if he was destined to perish under the sunlight streaming through the stained-glass windows, then there was nothing his little body could do about it.

Meantime, he would exhaust himself and sleep for a while and, when he woke up starved, he would cry some more and finally shudder to silence.

At last, he would learn that his tears would not bring his mother. He would learn that there was no milk and no semblance of comfort, yet his tiny brain would never comprehend the reasons. How could it when far older and far wiser brains would later fail to understand?

*

The church sat on a slight incline a mile from the centre of the town, and on a road where there was very little passing traffic. Despite it being a quiet Sunday - and despite there being nothing but the sound of birdsong on the still afternoon air – the baby's screams went entirely unnoticed.

His father would eventually miss him and go looking and he would find his dead wife and his hungry son and then it would just be the two of them to live in a world where there was no longer a God. The little boy would grow up never truly knowing his mother and have to be content with photographs and newspaper clippings to assuage the emptiness her absence caused.

At the beginning of the service, God had been present. He was there in the hearts and the minds of the congregation. He was there to receive their prayers and His presence was truly felt by everyone as they raised their voices in jubilant praise.

And, the voices raised in praise were loud because the church was unusually full for a Sunday in the middle of a month with no Saints' days nor Christian holidays to celebrate. Most of the families of the small town had gathered - with children scrubbed and in their best clothes and with parents and grandparents appropriately suited and booted – to take mass and to listen to a sermon on forgiveness and tolerance.

But, the usual sermon was not expected that Sunday.

The congregation had anticipated an exciting change to the message that was to be delivered because the priest was a visiting dignitary of sorts, and his being there was why the pews were filled, for once, to capacity.

Everyone had been keen to see and to listen to the priest who, only months before, had escaped from captivity in Syria. He'd been on the television and in the newspapers and they had all felt honoured that he'd chosen their church to share his lessons with.

The congregation was keen to witness the miracle priest express his forgiveness of his captors. They were curious to learn how he could even begin to preach such forgiveness. They wondered how he could bring himself to turn the other cheek, after everything he had been through. After all, the man had been kidnapped, tortured and starved. He had been humiliated and forced to deny his faith. How was the giving of absolution to such sinners even possible when almost every member of the congregation found it difficult to forgive even the slightest trespass against them?

No one learned the answer. They all died without knowing.

When the poison ravaged their bodies, some faced their God with a spotless soul and some did not, but all of them died without hearing the priest's story or understanding the true grace of forgiveness and – when their souls left their bodies, and they met their God – the act of forgiveness was still very much an enigma.

DAY ONE: EVENING

Lorrie had spent a quiet Sunday in her new apartment in Kensington. She was alone – she was always alone – and the day had passed in a blur of total inactivity. It was a rare day off for her and, instead of using the time to unpack the many boxes still taking up every inch of space in the spare bedroom, she had watched television in her pyjamas and drank copious cups of coffee, whilst wishing she'd made the effort to at least have a shower.

She wasn't depressed. She knew only too well what depression felt like and her miserable mood and lack of motivation was more to do with being utterly fed up, rather than the all-consuming, soul-destroying misery she'd experienced at the death of her son, and the overwhelming hopelessness she'd felt when she'd watched the man - who she had loved with all her heart - being cruelly murdered.

No, she wasn't depressed – not in the clinical sense – but, she *was* totally miserable. Some days – days when she was busy and in the thick of things – her misery dissipated, and she felt almost whole again. Thankfully, she refused to take much time away from work, which meant she was forced to shower and slap on some make-up and ensure that the clothes she wore were adequately ironed and, thus, staved off the innate compulsion to wallow in day-old sweat.

As she stared absently at the television, she wondered what is was that kept countless thousands of people engrossed in Sunday afternoon rubbish that failed to pass as the least bit entertaining? Although she'd channel-hopped all morning, she failed to recognise the irony of her disparagement of her fellow viewers and settled back against the cushions on the sofa and became engrossed in a programme about bed bugs.

For the next hour her mind was free from thoughts of Ollie, and the relief on her tortured heart was palpable.

When she *did* think of Ollie – and she thought of him often – she pictured her son as he would have been had he lived. He would have been approaching his twenty-first birthday and he, most likely, would have had a girlfriend and be quietly settling down into a fantastic post-PhD job. He would have lost all his nerdy, teenaged awkwardness and might even have matured out of his habit of self-inflicted social isolation. He would have got to know his real father and his years of living with a stepfather who was – to put it mildly – a psychopathic monster, would be behind him and a rosy and fruitful future would have been assured.

But, he was dead, and his killer was dead, and Sean was dead and – there but for the grace of God – she would be dead too.

Thinking of Sean was a different matter. She purposefully left all thoughts of him until she was alone in bed at night. She could never allow herself to picture him in her mind - or remember what they were to each other - during daylight hours, because, to do so, would put her on her knees.

Sean Kelly had been the love of her life. His death, at the hands of her deranged husband, affected her differently than the murder of her son. She had not witnessed her son's death, whereas she had been right there – front and centre – when Sean took his last breath. She thought that made a difference to how her brain coped with their murders.

Thoughts of Ollie's death consumed her waking hours and caused a deep-rooted sadness that seemed to be ingrained in her very DNA, but, she had good memories of her son - memories that sustained her and prevented her from dwelling too much on the horror of his passing.

With Sean, she'd had no opportunity to make good memories. She'd had no opportunity to truly put their past behind them and relish the second chance that fate had provided them. He'd been taken just as their love had reawakened - and before they'd had the chance to consummate it - so, she allowed herself only the dark hours to think of him and to picture what might have been.

The television programme she'd surprisingly been engrossed in finally finished, and she forced herself to get up and head for the shower. The day was nearly over, and she wanted to end it with clean hair.

Her mobile sent out its familiar ring-tone just as she began lathering shampoo into her mop of long blonde hair. Ignoring it, she allowed it to go to voicemail. It was Sunday – whoever it was could wait.

The caller decided that waiting was not an option and the mobile rang a second time. Cursing under her breath, Lorrie grabbed a towel and stepped out of the shower without rinsing off. She knew that her hair would be a tangled mess, and she tried not to make that fact irritate her so much that she would snap the head off whoever it was on the phone.

'Superintendent Sullivan,' she said. 'It's Sunday... This better be good.'

*

Police Constable Julie Cox and her colleague, Police Constable Sue Prince, had been despatched to the church following a frantic 999 call from a distraught father. His frantic call for help hadn't made much sense, so the information relayed to the two PC's had been scant and unhelpful.

Cox and Prince were newly paired and were still getting used to one another's foibles, but they got on well enough and had soon dropped into a comfortable working arrangement that suited both of them. They were beginning to anticipate each other's thoughts about particular situations and scenarios that they found themselves in and were relaxed enough to each allow the other the space to do their own thing, and to lead with what they were good at. Unlike most of their male colleagues, there was no sense of competition between them, and neither had any axe to grind when it came to be divvying up the tasks each 'shout' brought. This particular 'shout' was no different.

They found the man sitting on the church steps holding a squalling baby and sobbing his heart out. It didn't take a genius to surmise that he was the 999 caller.

Cox eyed her partner and gave a subtle shake of her head. They wouldn't approach just yet and, instead, took their time looking around, competently registering every detail of their surroundings and assessing for any obvious risk - just as their training dictated - and both noted the dozens of parked cars and the complete absence of any sound except the wailing man and the screaming baby.

By silent, mutual consent, both PC's finally ventured along the uneven path towards the church.

If the man noticed their arrival, and their journey towards him, he made no sign. He simply sat on the step, rocking backwards and forwards, gripping the child to his chest and seemingly completely lost in wrenching grief. There was more than a touch of hysteria in his guttural, pain-racked cries and - intermingled with the baby's incessant screaming – it made for a surreal tableau, and one that put both PCs on high alert.

Cox considered calling immediately for back-up and, if it wasn't for her genuine fear for the baby's safety, she would have been straight on her radio. But, she didn't want to do anything that would spook the man, so she approached slowly and hunkered down in front of him and gestured for Prince to try and take the infant.

'Sir, I'm PC Cox and this is PC Prince. Can you tell us what's wrong?'

Prince reached out and attempted to extricate the baby from the man's arms, but she was met with a fierce resistance.

'Sir?' Cox tried again. 'Can you tell me what's happened?'

Prince made another attempt at the baby, saying, 'Let me look after this little chap.'

Her words, and her attempt to take the child, met with a ferocious roar from the man that transcended even the high-pitched screams of the infant, so she was forced to drop her arms and step back lest her actions caused the baby harm.

PC Cox leaned in further. 'Sir,' she said, 'we're the police. Did you call us? We want to help. Can you tell us what's wrong here?'

He tried. Both Cox and Prince saw that he tried, but he couldn't form any words around the sobs that still tore at his throat and at a loss, Cox plumped herself down on the step next to him and gestured for her colleague to go and investigate the church.

When Prince was gone, Cox decided that calling for help was the only option open to her and used her radio to request an ambulance. She explained the situation and also requested that a senior officer attend the scene. She had no idea what had gone on at the church, but – considering the state the man was in – it wasn't something good.

Although neither the man nor the baby appeared to be injured, she decided to err on the side of caution. She realised that, just because there was no blood, it didn't necessarily mean that there was no injury, and something told her that she and Prince were going to need all the help they could get.

The minutes ticked by and she was glad that both the man and the baby were winding down. The noise had penetrated to her bones and she had to fight the urge to stand up and follow Prince into the church... anything to get away from the damnable racket.

She was uncomfortable on the step and, although the baby's cries - intermingled with the wracking sobs of the man - were reducing in volume, they were slowly doing her head in. She knew that she should say something – find the right words to penetrate the awful din and ease the man to silence – but she had no clue as to the reason for his distress and, therefore, no suitable words to end it.

It was with a profound sense of relief that Cox saw Prince step back out through the heavy wooden doors of the church. She exhaled – suddenly realising that she had been holding her breath – and pulled herself to her feet. Her eyes studied Prince closely and any relief she had felt at seeing her emerge was quickly replaced by alarm.

Prince's face was pale and she visibly trembled. Cox thought that she looked ready to chuck up the contents of her stomach and was troubled to note that she had to grab hold of the church wall to prevent herself from swaying.

Cox was at her side in a matter of seconds.

'What is it? Jesus, Prince... are you going to be sick? What the fuck happened?'

Prince opened her mouth to reply when they were both startled by a sudden scream. It sounded like a woman's scream, so both of them were surprised to learn that the sound came from the man on the steps.

Cox took a step away from Prince and turned fully on her heel – her concern over Prince momentarily forgotten.

'What is it?' she called down to him. 'Is it the baby?' But, the baby was wriggling like a giant worm in his arms and his crying was still rowdy and robust, so it wasn't the baby.

'They're all dead!' the man cried. 'My wife... all of them...They're all dead.'

Cox looked over her shoulder at Prince, and suddenly understood the reason for her partner's uncharacteristic wobbliness.

Prince nodded once and, her stomach giving up the ghost, placed her hands on her knees, leant forward and vomited up her, as yet undigested, Sunday lunch.

Cox thought about it for all of two seconds then made towards the church door. She had to see for herself. It was all very well the man screaming that everyone was dead, and it was all very well for Prince to chuck up all over the ground because of what she'd seen inside, but
none of it would make any sense until she'd seen it first-hand.

She was stopped in her tracks by Prince yanking on her arm.

'I'm going to check,' she protested, pulling herself away.

'No,' Prince returned. 'Leave it and call it in.' She gagged and wiped her mouth on the sleeve of her jacket. 'It's a crime scene. You need to call it in.'

*

Home Office Forensic Pathologist, Ricky Burton, stood at the entrance to the church and surveyed the scene before him. The last of the early evening sunshine still shone through the multi-coloured stained-glass in the windows and caused the bodies to look as if they were bejewelled, but the pretty colours and the sparkling sheen on the congregation's clothes did nothing to detract from the horror of the sight.

In death, the people who made up the congregation were grotesque. Their expressions were varied, but what they all had in common was a look of pained shock.

He thought that he had seen it all, but nothing could have prepared him for the sheer number of bodies ensconced on, and between, the pews.

He noticed that one woman was missing a shoe and he searched for it with fervent eyes. He might not be able to breathe life into the dead woman, but he would be damned if she would go to his morgue without both shoes.

He spied the errant shoe and made a mental note to ensure it was picked up later and reunited with its owner.

As his eyes continued to travel around the church, he noted the vomit-stained clothes and the evidence of desperate attempts that individuals had made to escape the confines of the pews. Bodies were bent and twisted and, at the end of one particular pew, he could see that one man had attempted to climb over the body of a woman before collapsing on top of her. It was all quite surreal, and the sights and the smells literally knocked the breath from him.

He couldn't quite believe it. *In a fucking church, for Christ's sake,* he thought to himself bitterly and, for the first time in his twenty-five-year career, he felt overwhelmed. He gave himself a mental shake, quickly detached himself from the gruesome reality, and went into full pathologist mode.

He noted the absence of blood, but also noticed that there was a subtle element of violence about the tableau laid out before him – the violence of the death itself and the violence of their struggle to elude it.

This was no massacre, he concluded, but death had not visited on the victims quietly or painlessly.

A hypothesis was already forming in his mind - one which he knew would be tested when he began the formal examination of the bodies – but all the signs were there, and he would be surprised if the post-mortems contradicted what he was beginning to believe had happened to cause the death of so many innocents.

Lorrie arrived at the church, stepped towards him and then stood silently at the forensic pathologist's side. Her silence told him that, she too, had had her breath stripped from her lungs.

For long seconds, Lorrie couldn't drag in even a tiny smidgen of air. *So many,* she thought... *and the children...* She blinked back the tears that threatened her composure and cleared her throat to rid it of a painful lump.

Ricky didn't turn to look at her. He kept his eyes locked on the scene before him, but he reached to his side and gave her arm a gentle squeeze.

Like Ricky, Lorrie thought that she had become immune to death. God only knew how close she had come to the many faces that Death portrayed, and, yet, the indignity and the sheer lunacy of so many slaughtered people in such a holy place was far beyond anything she had witnessed before.

She felt sick. All the coffee she had consumed was swishing about in her stomach and it took a sheer act of will not to vomit it all up. Contaminating the scene with the contents of her stomach would be an abomination - not to forget the fact that it would be hugely humiliating - so she swallowed back the bile and tried to focus on anything other than the almost paralysing nausea.

They made an almost comical spectacle – the pathologist so very short and so very round, and the police woman so very petite and so elegantly slim – yet there was no denying their formidable presence. Each seemed surrounded by an aura of superior authority that manifested in their posture and their bearing, and anyone looking at them could be in no doubt that they were the ones who would be responsible for ultimately making sense of everything... a responsibility no one else would ever willingly take on.

'I count at least eighty bodies,' Ricky said, still not looking at her. 'And, at least ten of them children.'

'Eighty?' Lorrie knew that he was probably on the mark, but she couldn't keep the shock from her voice. Eighty was such a significant number. It was a number that was usually reserved for victims of war or a terrorist attack, and certainly not for families worshipping in church on a lovely Sunday afternoon.

'Maybe more.' Ricky gestured with his head along the church aisle. 'I've got one of my lads doing an official count.'

Lorrie glanced to the side and then swept her eyes across the breadth of the church. The activity of the crime scene investigators was in sharp contrast to the stillness of the dozens of bodies, and the CSI's detached movements added to the bizarre atmosphere.

'So many, Ricky? Why so many?' She didn't really expect a reply, and went on, 'I don't understand how I can be seeing such a thing. It's a church, for fuck's sake.'

Her eyes fell on the body of a little girl – no more than six years old, she surmised – and her gaze automatically ricochet away in shock.

'What happened here? What, in God's name, happened?'

Ricky dragged up his gaze around to look at her. 'I imagine that it was the Cool Aid.'

'Cool Aid?' Lorrie stared for a beat, confusion creasing her forehead. 'What?'

Ricky kept his eyes locked on her face. 'Surely, you know about the Cool Aid? No...?' He shook his head. 'Well, I guess that it was a bit before your time. I'm referring to the 1978 Jonestown suicides - or murders depending how you look at it.' He sucked in a breath and went on, 'Over nine hundred members of the People's Temple - followers of cult leader, Jim Jones – drank Cool Aid laced with cyanide.'

'Jesus.'

'I don't think Jesus had anything to do with it then, and I don't think he has anything to do with *this* now. No – *this* was the devil's work.'

Lorrie took a moment to grasp the significance of Ricky's words. 'So – this reference to Cool Aid – you mean poison? You're telling me that they were all poisoned?' Her mind went blank. *What, the fuck*?

Ricky gave her a weak smile. 'That would be my guess, but...'

Lorrie blinked and re-focussed. 'You'll need to slice and dice to be sure?'

He nodded. 'It'll be a big job. I'll need to rope in some help.'

Lorrie could never understand why Ricky didn't employ a dozen pathologists - because he certainly had the work to keep at least a dozen of them busy - choosing instead to bring locums in whenever he and his two trusty partners were overwhelmed.

'You won't have room for all of them,' she said.

'No,' he agreed. 'I can take twenty. The others will have to be refrigerated elsewhere until I work my way through the first lot.'

Ricky was always Lorrie's first choice of pathologist. She rarely had much say in who was appointed but was always glad when it was Ricky. Although they had a love-hate relationship, he was undeniably the best forensic pathologist she'd ever worked with. She'd learned early in her career that working with the best was something never to compromise on and she was lucky, in that, she not only had the best pathologist, but also the best DI.

She looked across at her DI, and, when Detective Inspector, Simon Grant felt her gaze on him, he turned, and they locked eyes for a moment.

He was talking to the two PC's who had discovered the bodies. The two women still looked shell-shocked and Lorrie didn't envy them
their attempts to sleep without nightmares that night. They were both young and didn't have the armour necessary to protect them from the horrifying sight and smell of mass murder. But, Simon would make sure they were all right. He had a way with him – did Simon – and he would know exactly the right words to say to them.

As always, Lorrie felt the burden of responsibility weigh on her shoulders and, as always, she thanked God for Simon and Ricky. They formed part of *her* armour. They helped her bear the burden of command and helped stave off *her* nightmares.

Ricky spoke again, and his voice brought her eyes back to him.

'Sorry... what did you say?'

'I've confiscated the altar wine. If the poison is anywhere... it'll be there.'

Lorrie's eyes narrowed. 'If it's in the wine, then the priest did it, but... isn't the priest dead as well?'

'Dead as a dodo.'

She frowned. 'Murder-suicide?'

Ricky shrugged.

'Perhaps it's not poison.' Lorrie found herself hoping that it was something else. The thought of a man of God murdering his flock and then drinking his own poison was abhorrent.

'It's definitely poison,' Ricky affirmed.

Typical Ricky self-assurance, she thought. 'No need for the post-mortems, then?'

Ricky looked unimpressed. 'I'll treat that with the contempt it deserves.'

'But – if you're sure that it's poison...'

'I'm a scientist, Superintendent Sullivan. I always back up my hypothesis with facts. The post-mortems will give me my proof.'

'So, the priest?' She felt a distinct chill. 'I'm to focus on him?'

Ricky paused for a moment. 'Jim Jones committed suicide. He didn't drink the Cool Aid... preferring that only his followers should suffer the indignity of such a death. He shot himself instead. If it was
the priest then, at least, he went the same way as his followers.'

'I can't wait to discover the motivation for that.'

She caught sight of Simon weaving his way through the pews towards them. His expression warned of bad news. 'Here comes Simon bearing tidings,' she said. 'I think we'd better brace ourselves.'

Simon's step faltered as he drew near. The shit was about to hit the fan, and he hoped Lorrie wouldn't be tempted to shoot the messenger.

'Well?' She was impatient to hear what he had to say. 'You've tramped all the way over here with something interesting to share... I can tell by the frown on your face and the hang-dog look in your eyes, so spit it out.'

Simon tried to remove the frown, and only succeeded in looking manic. His eyes bounced off Ricky, before settling on Lorrie, and he had to virtually prize his lips open to speak. He said, 'Do you know who he is?'

The question caught both Lorrie and Ricky by surprise.

'Who?' They asked in unison.

'The priest. Do you know who he is... who he *was*?'

Lorrie shook her head, bewildered. 'Should we?'

Simon seemed reluctant to utter his next words. It wasn't often that he had information the Guv'' didn't have, and he only wished it was good news instead of the kind of news that was going to cause ructions. 'He's Robert Mackie,' he said. 'The dead priest is Robert Mackie.'

Lorrie's look of bewilderment didn't alter, and she looked at Ricky for a clue.

Ricky shrugged. 'Never heard of him. *Should* we have heard of him?'

'I don't believe you two,' Simon said, astonished at their ignorance.

'Don't either of you read the papers?' He shook his head in disgust. 'He's the priest who escaped from Syria.'

Lorrie felt the walls of the church close in on her. Her DI was telling her that their dead priest was a national hero. The man was virtually a saint, and she had been just about to consider him as her number one suspect. Scully would have a nervous breakdown when she told him.

She eyed Simon with uncertainty. 'You're sure?'

Simon nodded. 'One hundred percent.'

Ricky looked from Simon to Lorrie and frowned. Things had just become a whole lot more complicated and he took that as his cue to go about his business and leave them to the task of working out how they were going to get away with naming the hero priest as their prime suspect. *Good luck with that*, he thought, as he walked away.

DAY ONE: NIGHT

Restraint was not one of Lorrie's better qualities so, when Commander Scully ordered her to refrain from pursuing the priest as a suspect, she had to bite down hard on her tongue to stop herself from verbally annihilating him.

He had the audacity to stand in *her* office and dictate how she was to lead on *her* investigation. If it wasn't so tragic, it would almost be amusing.

It was obvious that the buffoon would never learn, and Lorrie despaired of his inability to realise just how stupid he actually was as a human being, and certainly as a senior police officer. His numerous attempts at trying to make out that he had the slightest inkling of how best to lead an investigation was the butt of many a joke, but Lorrie knew he was deadly serious and that no one would be joking about it – not this time.

Commander Scully had slithered his way up the ranks without very much experience at the front line, but that didn't stop him from believing he knew best. His interference was legendary and, as Lorrie didn't suffer fools gladly, it took an enormous effort to remain civil in his presence – an effort she usually failed to deliver on.

He was a fool, but he was also a very powerful fool, and his word was usually law. It would take a virtual act of parliament to supersede any order he gave, and that fact – coupled with his unwavering sense of righteousness – meant that Lorrie was well and truly snookered.

If it was anyone else but Scully, Lorrie knew that she would have been able to reason with them. She would have presented her thoughts, added what evidence – circumstantial, or otherwise – that she had to hand, and been listened to with respect. But, it *was* Scully, and he certainly wasn't a fan of hers. Lorrie would go so far as to say that the Commander hated her, so there was nothing she could do, and nothing she could say, that would persuade him to accept her judgement and pull his horns in. Of course, that didn't stop her from trying.

She forced some reasonableness into her voice and went as far as softening her tone to include a hint of deference. Unfortunately, Scully was itching for a fight and her attempts to reason with him fell on deaf ears. She wasn't naïve enough to believe that he would back her decision to investigate Mackie, but she did think that he would at least listen before shutting her down.

She knew that Scully didn't rate her in any positive way, and she had known for some time that he believed her success was more luck than judgement. The fact that he resented the hell out of her close relationship with the Assistant Commissioner didn't help. The AC's mentorship of her did nothing to encourage him to give her the respect that her rank deserved, and he took great pains to ensure he rattled her cage at every opportunity. She knew that, as far as he was concerned, she was far too big for her boots, and she also knew that he would be quite happy to use the priest as an excuse to knock her down a peg or two.

Lorrie's first mistake had been putting a photograph of Mackie on the wall in the major incident room. Her second mistake had been putting the label of *Prime Suspect* above it. She should have been more circumspect - waited until she'd informed Scully of her misgivings about the priest – but she'd thumbed her nose at the Commander and he'd been quick to hot-foot it from his office to confront her.

After their initial war of words – albeit that Lorrie had tried her best to be civil – a silence had descended between them. It was as if they both needed a few moments to gather their strength for the next round of argument.

Finally, Scully looked at her, and said, 'I'm not changing my mind, and you can take that snarky expression off your face, Superintendent. I don't give a shit what *you* believe... I don't give a shit what evidence you *think* you've got... lay off the priest. He's *not* a suspect, *and never will be* a suspect... Got it?

Lorrie's thin layer of self-control evaporated. 'You can't order me not to investigate him,' she challenged, affronted by his gall. 'He may be the only one who had access to the wine.'

'You know fuck-all about the wine,' he snarled in return. 'Until it's examined, no fucker knows *anything*, and I'll not have you jump to conclusions and besmirch a man's good name for no reason.'

Lorrie looked at him askance and fell silent once more. His reasoning was absurd. She thought that he must realise – even before forensics started reporting, and even before Ricky had completed the first of the post-mortems – that the investigation couldn't afford to be stalled by him or by anyone. Sitting on their hands was never an option where murder was concerned, and, denying the possibility that a person was a suspect simply because he was something of a celebrity, would be extremely ill-advised.

Of course, the Commander had his eye on what the press might do if they got a hold of Lorrie's suspicions about Robert Mackie. Scully was, first and foremost, a political animal. There was no way he was going to countenance anything that put him in a bad light - and hanging the priest out to dry was one sure way of doing just that.

'The man's a fucking hero,' Scully went on. 'A *national* hero who survived the rigours of torture, and God knows what else at the hands of those terrorist bastards, and *you* want to malign him? Well, not on my watch, madam.'

Lorrie tried again. 'But, sir, we're also going to investigate the other priest... the one who actually *belongs* to the church? We might not even have to look too far into Mackie. He was just a guest for the day.' She tried a smile – almost choking on the effort - and added, 'We could rule him out with a few perfectly placed questions put to the other one.'

Scully wasn't moved by her attempt to reassure him, and her smile only succeeded in exacerbating his foul mood. He set his face. 'Have you any idea of the ramifications of blindly accusing a man of God of murdering his flock? Do you? I think not. You don't have the sense to realise what your cack-handed investigation would bring.' He paused a moment, then said, I don't think you should waste any time looking into *either* of the priests. Leave them both the fuck alone.'

Lorrie shook her head in disbelief. The stupid bastard was now ruling out questioning the other priest. What next, she wondered... bury the whole thing and do no investigation at all?

'Eighty-two people died, sir... including thirteen children. Do you understand the ramifications of that?' She failed to keep the anger from her voice. 'You're hamstringing me.'

Scully threw her a look of pure hatred. 'You've got a smart mouth, Sullivan.' He moved towards the door and pulled it open. 'You'd better watch your tone with me. Your impertinence is beginning to grate on my nerves. I've given you my orders and I'll hear no more on the subject.'

He stepped out into the corridor. He was obviously finished with her and she decided to remain seated behind her desk rather than follow him to argue her point further.

She wondered – not for the first time – why she engendered such hatred from Scully and his cronies? It wasn't as if she was a threat to them. Yes, she was much smarter, and, yes, she had the ear of the AC, but it had to be more than that, surely? She had once believed that it was merely a sex thing – a mix of chauvinism and misogamy on the part of her male superiors – but, to *actually* hate her meant that there was something much more sinister going on in their tiny little minds.

She wished that her Chief Super' had been there with her. Bernard Fredrickson might be subordinate to Scully, but he wouldn't have allowed such a tiny thing as the line of command to stop him from wiping the floor with the Commander. He wouldn't have tolerated Scully's words or actions, and certainly wouldn't have agreed to leave the two priests out of the investigation. Fredrickson was afraid of no one, and - because his job was rock solid – Lorrie knew that, regardless of any insubordination, Scully couldn't touch him and wouldn't have the balls to take him on.

It had taken Lorrie quite some time to like and feel comfortable with Fredrickson. She was so used to being put down and patronised by her superior male colleagues that, for a long time, she neither trusted nor appreciated him. He'd waltzed into her life when she was at her most vulnerable, and, time and time again – since the first moment they'd met - he'd shown her that he would always have her back. Through his words and actions, he'd proven himself to be a loyal and trusted ally and – if truth be known – she believed that he also had a soft spot for her. He was a bit of a dandy, and his sense of humour left a lot to be desired, but he was a good officer, a good boss and was fast becoming a loyal friend. The fact that she often caught him staring at her with deep longing was neither here nor there. She wasn't interested in him in *that* way and she knew that he had the sense to realise that she was out of bounds. She was pleased and relieved when he didn't allow his feelings to interfere with their working relationship, and she lived in hope that he would find someone else to moon over.

It was unfortunate that Fredrickson was currently in hospital having his appendix removed. His timing was less than ideal, but there was nothing to be done about that. She couldn't exactly blame him for an appendix that had been on the brink of rupturing and – bad timing or otherwise – she couldn't, at the moment, rely on him for support. She hoped, however, that once he heard about the situation at the church, he'd contact her and offer some words of wisdom – especially regarding Scully's outrageous demands.

She allowed a few minutes to pass before leaving the office and making her way along the short corridor towards the major incident room where her team was busy beavering away on the case.

Considering the serious crimes that landed in their laps, it was a small team, consisting of Simon Grant, her DI, and three detective sergeants – Lovell, Baxter and Powell.

A variety of uniformed officers were seconded in and out of the team's orbit, as and when required, and there were currently six constables and one sergeant assisting with enquiries – with more promised. For a crime of such magnitude, Lorrie expected at least another fifty officers to be roped in to lend a hand. They would be seconded in from a variety of teams – MIT, traffic, logistics - but she wasn't going to hold her breath waiting on Scully approving the temporary transfers. She knew that he would drag his feet. The additional resources would come, eventually, and – until then – they would have to make do.

PC Cox and PC Prince were amongst the uniformed officers lending a hand. Both had requested the assignment. Having discovered the bodies, they were determined to help find the killer and Lorrie was glad to have them. She knew that the best way of getting a good night's' sleep - after the trauma of stumbling upon so many victims - was in having the satisfaction of nailing the bastard that did it. Experience told her that Cox and Prince would work doubly hard to achieve that goal.

Whenever there was a serious crime, that required the specific expertise of Lorrie and her team, they all worked gruelling hours. It was already ten o'clock and not even a small dent had been made in the long list of things that required their urgent attention. She'd already briefed them, and she planned to do a second, more formal briefing, shortly.

Lorrie entered the incident room and immediately caught Simon's eye. He trotted over to her and, in a low voice, asked, 'Is it true? Has Commander Scully warned us off the dead priest?'

'How the fuck?' She shook her head in amazement. 'Do you have my office bugged?'

Simon looked uneasy. 'It's true, then?' He couldn't quite believe it. 'Is Scully off his head?'

'No.' She shook her head. 'He's just stupid.'

Simon stared at her. He never ceased to marvel at her ability to work with pricks like Scully. 'You didn't agree, did you? I mean...'

'I know what you mean, Simon,' Lorrie returned a little sharply. 'And, no – I didn't agree with him, but...' She shrugged. 'What choice do we have?'

Simon knew that the Commander thwarted the Super' at every turn, but he trusted that she could always outsmart and out manoeuvre him. He knew that it would take more than the likes of Scully to get the better of her. Lorrie would have a plan about the priest. Lorrie always had a plan.

'So?' he ventured. 'What should we do?'

'Our jobs, Simon. We'll do our jobs, and speaking of doing our jobs... where are we up to?'

'Well...' A look of utter dejection flashed across his face. 'We've identified nearly all of the victims. We've got names and addresses for all but a dozen of them.' He sighed and swiped a hand across his eyes. 'They're all families... husbands with their wives and kids... grandparents. Whole families wiped out.'

Lorrie tried to summon a brave face. She felt like crying, but that would be the completely wrong thing to do. She had to remain stoic – even in the face of such a devastating tragedy.

'Not whole families,' she said. 'There's that man and his baby. What's his story?'

Simon didn't immediately comprehend her meaning, and he had to think a moment. Finally, he said, 'Dicky tummy. He said he couldn't move far from the toilet, so gave the church a miss. When his wife didn't come home, he went looking.'

'You believe him?'

'Actually, I do. You can't fake that level of shock and grief.'

Lorrie was sceptical. It was her nature to be suspicious and – shock or not, grief or not – she would have the man questioned again.

'The priest... the live one,' Simon continued. 'He planned to be at the church when Mackie gave his sermon, but he was called away to the hospital to give the last rites to a dying parishioner. His alibi is solid.'

'But, he could have poisoned the wine earlier?'

'I suppose.' He frowned and ran a weary hand through his hair. 'You seem pretty sure that it was poison, and you seem just as sure that the communion wine was doctored.'

She shrugged. 'I trust Ricky's instincts.'

'What about motive? Why would either priest want to poison anyone? It doesn't make any sense.'

'No, I agree... it doesn't.'

Simon sighed. 'There's not a great deal we can do until the forensics start coming in. I'm thinking of sending everyone home. We're all knackered.'

'Okay. Sure.' She glanced at her watch. 'I was going to brief everyone on the Mackie situation, but it can wait until the morning.' She glanced at her watch a second time. 'It's late, but I think we should both go and see what Ricky can tell us. The first couple of post-mortems should be concluded by now.'

Simon nodded and moved off to let everyone know that they could go home, and, just as Lorrie made to return to her office to collect her things, she spied a familiar figure exit the lift.

Bernard Fredrickson looked like death warmed up. His face – usually pale – was gaunt and held a deathly pallor that suggested that he was in extreme pain.

He wasn't a handsome man. He was too thin and too rangy to be described as good looking, but, nonetheless, he was attractive. It was his mind, Lorrie had concluded some months before, that attracted people to him. Fredrickson's mind was deadly sharp, and he could analyse every single clue in a case with an effortless precision that left everyone in his wake. He was unlike any other Chief Superintendent she had ever known or worked with. He was pragmatic and loved nothing more than rolling his sleeves up and getting stuck in. He loathed sitting behind a desk and could usually be found right in the thick of things. At first, she had resented his presence – believing he was undermining her authority by hovering at her shoulder - but, later, she had come to depend on his constant presence.

'Sir?' She was shocked at his sudden appearance. She stood rooted to the spot as he attempted to male his way towards her.

'You should've called me,' he said breathlessly. 'I had to find out about this church thing from the news.'

As she witnessed him tottering on shaky legs, she was spurred to action. She rushed to offer him a steadying hand, and grabbing an arm, said, 'What the hell are you doing here? Surely they've not discharged you from hospital already?'

He pulled his arm from her tight grip and placed a hand on her shoulder.

'Keyhole surgery, Sullivan. They kick you out as soon as you open your eyes and squeeze out a piss.'

'But... you look like shit. You should be at home in bed.'

'Plenty of time to lie abed after we catch this fucker.'

He allowed her to lead him to her office - grateful for the support her body offered.

'Fill me in on everything,' he said, sinking down into one of the chairs. Not that I imagine you have much.'

Lorrie took a seat opposite and sighed. 'Hardly a thing, Guv''. Once I pop over to Ricky's place, and get the lowdown on the bodies he's managed to slice and dice, I'll be calling it a night.'

'Well, leave me with what you've already gathered, and I'll give it the once over.'

'Well,' she reached over to the desk and picked up a manila folder. 'If you insist. Everything we have is on computer, but you can look through this. It has the provisional statements from the man who discovered the bodies and who made the 999 call. There's also statements from the two PC's called to the scene. There's information on the priest's alibi and details on most of the victims.'

'That's it?' He was disappointed. 'Nothing from forensics?'

'A few bits and pieces on file, but you'll have to log-on to have a detailed look, but be warned, there's nothing much to see.'

'What about the priest who died with the rest? I hear he was quite the celebrity.'

Lorrie threw him a wry look. 'I think it's worth taking a very close look at him, but...'

'But?'

'Scully, sir.'

'Don't tell me,' he grimaced. 'Scully is balking at you poking through this celebrity priest's life?'

She nodded. 'He warned me off.... It won't make good press, you see?'

He nodded, understanding. 'Right... well, there's nothing stopping me having a nose around, is there? It's not as if he's warned *me* off. I can plead total ignorance.' He pulled himself to his feet and staggered around the desk to sit in front of Lorrie's computer. 'I'm sure there's a few of my army contacts who can fill me in on what went on with our priest in Syria. I'm going to see if I can get access to the de-briefing interview notes.'

'That would be a good start.'

'And, I'll try and dig underneath the official story and see what muck I can find.'

'Very good, sir.' Lorrie smiled and, with a final glance to reassure herself that he was comfortable, she left him to it.

*

Ricky's lab was housed in a large glass and steel building that boasted a number of state-of-the-art autopsy suites. The renowned forensic facilities were the envy of every other forensic pathologist in the country and Ricky always made good use of them. He never failed to provide the evidence that would not only stand up in court, but that often led to new innovations in forensic science being heralded in prestigious publications such as *The Lancet* and *The Journal of Forensic Pathology*. He had resources at his disposal that would ensure that all the eighty-two victims were autopsied under his expert supervision and, even though he wouldn't perform all of the post mortems himself, each and every one of them would require his approval before they were signed off. He was known for checking and double-checking results, and no pathologist under his supervision escaped his scrupulous critique of their work.

Security at the lab was discreet but rigorous. Ricky handled most of the Met's cases and it had been known for various people of the criminal persuasion to attempt to break into the lab to destroy evidence. Ricky didn't take any chances, and both Lorrie and Simon's credentials were given a very critical once-over before they were allowed into the building.

They found Ricky finishing up at one of the dissecting tables. A small child – perhaps eight years old – lay quiet in death on the table. Evidence of the post mortem was a grievous affront to their eyes and Lorrie had to blink rapidly to prevent tears forming.

'Poor wee mite,' Simon said thickly. 'I hope he didn't suffer?'

'I wish I could say that he didn't,' Ricky replied. 'But there's evidence to the contrary.' He stripped off his gloves and threw them into a biohazard bin. 'He bled out internally and I can only imagine his pain.'

Lorrie studied the pathologist. He was obviously terribly upset and that wasn't like him. Ricky had lived with the dead for more than twenty years and she was disturbed to find him so affected.

Ricky was aware of her eyes on him and he pushed away his bitter thoughts and pasted on his professional expression before continuing. 'The poison was probably a rodenticide but – to kill so quickly and with only a sip for each victim – the concentration must have been off the charts.'

'A rodenticide?'

Ricky turned his eyes on Simon. 'Rat poison.'

'And, a sip could kill?'

'Not normally. There's usually nausea, vomiting, cramps, convulsions… and death isn't instantaneous. It was probably mixed with something else... either that or, as I said, it's the concentration. We'll know more when toxicology results come through.'

Here we go again, Lorrie thought. Her first case with the National Major Crimes Unit at the Met' – the case that her psychopathic husband, AKA the Reaper, masterminded – involved an unknown poison that had them all baffled for far longer than it should have.

Ricky read her mind. 'It's not as complicated as the Reaper case,' he said. 'And, I learned a lot from that diabolical debacle. No poison will go undetected or unidentified for long on my watch... not this time around.'

Lorrie paced the length of the room. She tried to gather her thoughts and work out the questions she needed to ask, but the prevalence of the sickly smell of death, combined with an array of chemical aromas, was beginning to make her feel sick and she found that she couldn't think clearly.

Luckily, Ricky wanted to leave the autopsy suite to rid himself of his protective clothing and Lorrie and Simon wasted no time in following him from the ghastly room.

As they waited in his office for him to shower and change, Lorrie and Simon lapsed into an exhausted silence. Midnight was fast approaching, and they were both so very tired. They would be lucky if they managed to snatch a few hours' sleep before it was time to begin climbing the investigative mountain once more.

The thirty minutes they then spent talking to Ricky, and picking his brain, elicited no information that was worth keeping them from their beds.

For the record, Ricky confirmed that poison was, in fact, used to kill the congregation - certainly those victims who had already been autopsied - and there was no doubt that the remaining autopsies would show the same damnable evidence of poisoning.

Other than that – and the fact that every victim had suffered violent spasms that left them incapacitated – there was nothing else to learn from the post mortems.

DAY TWO: MORNING

Chief Superintendent, Bernard Fredrickson had an unwelcome habit of turning up unannounced on Lorrie's doorstep at the crack of dawn. The first time she'd met him was on her doorstep at an ungodly hour, and when she was ill-prepared for visitors. She didn't appreciate his inopportune visit then, and she didn't appreciate it now.

Three hours of sleep was not sufficient to put her in a good mood and, when her doorbell rang at five o'clock, she seriously considered murdering whoever her visitor was.

Fredrickson gave a quiet nod and ignored her furious expression. He knew she'd get over her pique, and anyway, he was thick-skinned enough not to let her mood or her expression affect him.

'I suppose you want coffee?' Lorrie said, giving in to the inevitable.

'No, thank you. I'm all coffee'd out. I must've drank a gallon of the horrid stuff through the night.' He stepped across the threshold and headed towards the kitchen. 'A cup of tea would be lovely, though.'

Lorrie wrapped her dressing gown tight around her body and followed him. She could see that he was still unsteady on his feet and her mothering instincts took over and she harried him down and into a chair and set about making him the desired cup of tea.

'Plenty of sugar, please,' he said. 'I need the energy boost.'

'Have you been up all night?'

'Yes, but I'm used to all-nighters.'

'You should take better care of yourself. All-nighters after an operation is just bloody stupid.' She slammed the mug of tea down on the table. 'I'm taking you home once you drink that.'

He took a sip of the scalding drink. 'Don't you want to hear what I found out about Mackie?'

'Well, I'm quite sure you can multi-task.' She gave him a tight smile. 'Drinking tea and talking shouldn't trouble you too much.'

'I'm beginning to understand what Scully sees in you,' he said, his lips twitching. 'You've got such a lovely way with you.'

'You always catch me at my best,' she returned. 'So... what have you dug up on our priest?'

Fredrickson nodded briefly. 'Right... well, he went to a refugee camp just outside Syria – at Suruç- primarily to help with one of the refugee programmes.'

'Primarily? Was there another reason?'

He shrugged. 'Probably, because he spent a great deal of his time outside the camp.'

'Doing what?'

He pulled a face. 'Nothing that you would expect a priest to do.'

'I'm almost afraid to ask.'

He took another sip of tea, then snorted. 'He was enamoured of one of the French aid workers. Their relationship was intense and, according to one of my sources, he promised to de-frock himself and marry her.'

She let out a slow whistle. 'Naughty, naughty.'

'I know.'

'Then, he was kidnapped?'

He nodded. 'The stupid bastard crossed the border into Syria and was dragged off the street by rifle-toting extremists and held for eighteen months in some hell-hole north of Izra.'

'Why him? Why take a priest?'

'Probably because he embodied everything the extremists hated... and, he wasn't exactly faithful to his calling. They didn't respect his faith, nor his morals.'

Lorrie thought a moment. 'Why would he venture into Syria?'

'Now, that is the six-million-dollar question.' He shook his head slowly. 'Mackie seems a bit of an enigma. My sources tell me that he often went across the border and always alone.'

'What did he have to say about it? Surely they questioned him?'

He nodded. 'They questioned him relentlessly. No one could quite believe how easily he escaped, and how well-nourished he was when he was found. He said he was traumatised and couldn't remember why he made the trips across the border, except to say that he was probably doing God's work.'

'Was it ISIS who took him?'

'So, it seemed.'

'You're not convinced?'

He shrugged. 'Nothing quite added up.'

'Was his escape from captivity suspicious?'

'It was certainly looked into.'

'And..?'

'And... nothing.'

She raised an eyebrow. 'So, not suspicious?'

'I didn't say that.'

'So, suspicious, but nothing anyone could put their finger on?'

'That sums it up.'

She picked up on his reticence. 'What aren't you telling me?'

He sat motionless, thinking. It was obvious that he was at war with his thoughts. Finally, he sighed and said, 'As I said, he was well nourished when they found him, and there were no signs of any ill treatment. That raised a few eyebrows. He'd been gone for eighteen months, and it was expected that he'd be in much worse shape. He said that his captors – after the first few months – treated him kindly.'

'That doesn't sound credulous.'

He shrugged. 'It was difficult to challenge him. The de-brief was thorough, but he ran rings around them.'

'I'm liking him more and more as our prime suspect.' She sat down at the table and placed her head in her hands. 'Scully is going to have a fit.'

'Fuck Scully.'

'That's easy for you to say.' She raised her head to look at him. 'He's scared of you. Me? He'll chew me up and spit me out if I take this to him.'

'You won't have to. I'll deal with Scully.'

Her eyebrows snaked up her forehead. 'Can I be a fly on the wall when you talk to him?'

'Best not,' he returned. 'I want to leave him with a little dignity.'

'I promise not to smirk.'

'No.' He shook his head emphatically. 'I want him to believe that investigating Mackie is his idea. When he comes to you with the suggestion that you escalate Mackie to prime suspect status, I want you to look appropriately surprised and thank him profusely for his wisdom in the matter.'

'I can try,' she smiled.

'You can do more than bloody well try, Sullivan. You can kiss his arse, and tell him how insightful he is, and thank him for his astute leadership.'

'Yeah, right.'

*

Lorrie was in her office scrolling through articles on the internet pertaining to the Syrian refugee camp at Suruç when, almost on cue, Scully arrived.

His piggy little eyes studied her for a moment and, if he was perturbed at her lack of response to his entrance, he made no sign.

Lorrie allowed a few moments to pass before she closed the lid of her laptop and finally acknowledged him.

'Good morning, sir. What can I do for you?'

She watched as his face screwed up in obvious distaste with what he was about to say, and it took a monumental effort on her part not to smile with satisfaction.

He cleared his throat and drew his shoulders back. 'I've been thinking,' he began. 'I've been thinking about the priest and I've concluded that it might be wise, after all, to look into him. Leave no stone unturned, eh? That's the wisest thing.'

'Thank you, sir. I'll get the team onto it right away.'

'Yes, right...' His discomfort was palpable. 'Only, keep it low-key. I don't want his face plastered all over the front pages as our main suspect - just in case it doesn't come to anything.'

'Of course, sir. Whatever you say.'

Something was amiss, and Scully wasn't an idiot. 'Are you taking the piss, Sullivan? All this *yes sir* bullshit.'

Her expression remained neutral. 'No, sir,' she said. 'Of course not, sir. I'm just pleased that you came to your senses with regards to Mackie.'

'Came to my senses?' he spluttered, suddenly red in the face. 'I've a good mind to...'

Lorrie stood up and her quick movement startled him into silence.

She said, 'I'm busy, sir. Do you mind if I get on?' She gave him no
time to respond, sidled past him, and left the office.

Scully quickly followed her and was about to make a grab for her arm, when he spied Fredrickson wincing his way along the corridor towards them.

Ignoring Scully, Fredrickson said to Lorrie, 'Get the team together for a briefing. It's about time we kick-started our enquiries into that dead priest.' Then, turning his eyes on Scully, said, 'I take it you've appraised Superintendent Sullivan on your change of heart?'

Scully merely nodded. He didn't trust himself to speak.

'Good,' Fredrickson said. 'Let's be having you, Sullivan.' He took her arm and steered her away from the seething Scully.

Lorrie felt the weight of him on her arm and knew that he was struggling to remain on his feet. She wished that he'd agreed to let her take him home. She modified her step to allow him to take his time, and gently led him towards the major incident room where, she hoped, her team had gathered.

Fredrickson sucked in a painful breath and said, 'I see you've managed to piss Scully off again. Do you never learn?'

'I was very polite and deferential,' she hissed up at him. 'It's not my fault that he reads insult into everything I say. The man's skin is much too thin.'

They reached the major incident room. Fredrickson stopped out-side the door to catch his breath. He attempted to disguise his pain, but evidence of it was clearly etched on his face and completely unmissable.

'I'll say it again... You should be at home in bed. I can handle this
without you.' She pushed open the door and stepped through, adding, 'I don't need a babysitter.'

Fredrickson dropped his hand from her arm and entered the room under his own steam.

Lorrie glanced at him and mumbled *idiot* under her breath then followed him through the door and across the long room.

Simon was leaning over one of the desks, studying a computer screen, and didn't notice Fredrickson and Lorrie approach. He was engrossed in scrutinising a CCTV image and almost jumped out of his skin when Fredrickson slapped him on the back.

'Jesus, sir,' he exclaimed, straightening up and taking a step back from the desk. 'You scared the shit out of me.' His eyes moved across to Lorrie. 'You ready for the briefing?'

She nodded. 'As ready as I'll ever be.' She turned and slapped her palms together in a clap to get the attention of the officers in the room.

'Right, everybody,' she said, moving to the end of the room and standing in front of a large, multi-media screen. 'Gather round.'

Fredrickson chose not to walk another step and gently eased himself into a chair. Simon eyed him briefly and then went to join Lorrie.

The major incident room had undergone a transformation since the previous night. Someone had obviously been busy.

Almost one full wall was taken up by large photo boards. Unless there was a current case, the photo boards were usually glaringly empty, and the sheer number of photographs took Lorrie's breath away. The boards were old-fashioned. Most major incident rooms across the country made use of multi-media technology to produce images of the victims, but Lorrie insisted on paper photographs and hand-written notes on the boards.

The macabre display of dozens of photographs of the victims, pinned up and framed by an assortment of scribbled notes, took up one full wall. Each photograph had a name and an arrow linking them to family members. They were mostly post-mortem photographs because access to any others had proven difficult. Who could you ask for a photograph of the deceased if the people you needed to ask were also pinned on the boards?

The photographs of the children were particularly poignant, and Lorrie's heart broke when she noticed the grey faces of three children from one family.

She sighed and tore her eyes away. 'What were you looking at on the computer?' she asked Simon.

Simon shrugged and shook his head. 'Not a great deal,' he said. 'You know that the church was situated off the main road in a quiet spot?'

Lorrie nodded and urged him on with a flap of her hand.

'Well, I'd hoped there would be some useful CCTV from around and about, but the church is too far off the beaten track.'

'But, you'd be able to track the traffic? I mean... see the cars turn off from ... what's the name of the main road?'

'Cooper Road.'

'Yes,' she nodded. 'Cooper Road. You'd see the cars head off towards the church?'

'Seen and counted off, Guv".'

'I suppose you checked them against the cars left in front of the church?'

Her question offended him. 'Really? You didn't just ask me that?'

'Sorry. I know that you're thorough, Simon.'

He made a sound in the back of his throat and said, 'No extra cars. Every car accounted for.'

Their conversation was interrupted by a not too subtle clearing of a throat. 'We're all ready for you, Guv".'

Lorrie smiled at DS Lovell and dragged in a breath. She gave the room her full attention and was surprised to see that the numbers in her team had grown significantly since the previous day.

Fredrickson had obviously brow-beat Scully into authorising the extra manpower. She wondered how many times – before the case was solved – she would be grateful for the Chief Superintendent's interventions? She threw him a brief look before turning her full attention to the room.

She took in the faces that she recognised, and those that she didn't, and felt herself relax. She knew that she didn't have much to say but was relieved that it didn't include the order not to investigate either of the priests. That was the first order of business, and the second was to re-interview the man – Davidson – who was first on the scene.

Ten minutes later – after Simon had relayed instructions for everyone's individual roles – the business of finding the killer began in earnest.

DAY TWO: AFTERNOON

Ricky Burton snapped on a new pair of gloves and, with tired eyes, surveyed victim number twelve. She was the mother of the baby found alive in the church, and hers would be the eighth body he'd had to cut open to confirm the cause of death.

He tried not to think about the baby left motherless by some unknown deranged nut-job, but he found it hard to look at the woman without imagining how the little rug-rat was going to cope without her.

Sometimes, Ricky thought that working with the dead had stripped him of his ability to emphasise with the living, but this woman, this mother – and the child he had autopsied earlier - reminded him just how much life was continually disrupted by the cruel death of the innocent. He thought that, becoming jaded and immune, would be worth the hit to his soul because he would then, at least, be free from the almost constant regret he felt at the futility of life itself.

The other four bodies had been autopsied by his colleague, Mira Santosh, and, between them, they planned to autopsy another four before the day was out. He'd succeeded in roping in another three Home Office approved forensic pathologists to help with the others, but it was still going to be many days and nights before the last body was examined.

He shifted his gaze from the body and looked across the table at the young PC standing uncomfortably waiting.

'You look a bit green around the gills, PC Cox, and I've not even started.' He smiled to show that he wasn't being cruel. 'Superintendent Sullivan must really rate you to send you here to observe me.'

'I don't know about that,' she replied, blushing. 'I think she just wanted to find me something to do.'

'That doesn't sound like the Lorrie Sullivan I know. She doesn't just find something for her officers to do. She told you to observe this autopsy because she trusts your eyes and trusts that you'll accurately report back to her everything of relevance.'

'She has you for that.'

'That's as maybe, but she likes a second opinion.'

Cox smiled. 'I don't think my opinion will be very well informed. I've never observed a post mortem before.'

'Well, I can't say that you're in for a treat.' He picked up a large block and manoeuvred it, so it lay under the woman's back, causing the chest to protrude upwards and the arms to drop back.

'I've already carried out the visual examination and noted everything, and it's just the slice and dice left to do.' He picked up a scalpel. 'I'm going to make the 'Y' incision and then reflect the skin to expose the ribs. It won't be messy, because she no longer has a blood pressure, but – when I use the Stryker saw to open the chest cavity – you might get a little bit light-headed.'

'I'll be okay... I think,' she replied on a swallow.

'Well, if you think that you're going to be sick... try to aim your vomit away from me and the body.'

Cox nodded and took a step back. She didn't think that she would be sick, but the smell was already beginning to give her the urge to gag, and, as far as she was concerned, the further away from the table and the body, the better.

Ricky switched on the overhead microphone and began outlining the procedure for the official record. His voice was low, but clear and precise.

The 'Y' incision took a matter of seconds and, a few seconds later, the woman's ribs were exposed.

He used the saw to cut through the ribs on the lateral sides of the chest and then used a scalpel to remove the soft tissue attached to the posterior side of the chest plate. He removed the chest plate and exposed the heart and lungs.

'All of the organs will be weighed and measured,' he said to Cox. 'We've already taken blood samples, but we'll take tissue samples as we go along.'

Cox needed to talk – anything to take her mind off the gruesome
procedure. 'She's the mother of that baby we found screaming its lungs out in the church?'

He nodded solemnly. 'You found the bodies?'

'Yes, me and my colleague – PC Prince. She's been sent to sit with the husband. I think that I'd much rather be here.'

'I can understand that. He must be distraught... poor man.'

Ricky removed the heart and lungs and began to dissect and reflect the abdominal muscles, exposing the abdominal organs.

'What did you make of him... the husband?'

To her credit, Cox didn't immediately answer. She wanted to think about it. What, exactly, was her opinion on the husband?

'I don't really know,' she said, at last. 'He shut down on us as soon as we discovered the bodies. He's not been fully questioned, yet.'

'I don't suppose he'll have very much to say.'

'No.' She shook her head. 'I don't suppose he will.'

*

PC Sue Prince was – as Cox had intimated – at the home of the victim's husband. As soon as Superintendent Sullivan had discovered her Family Liaison experience, she'd been ordered to support, observe and report back anything he said and did.

As far as Prince was concerned, Alexander Davidson was a strange one. He completely ignored her presence in his home and, despite the death of his wife and the other members of the congregation, he went about his business as if the whole thing no longer touched him.

Gone was the distraught man she'd found cradling his baby on the steps of the church. There were no more tears and no longer any semblance of grief. It was shock, she supposed – giving him the benefit of the doubt – and she was sure that the horror of it all would soon slam into him once more and drop him to his knees.

The baby was a darling and content enough in the care of his grandmother. Maxine Davidson – Alexander's mother – was, thankfully, staying with her son and grandson, and Prince was glad of her company. If she'd been alone in the house with the husband and the baby she believed that she would have slowly gone off her head.

'Cup of tea?'

Prince snapped out of her reverie and nodded. 'That would be lovely, thanks.'

'Sugar?'

'No sugar, thanks. Do you want me to take the baby?' She held out her arms. 'He's such a beautiful little thing.'

Maxine handed off the baby. 'I didn't get to see him much. His mother...' Her lips trembled. 'Well, best not to speak ill of the dead.' On those words, she turned and marched away to the kitchen, leaving Prince with a thousand questions.'

*

Father Malcolm Young sat in the interview room portraying all the signs of his inner devastation. He was pale, drawn and utterly bewildered. Lorrie watched him on a monitor in the observation room and studied his features.

Malcolm Young was in his fifties and looked at least a decade older. His face was an unhealthy shade of red and broken veins crawled like insects across his nose. Lorrie knew immediately that the man was a drinker.

'He seems genuinely shocked,' Simon said. 'I don't think he's faking.'

'No?' Lorrie wasn't convinced. 'I'm reserving judgement.' Ever since her husband had pulled the wool over her eyes, as to the extent of his depravity, she'd taken her time in drawing conclusions about a person's character. Everyone, she had reluctantly concluded, had the capacity for great deception.

'He *does* have an alibi.'

'Yes, but that means nothing. He had access to the wine.'

'I can't see it, Guv". He's not our man.'

'Perhaps not, but we're still going to grill him.' She made for the door. 'You coming?'

Father Young made to stand when Lorrie walked into the room.

'No. Sit,' she said. 'No need to stand on my account.' She placed a large folder on the table and sat opposite him. 'I'm Superintendent Sullivan. I'm the lead investigating officer, and this is Detective Inspector Grant.'

'I can't say that I'm pleased to meet you... not under these circumstances.' He shifted forward in his chair. 'I want to help. Tell me what I can do to help.'

'You can start by explaining to me why you weren't at the church for the service yesterday.'

He was taken aback at the tone of the question. 'Well... well, I think that I explained all of that to one of your officers.'

'Explain it again, please.' Lorrie kept her expression neutral. 'Humour me.'

For a moment it looked as if he was going to refuse, then he sighed and nodded his head. 'Of course. Well, I was meant to be there. Father Mackie was only meant to address the congregation briefly, and I was supposed to run the service. I received a phone call from the daughter of one of my parishioners... Sandy Thomas. She said that her father was fading fast and asked if I could visit him in hospital and give him Holy Communion and the sacrament of the last rites. Of course, I went. Father Mackie was very obliging and agreed to do the full service.'

'Including Holy Communion?'

He nodded. 'Yes. He was very obliging.'

'You didn't return to the church from the hospital?' Simon asked

'No. Sandy... Sandy Thomas... She doesn't have any siblings, and her mother died last year, so I stayed with her until her father passed.'

'And, afterwards?'

He dropped his eyes. 'I took her for a drink.'

'To a pub?'

'She needed a drink to steady her nerves.' Lorrie noted his defensive tone. 'I didn't know,' he went on.' He lifted his head and Lorrie could see the unshed tears in his eyes. 'If I'd only known...'

Lorrie allowed him a few seconds to compose himself, then said, 'Tell me about Father Mackie. How did he come to be in your church yesterday?'

'He was staying with me. We were friends... we'd been at university together – back in the day – and we reconnected after... well, after all that carry on in Syria. He was about to be given a new parish and was biding his time before moving to Birmingham.'

'How long had he been staying with you?'

'About a month.'

'And, was this the first time he was to address your congregation?'

He nodded. 'He kept himself to himself. It took him a bit of time to adjust to being back in the country and, although he attended church, he always sat at the back and never spoke to anyone. I was surprised when he offered to address the congregation. He said he wanted to preach forgiveness. He said that the whole world needed to learn forgiveness, and he wanted to start getting the message out with my congregation. I had no objections... In fact, I thought it was just the thing to get him back on his feet.'

'He'd been struggling?'

He turned his eyes to Simon. 'I think so, yes. He was worried about how he'd cope in his new parish. He'd been away such a long time.'

'Not that long,' Lorrie put in. 'Only about two years.'

'Long enough,' he returned.

Lorrie changed the subject. 'Did he have any other friends?'

'He was a bit of a loner – even before Syria. He didn't mention any friends in particular.'

'Did he talk about a female friend he had amongst the aid workers?'

'No, but he wasn't one for discussing such things. He could've had
dozens of friends, and I wouldn't necessarily have known about them.'

Lorrie let that sink in. She was having a difficult time understanding Father Young's relationship with Mackie. On the one hand, Mackie seemed to have turned to him for support after his imprisonment in Syria, and had stayed with him for several weeks, but - on the other hand - he refused to share anything with him about his friendships. She wondered what else he had refused to share with Young?

'What did he do with himself – day to day?'

Father Young shrugged. 'I didn't keep tabs on him.'

'He never mentioned what he did when you were going about your business?'

It was beginning to dawn on the priest that Father Mackie was a person of interest far beyond what he expected the interest of the police to be.

'You're acting as if he's a suspect,' he said. 'Surely, you don't think that he had anything to do with... anything to do with those poor people's deaths?'

Neither Lorrie nor Simon reacted to his words, and it became abundantly clear to him that Father Mackie was, indeed, a suspect.

'You can't be serious?' His shock was clear. 'He was a man of God. He would never...'

'He wasn't a man who held his vows sacred,' Simon said. 'He certainly wasn't celibate.'

'That's ridiculous.' Father Young seemed to shrink inside his skin and, against every rule of human biology, his ruddy cheeks paled. 'He was very devout. He was a very devout man and he wouldn't... he wouldn't...'

'We know of at least one woman who he was more than friendly with,' Simon put in gently.

'No. 'He shook his head vehemently. 'I don't believe it.'

'Believe it, or not,' Lorrie returned. 'Nonetheless, it's true.'

This time, she gave him no opportunity to compose himself, and fired the next question at him before he could draw his next breath.

'Who had access to the communion wine?'

He stared at her for long seconds, digesting the question, before

saying, 'I don't understand. What has the communion wine got to do with anything?' He was genuinely perplexed.

Lorrie opened the folder and withdrew several photographs. She spread them out and he immediately saw that they were pictures of

several of his congregation, laid out and posed on mortuary slabs.

'All poisoned,' she said, removing several further photographs and fanning them out under his nose. 'All of the post mortems haven't been completed yet, but so far every one of these people were poisoned. We expect the same result on all future autopsies.'

Simon felt sorry for the priest. Lorrie was giving him no quarter and he could see the damage she was doing to him. But, he knew that her way was the best way and he bit back on his pity.

'Even the children,' she went on. 'Even the children were poisoned and they suffered, Father. It was a cruel death for all of them.'

He couldn't tear his eyes from the photographs. He knew those people. He'd baptised some of them, married some of them and comforted them in times of grief when he'd buried one of their loved ones.

'Dear Lord,' he said quietly. 'Have mercy on their souls.'

It was as if Lorrie didn't hear him or notice the plaintive sound of his voice. 'Back to the wine,' she said. 'Who had access?'

'I... I...' The priest pulled himself to his feet. 'I can't stay here. I have to go.'

'Sit down, Father. We only have a few more questions,' Simon stood and leant over the table. 'Bear with us. It's important.'

But, Father Young didn't sit back down. He seemed confused, and his colour had all but leeched from his face. He moaned, and it was the first sign that all was not well with him. Both Simon and Lorrie became alarmed, and both reached out for him, just as he clutched his chest and crashed to the floor.

DAY TWO: EVENING

PC Sue Prince headed back to base. Her stint as FLO was over and, instead of going home for a nice cup of tea and a take-away with her husband, Robert, she decided to go back to New Scotland Yard and catch up on what she'd missed. She arrived just in time for the evening briefing.

The room was packed, and she only just managed to squeeze in at the back, between two overstuffed sergeants, before the doors were closed and the briefing began.

Lorrie looked around the room before her eyes settled on PC Cox. 'Ah... Cox... just the woman.' She smiled at the young PC. 'What do you have for us?'

'Ma'am?' Cox blushed as all eyes turned on her.

'Anything from the post-mortem?'

'Nothing new, Ma'am...'

'Please,' Lorrie interjected, raising an impatient hand. 'Don't *Ma'am* me. Guv" will be fine.'

'Yes, Guv". Sorry, Guv"... Nothing new, Guv".'

A few sniggers around the room were quickly stifled by a hard look from Lorrie. 'Nothing new? Can you expand on that for the benefit of the newbies in the room?'

Cox felt like a rabbit caught in the headlights. She felt dozens of pairs of eyes boring into her from all directions. 'Em... well... I observed the post-mortem of one of the female victims. She was twenty-nine years old, a mother... that was her husband and baby PC Prince and I met at the church.' She threw a quick glance in Prince's direction.

Lorrie nodded encouragement. 'Go on.'

Cox smiled and continued. 'She was in good physical shape - considering she was twelve weeks post-partum – but her stomach was turned to mush by the poison and there was evidence of severe internal haemorrhage.'

'The same rodenticide was confirmed?'

'Yes, Ma'am... Guv".'

Lorrie ignored her faux-pas and surveyed the room once more. Catching sight of PC Prince, she said, 'Come nearer the front, Prince. I want to hear from you next.'

PC Prince pushed her way forward, and, when she was as close to the front as possible, looked expectantly at the superintendent.

'You spent the afternoon with the victim's husband?'

Prince nodded. 'His mother and baby were there.'

'Yes – how is the baby?'

'None the worse for his ordeal, Ma'am... I mean, Guv".'

'And, the husband... what's his name?'

'Davidson.' Her brow furrowed, and she added, 'He's a strange one.'

'Strange... in what way?'

Prince shrugged. Well, he seems to have recovered rather too quickly from his grief. He was hysterical and inconsolable earlier - when me and PC Cox arrived at the scene – and, suddenly, he's acting as if nothing bad happened.'

'I wouldn't put too much stock on that meaning anything,' Simon put in. 'Grief's a funny thing.'

'Yes, sir.' Prince was mortified at what she perceived as criticism from the DI. 'It's just that...' She searched for the right words. 'He was carrying on as if he wasn't that bothered, and his mother... well, it was clear that there had been no love lost between her and the victim.'

'That's mother-in-law's for you,' a voice heckled from the back.

The room erupted in laughter and Lorrie allowed it to continue for a few moments before holding up her hand for silence. It was common for officers involved in investigating heinous crimes to use humour as a means of coping. Lorie knew that they didn't mean any disrespect, but she was going to keep a firm hand on any outbursts.

'Do you know why their relationship wasn't friendly?' she asked Prince, her interest piqued.

'No, Guv". She was pretty tight-lipped.'

'Okay, we'll park that for the moment, but we won't let it go. See what you can draw from her tomorrow.'

'Yes, Guv'.'

Lorrie turned to the large photo boards. 'There's still a couple of dozen post-mortems to be done but it's pretty clear that a highly concentrated rodenticide was used to poison this innocent flock. We've confirmed that the Communion wine was doctored, and the two priests who had access are dead.'

Prince was the only one in the room who hadn't been informed about Father Young's heart attack, and she looked across to Cox with a question on her face. Cox shook her head and mouthed 'I'll tell you later.'

Lorrie continued, 'My gut tells me that Father Young had no idea
about the poison, but I'm not ruling him out completely. My gut has
been known to be wrong on more than one occasion.'

'My gut tells me the same thing, Guv",' Simon put in. 'I think we should concentrate our efforts on Father Mackie.'

'Yes... Father Mackie.' She bent and picked up a sheaf of papers. 'I want everyone to study this profile on Mackie. Fortunately, DCS Fredrickson has one or two friends who were able to give us pertinent information on the good Father, and it makes for interesting reading.'

She handed the papers to Simon. 'We're confirming him as our prime suspect, and there are a few areas of his life that still require a good going through.' She looked across to DS Lovell. 'Sonia will work on that with DI Grant and, as for the rest of you...' Her eyes swept once more around the room. 'We won't take our eyes off the possibility that someone else is the killer. I want every family member of the victims - those who weren't at the church and who are still alive – questioned and their lives investigated. Powell and Baxter will lead on that.' She paused for a moment to gather her thoughts. 'The rodenticide needs to be tracked. It's not the sort of thing found in any common or garden cupboard, so let's find out where it came from, and let's also try and find out if anyone had been hanging suspiciously around the church over the past few days.'

Briefing over, and tasks assigned, Lorrie left them to it and made her way back to her office.

Scully was waiting.

Lorrie wondered what form of abuse the Commander was about to subject her to and prepared herself for the worse. He had a malicious gleam in his eyes that suggested to her that he was gearing up for a right go at her, and she took what support she could by leaning back against the door.

'I hear you killed the priest,' he said, and she was surprised at the lack of rancour in his voice. 'That was quite something, Superintendent, and I think it might just be the final straw to break that pretty little back of yours.'

She tried her best not to antagonise him. 'He had a heart attack, sir.'

'Yes, a heart attack... indeed.' His face split with a wide grin. 'But,
one caused by your cruel and unusual treatment of him.'

'I beg your pardon?' She reared forward off the door and almost
staggered towards the desk, behind which he sat grinning and gloating like a big fat cat that had just snatched all the cream.

'There's already been a complaint lodged against you, I'm afraid. The Assistant Commissioner has it in front of her as we speak.'

It was Lorrie's turn to grin. 'The AC will see it for what it is... a malicious attempt to discredit me. She'll want to know who it was that put the complainant up to it. Will she have far to look, sir?'

Scully's grin wavered. 'No one put him up to it. The Bishop has every right to be concerned about your tactics, Sullivan.'

'So, it was the Bishop? How did he know what tactics I did, or did not, use in my questioning of Father Young?'

'I wouldn't know. Perhaps you have a spy in your midst?'

'Oh, there's a spy all right.' Her grin dropped to a sly smile. 'You're friends with the Bishop, I believe?'

Scully had the sense to ignore the implication. 'You'll be taken off the case, pending an investigation. I'm bringing in someone to take your place... someone who knows the rules.'

Lorrie wasn't worried. The AC would kick Scully's arse, and see him sacked, before she would countenance such a thing.

It was as if Scully read her mind. 'Don't imagine for one moment that Annie Gordon will come riding in on her white charger to rescue you. A complaint from the Bishop – malicious, or not – carries a lot of weight, and, after all, a man died, Sullivan. I may not be able to have you terminated, but what I *can* ensure is that you're kicked off this case.'

'That wouldn't be fair, sir. I didn't do anything wrong. The man was obviously very ill.'

'Be that, as it may,' he said. 'You're off the case – as of right this minute.'

There was no point in engaging any further with the tin-pot dictator sitting behind her desk. He obviously thought that he held all the cards, but he'd forgotten all about Fredrickson. Fredrickson wouldn't stand for any of it.

As if her thoughts had conjured him up, Fredrickson pushed open the door and stepped into the office. His expression told her that he already knew what Scully had done, but the look in his eyes robbed her of any hope that he'd come to put Scully straight.

'Ah, Chief Superintendent Fredrickson... just in time,' Scully ex-
claimed. 'Perhaps you can confirm the Superintendent's position because, frankly, I don't think she believes me.'

Lorrie looked from Scully to Fredrickson and felt the blood drain from her face. He'd been nobbled. It was as plain as day.

'Would you give us a minute, sir?' he asked Scully. 'I'd like to speak to Superintended Sullivan alone... if you don't mind?'

'Mind?' Scully pulled himself to his feet. 'Of course, I don't mind. I'm already late for an engagement. Drinks with the Bishop.' With that, he almost bounced from the room.

'You gutless...'

'Now, now, Sullivan – no need for name calling. I had no choice but to go along with it.'

'I did nothing wrong. He and that slimy friend of his set me up.'

Fredrickson felt sorry for her. She'd had more than her fair share of bad luck... not the worst of which was having Scully hell-bent on ruining her. Everything in her life was so damned hard and she didn't even have the solace of being left alone to do her job without arseholes like Scully putting the boot in. Nevertheless, she was well and truly fucked this time. He had no doubt that an investigation into the Bishop's complaint would prove to be unfounded, but that would take weeks, and meantime, he had no choice but to follow protocol and support the decision to temporarily remove her from the case.

'That priest was a heart attack waiting to happen. I wouldn't be surprised to find that the post-mortem shows a liver that's well pickled and arteries so clogged with shit that it was a miracle he hadn't dropped dead long before he found himself in my interview room.'

Fredrickson nodded. 'You're probably right, but...'

'Yes, I know,' she sighed. 'I'm not blaming you. I'm sorry I called you gutless.'

'I've been called much worse.'

'I'll bet, but it was uncalled for'

'There's one piece of good news,' he said, smiling. 'I've managed to put the kybosh on Scully's replacement for you.'

'Who did he have in mind?'

'DS Ian Grosvenor, from Vice.'

'You've got to be fucking kidding?'

He shook his head. 'Not kidding.'

Lorrie blew through her lips. 'He wouldn't have a clue.'

'No, and that's why the AC and I pulled the rug. Scully doesn't know yet and, when he does, we might hope that he follows Father Young's example and have a heart attack.'

Lorrie was shocked. 'That's going a bit far. I don't want him dead.'

'No, neither do I... not really. Perhaps just a small heart attack – enough to put him in a hospital bed for a few days.' He smiled to show that he didn't mean it. 'Anyway, I've promoted DI Grant. He'll be the lead on this.'

'Oh, thank God for small mercies.' She let out a long sigh of relief. 'I only hope he's strong enough to endure Scully's wrath.'

'I'll have his back.'

'Yes, I know you will and, anyway, Simon's a lot tougher than he looks.'

*

Simon took the news with stoic resignation. He was surprised not to be taken off the case alongside the Guv'' because, after all, he'd been in the room when the priest dropped like a stone to the floor. No doubt he would be questioned as part of the investigation and, no doubt, Scully would be up to his eyes in trying to get him to screw over Lorrie, but neither of them had done anything wrong, and the sooner everyone knew that then the sooner he could get out of Scully's firing line.

Lorrie eyed him speculatively and said, 'No one's out to get you, Simon. Scully wants my head on a spike, not yours. Stop worrying and simply get on with the job. You covered for me for six months when I lost Ollie and Sean and – by all accounts – you did a damned fine job.'

Simon smiled at that – albeit reluctantly – and said, 'That was different. I didn't have to track down the killer of over eighty people, and I didn't have the unenviable task of blackening a dead hero priest's name.'

Lorrie kept her voice cheerful. 'I'll still be around,' she said. 'Just

because I'm no longer SIO, doesn't mean I'm going to abandon you. I'll be in my office every day, and you can come and pick my brains anytime you take the fancy.'

'Thanks, Guv''. I might just take you up on that.'

They dropped into an awkward silence. It was an unusual situation for both of them and navigating through what was going to be very troubled waters was not going to be easy.

'Have you thought about promoting one of the sergeants to acting DI?' Lorrie asked. 'I know it will probably only be for a couple of weeks, but one of the team should have the opportunity. Acting DI on such a high-profile case would do wonders for one of their CV's.'

Simon seemed genuinely pleased at the suggestion. 'I didn't think it would be worth it - not for such a short time – but, I think you're probably right.'

'I'm *always* right,' she said, smiling. 'Who do you have in mind?

'Lovell, of course. It goes without saying.'

'Yes, she's a good officer, and an excellent DS, but both Baxter and Powell have merit.'

He nodded. 'I don't dispute that, but they're followers, and Lovell is a leader.'

'I've seen her leading you by the nose on more than one occasion. You *do* know that she's mad about you, don't you?'

He blushed to the roots of his hair. 'We're just colleagues. We respect each other.'

'Oh, I know there's been no hanky- panky, Simon. Relax. I'm just pulling your leg.'

'Right,' he said, making no further comment.

Lorrie knew that she had embarrassed him. It was an open secret that DS Lovell was in love with the DI, and it was thanks to their utter professionalism that the matter hadn't really raised any eyebrows, but eyebrows might be raised should he promote her above Baxter and Powell.

'Think about one of the others,' she said. 'Don't complicate things for yourself.'

'I'll take your opinion under advisement,' he replied, grim-faced, 'but the decision is mine and mine alone.'

Rather than being put out by his response to her suggestion, she was secretly pleased. She liked when Simon showed a bit of gumption. It meant that he wasn't going to be a pushover and – bearing in mind the shit that Scully was going to throw at him – gumption was going to be sorely needed if he was to survive the next few weeks.

From the corner of his eye, Simon noticed Cox and Prince approach. They were both tip-toeing over as if afraid that they were entering the lion's den, and he turned to them and gestured for them to put a move on.

'You have something?' he asked.

'I... we... well, sir, we don't rightly know.' Cox turned to Prince and pleaded with her eyes for her to say what was on their minds.

Prince cleared her throat, threw back her shoulders, and dived right in.

'We've both been studying the list of victims, Guv', and we think there's someone missing... someone that isn't on the list of people we're to question.'

'Oh, and who might that be?'

'The churchwarden, sir.' That was Cox. 'We checked and there definitely is a churchwarden employed at the church. He looks after the building and everything in it. You don't usually see churchwardens employed in catholic churches – not these days, because it's usually the Anglican churches that have them – but we checked, sir.' She wound down and dropped her eyes.

Both Lorrie and Simon stood open-mouthed at the critical piece of information brought to them by the two inexperienced PCs.

Prince dived in once more. 'We took the liberty of finding out who he is, and where he lives.' She handed Simon a scrappy piece of paper.

Simon's hand trembled as he extricated the paper from Prince's fingers.

'Thank you,' he said. 'Good work.' He then stood, motionless and expressionless as the two women nodded, turned on their heels and
walked away.

'Shit.' Lorrie mumbled. 'How the hell did we miss that?'

'There was no one to tell us. Father Young might've mentioned it, if his heart hadn't burst in his chest before he had a chance to.'

Lorrie chewed on her lip. 'It does beg the question...'

'What question?'

'Why hasn't this churchwarden made himself known to us?'

'Yes,' he nodded thoughtfully, glancing at the words scribbled on the
paper. 'I think we better pay this man a visit.'

'Not me,' she said. 'Take Lovell. You can give her the good news about her promotion on the way.'

DAY TWO: NIGHT

'You're not serious?' Sonia Lovell slammed on the brakes and turned to look Simon fully in the face. 'You really mean it?'

'Jesus fucking Christ, Lovell! You can't stop here. You'll get us both killed.'

White-faced, he looked behind him, out the rear window, and satisfied that there was no danger of being rear-ended, turned back and said, 'Yes, I meant it. You're acting DI ... or you will be as soon as I clear it with Fredrickson.'

Sonia gaped at him in wonder. He had chosen her over Baxter and Powell and, for that, she was both shocked and deliriously pleased.

'Can you move, please?' Some colour had returned to his face. 'And, no more crazy emergency stops.'

'Yes, Guv.' She accelerated and moved off. 'Acting DI,' she said to herself. 'I can't believe it.'

'You deserve it,' he said. 'You're the best DS I've ever worked with, and you'll make a great DI. I know it's only for a few weeks, but it'll set you up for a proper promotion.'

They sat for a moment in silence. 'Thank you.' Sonia said. 'I appreciate your faith in me.'

Simon wasn't one for outward displays of emotion and, for the first time in his life, he wished he had the ability to fully express his gratitude to the woman who had extricated him from more than a few sticky situations. He depended on her to do the thinking for him during the times when he couldn't see the wood for the trees, and her thoughtful, on-the-button advice had always proved to be the catalyst for his success in matters pertaining to the many cases they'd worked together. He was a better investigator, a better DI because of her, and promoting her was the only way he was able to show his appreciation.

Lovell got the car moving again. They arrived at the churchwarden's address, and quickly noted the car parked in the driveway and the illuminated windows.

'He's obviously at home,' Sonia said. 'How do you want to play this?'

He shrugged. 'Let's just see where he leads us. I can't see how he'll manage to convince us of a reasonable excuse for not getting in touch,

but... let's just hear him out.'

'Softly, softly, catchee monkey.'

'Exactly.'

They climbed from the car and made their way up the drive to the front door.

'We don't know much about him, do we?'

Simon shook his head and rang the bell. 'Nothing, really.'

'Those two PCs are stars.'

'You can say that again.' He pushed the bell a second time, leaving his finger on it for a few extra seconds. 'They showed us up, big time.'

'Try banging on the door.'

Simon raised his fist and hammered.

'I'll see if I can spot anything through the lounge window.'

Sonia moved off whilst Simon continued hammering on the door. He soon gave up and followed Lovell across the front of the house.

'I think I see him,' she said. 'There's just enough of a crack between the curtains, but I'm not sure.'

Simon rapped on the window, calling out, 'It's the police, Mister Pertwee. Open up, please.'

Nothing – no sound and no movement from within. Simon rapped again.

Sonia leaned forward and pressed her nose up against the glass.

'There's definitely someone in there. I can just about make out a pair of legs.'

'Something's not right. We've made enough noise to wake the dead. I don't think he's ignoring us.'

Sonia straightened up and stepped back from the window. 'Are we going in?'

Simon nodded. 'Call for back-up. I've a sick feeling in the pit of my stomach.'

'You and your stomach, but I've learned to trust your stomach.'

'Except for the times when I've had an iffy curry.'

'Yes, except for those times.' She reached in her pocket and pulled out her mobile phone. 'I'll send for the cavalry.'

While they waited on back-up to arrive, they walked the perimeter of the house, trying all the downstairs windows and checking if the back door was unlocked.

'He might need help,' Sonia said. 'Perhaps we should just go ahead and break in.'

'You've read my mind. Let's do it.' Simon reached down and picked up a hefty rock from the garden. 'This should do the job.'

He took off his jacket and wrapped one sleeve around his right hand and then proceeded to smash the window in the back door with the rock. Reaching in, he managed to turn the key in the lock.

Once inside, they made their way through the kitchen and found themselves in a long, gloomy hallway. Muted voices could be heard coming from a door to their left, and they simultaneously stiffened at the sounds.

'I think it's the television,' Sonia whispered.

'Why are you whispering?' Simon retorted, loudly. 'Smashing that window gave us away, don't you think?'

She grimaced and nodded.

The door to the lounge opened with a loud squeak and, when it was fully open, Mister Pertwee was in full sight.

'He's definitely dead,' Sonia said. 'I'll get onto forensics.'

'Okay.' Simon stepped back from the door but kept his eyes firmly on the body. 'Been dead a while, I think. More than a day, I'd say.'

Sonia agreed with a nod and turned to make the phone call that would summon Ricky Burton and his team.

*

Lorrie poured herself a glass of wine but, instead of drinking it, she savoured its aroma and then placed it on the kitchen table. She allowed herself the occasional glass of wine, but never when she felt stressed or depressed. Her previous tussle with the demon drink was still a scary memory, and she was wary of its enticing charm.

Being taken off the case had hit her hard. All she had in her life was her job and, without it, she knew that she would fade and eventually disintegrate into a non-person. It was a sad reflection on just how lonely and dysfunctional she had become since her husband had all but destroyed her, and, what was sadder still, was that there was nothing she could do to change things.

Lorrie had a horror of being completely alone. Her team had become her family, and, although as a rule they didn't socialise, just knowing they would be there when she stepped into work was enough to make her feel that she wasn't entirely on her own. If Scully had his way, he'd take them away from her. He'd cast her out and that would be the end of everything.

She'd been a bit rough on Father Young – she knew that – but she hadn't been responsible for his death. Perhaps she should've known that he wasn't well, and postponed the interview, but that wasn't something she could be held accountable for. He hadn't seemed unwell. He didn't complain of anything. *She wasn't a fucking doctor, for Christ's sake!*

The wine seemed to call out to her and she absently reached for the glass. The first swallow was like nectar and, before she was tempted to take a second, she marched over to the sink and poured it down the drain.

Her apartment looked out over a main road and the noise of the traffic drew her to the window. Looking out onto the busy world eased her mind a little and she felt herself relax.

She was thrown out of her reverie when her mobile chirped in her bag. It was Simon.

'You shouldn't be telling me this,' she said. 'I'm off the case – remember?'

'Fuck that for a game of soldiers,' Simon snapped down the phone. 'No one's ordered me not to talk to you, and, until Scully gets around to it, I'll do what the fuck I want.'

Lorrie was taken aback by Simon's tone. He very rarely ever got rattled and he rarely, if ever, swore at her.

'Okay… tell me,' she said. 'Tell me everything.'

*

Fredrickson headed her off at the pass.

'Stay out of the major incident room,' he said sharply. 'Scully is skulking the corridors, and he'd like nothing better than to have an excuse to suspend you.'

'What's he doing here at this time of night? It's well past his bed-time.'

'He got wind of the Pertwee situation.'

'Really? I'm beginning to think that man either has supernatural abilities, or he has a spy planted in my team.'

'I'd go with the spy scenario,'

Lorrie leaned back against the wall and looked up into Fredrickson's face, searching for a clue that he was joking. She couldn't countenance the notion that Scully had turned one of her team.

'I'm not sure I meant that,' he said, noting her shock. 'Let's just settle for supernatural abilities. It's much more believable.'

It took a moment of recovery before she could ask, 'What's the story on Pertwee? Simon didn't say any more than he found him dead.'

'I don't know much more than that myself.'

'Come off it… you *must* know more than I do. You've not been kicked to the kerb.'

'Okay,' he sighed, 'but, you didn't hear this from me.'

Lorrie straightened up from the wall, all ears.

'He was found, slumped in his armchair, with half a bottle of Communion wine on the table next to him, and with an empty glass on the floor at his feet.'

Lorrie opened her mouth to speak and then snapped it closed again. She had a million questions all fighting with themselves in her brain and she couldn't separate them sufficiently to ask one.

'Obviously, Simon is treating the death as suspicious. Ricky already has the body, the wine and the glass, so it's only a matter of time before we'll have the answers to all of the questions you're dying to ask.'

'I should be reinstated,' she said. 'I'm needed.'

He shook his head. 'That's not going to happen, Lorrie. Anyway,' he went on, 'you should show more faith in the Acting Superintendent. He's doing all right, so far.'

'I'm sure he is,' she retorted, a little harsher than she intended.

'It'll all work out,' he said, attempting to soothe her rancour at the injustice of it all. 'This investigation is nothing more than a farce and it'll be done and dusted before you know it.'

'If it's such a farce, why has the AC countenanced it?'

'Because, she doesn't have a choice. I'm sure that Scully hoped she'd kick up a fuss and refuse his request that you be taken off the case.
That would've played right into his hands, and Annie Gordon is much too clever to allow him the pleasure of having *her* investigated.'

His words made sense, but they failed to reassure her. She had visions of never being allowed back, and the thought of being sent to some backwater and plonked behind a desk filled her with dread.

'I'm going to have him, you know?'

'Who... Scully?' She made a derogatory sound in her throat. 'Many
have tried, and just as many have failed miserably. He's made of Teflon.'

'He's not as invincible as you might think. He's made a lot of enemies, and he's beginning to make mistakes. The one big mistake he *has* made, is in making an enemy out of *me*.'

'I suggest that you watch your back,' she said. 'He's outlived a few good men.'

'Well, this is *one* good man who will see him off. He's bitten off more than he can chew by coming after one of *my* officers.'

'Thanks, sir. I appreciate your support.' She looked into his eyes and immediately wished that she hadn't. There was something there, in their depths, that frightened her. She thought that it was more than a mere shadow of attraction for her. She thought that it was love, and that scared the shit out of her.

He gave a wry smile, and said, 'Once upon a time, you were suspicious and aggravated by my support.'

'Well, a lot of water has gone under the bridge since then,' she replied, avoiding his eyes. 'I know better, now.'

He nodded, then realising that she couldn't see the nod, said, 'I still get the feeling that you don't completely trust me.'

Lorrie lifted her eyes and studied his face. It was a kind face, a completely open face, and she suddenly felt guilty about her fear of his feelings for her, and actually began to question her interpretation of the expression in his eyes.

'I trust you,' she said.

'But?'

'But, nothing,' she returned firmly. 'I trust you completely.'

He wasn't convinced, but he let it pass. 'There's no point in you hanging around. You should go home,' he said. 'I'll make sure that Simon fills you in tomorrow.'

There was no point in Lorrie arguing to stay. She had no role to play, and her presence would probably just make everyone uncomfortable, so she left them all to it and went back to her empty apartment and her empty life.

DAY THREE: MORNING

Julie Cox arrived home at the crack of dawn and immediately rushed upstairs to the bedroom. Her husband of a mere two weeks would be awaiting an explanation about why she'd been out the whole night, and she was anxious to share everything with him...or as much as she was permitted to share.

He was used to her working regular hours. She worked shifts, but you could normally put the kettle on for her arriving home. Her new job wasn't going to be like that, and she was sure that Richard would understand. Her Richard was nothing if not understanding and supportive of her career, and she counted herself lucky that he didn't have an axe to grind about her being a police officer.

He was awake and welcomed her with a kiss. 'You must be knackered,' he said.

'I'm too excited to feel it,' she replied, stripping off her uniform and walking through to the en-suite in her underwear. 'Prince and I were indispensable today,' she called over her shoulder. 'I don't care what they say about us uniformed officers... we rock.'

She turned on the shower and, whilst the water warmed, turned to the sink to brush her teeth.

She had no qualms about continuing to talk with a mouthful of toothpaste. She said, 'This case has us all baffled and I don't know how we're going to get on with Superintendent Sullivan being reassigned. The acting Super' seems competent enough, but there's no one to hold a candle to Sullivan.'

'That sounds like a touch of hero worship,' he called back. 'Should I be jealous?'

She stood in the door, toothbrush in hand, and said, 'No, my darling... you're my one and only hero.'

'Come to bed, then and never mind the shower.'

She thought about it for all of two seconds before taking a running jump and landing beside him.

'I wish I could join the team permanently. *Detective* Constable Cox sounds *much* better than plain old *Police* Constable Cox.'

'I'm sure – if that's what you want – it'll happen.'

Julie grinned up at him. 'It will, won't it?'

He nodded and kissed the top of her head. 'Superintendent Sullivan had better look out, because my Julie will fill her shoes one day.'

'Oh, Richard, you *are* funny. She's ancient... must be forty if she's a day. She'll be retired and gone before I reach the dizzy heights of Superintendent.'

*

The ancient Lorrie Sullivan was staring at her reflection in the mirror and scrutinising the brand-new wrinkles at the corner of her eyes. She was getting old and wouldn't see forty again. At the exact moment PC Cox was discussing her with her husband, Lorrie was contemplating a future as a lonely old woman.

She scowled at the wrinkles and slapped some moisturiser on her face. She wished that she'd been born on the plain side of beautiful. Her looks had been more of a hindrance than an asset in her job, and now that she'd seen the look in Fredrickson's eyes, she wished that she'd been born pug ugly, and wished that she'd been prone to running to fat. Plain, fat women were more respected on the job, whereas someone with her looks and her figure seemed to evoke either lust or hatred, and never seemed to get the respect earned from a job well done.

She wondered why she was frightened of Fredrickson's feelings for her. She liked him – she couldn't deny that – but he was her boss and she wasn't remotely interested in him in *that way*. She'd learned her lesson a long time ago about having a relationship with a colleague who also happened to be her boss, and she wasn't about to repeat that long-ago mistake.

But, it wasn't a mistake, she admonished herself. Admittedly, until Sean had walked back into her life, she'd always felt that their love affair had been misjudged and misguided - with the only thing coming out of it that was worthwhile being the birth of their son, Ollie – but she'd always loved Sean. She knew that she would never love another man as much as she'd loved him, and that fact was the crux of her fear of Fredrickson's feelings for her.

She had no doubts but that she could crush him. If she succumbed to her loneliness and assuaged the loneliness she saw mirrored in him by having an affair, she would end up destroying him. She might be vulnerable, but she didn't think that she was wrong when she determined that he was much more vulnerable than she was.

She wondered what the sex would be like and blushed at the thought.

No, she wouldn't use him for company or for sex. She wouldn't cleave his chest open and suck out his heart. She didn't want that. She liked and respected him too much to use him.

So, what to do, she wondered? *Not think about it,* she concluded with a shake of her head.

She completed her ablutions and went back into the bedroom to search for her phone. It was early – not yet six o'clock – but she was wide awake, and she had no sympathy for anyone who wasn't.

She found her phone, buried beneath the pile of clothes she'd discarded on the bed earlier and keyed in a number she knew off by heart.

'Ricky, it's me,' she said. 'I have a few questions for you.'

On the other end of the phone, an exhausted Ricky Burton bit back the tirade of expletives that had formed on his tongue and sighed.

'What questions, Lorrie? What questions could you possibly have at six o'clock in the morning?'

'Questions about your post-mortem on the churchwarden.'

'Pertwee? How is that any of your business? In case you've forgotten, you've been taken off the case.'

'Only in body, my dear Ricky, never in spirit.'

'You know that I can't tell you anything, right?' Despite his denial, there was a hint of resignation in his voice. 'I'd run the risk of losing my contract with the Met.'

'Rubbish. The only person who'd care a jot that you spoke to me would be Scully and *I'm* not going to tell him, are you?'

'I never speak to Scully – not if I have any choice in the matter – but, that's beside the point. He'd find out.'

'Don't be such a wimp. Since when did you care about breaking the
rules?'

'All the bloody time, Lorrie.'

'Yes, that's as maybe, but you'll break them now ... for me.'

'I can't, sorry.'

'Please, Ricky.'

The phone went silent and then she heard him say '*Fuck.*'

'Thanks... I owe you one,' she said, letting out a breath.

'What do you want to know?'

'Everything. I want to know everything.'

*

Simon was surprised to see Lorrie at her desk so early in the morning. He couldn't imagine what she thought she had to do that was important enough to have her drag herself into work at such an ungodly hour.

'I've spoken to Ricky,' she said, before he had a chance to wish her a 'good morning."

'Ricky? Why?'

'Because he's the man with all the answers,' she replied.

'Answers that he's not supposed to share with you.'

'I had to drag them out of him. He can be such a pussy.'

'What did he tell you?' Then, quickly – 'No, I don't want to hear it from you. You've compromised yourself enough without discussing his findings with me.'

'Hark at the man who phoned me and said he'd do what the fuck he likes. What happened to *that* man, Simon?'

'He came to his senses.'

'Chickened out, more like.'

'That's not fair, Guv'. All this cloak and dagger shenanigans won't bode well for either of us. You have to keep your head down and your nose out or Scully will finally have his wet dream.'

'Nice metaphor, Simon.' She stood up from behind her desk and gestured for him to close the office door. 'Scully never gets out of bed before nine, so there's no chance that he'll catch us talking about the case. Stop worrying and sit down.'

'I don't want to sit down,' he said petulantly. 'I want to go and find Ricky and hear from him first-hand.'

'Suit yourself,' she returned. 'I won't stop you.' She returned to her seat and switched on her computer – completely blanking him.

Simon was at odds with himself. On the one hand, he wanted so very
Much to protect her by keeping her at arm's length from the case but, on the other hand, he knew that Scully was wrong, and that Lorrie had every right to work every aspect of the case. The fat bastard was out of order, and Simon really didn't want to make matters worse for Lorrie
by abiding by the vindictive Commander's rules.

'Okay,' he said.

Lorrie glanced up at him. 'Okay, what?'

'Okay, you can tell me what Ricky said.'

'Are you sure? I don't want you to compromise yourself.'

'Well, what the fuck... it's only a job.'

'Good boy.'

He ignored the '*good boy*' jibe. 'So, what did Ricky have to say, and why didn't he contact me with his findings? I'm the SIO. He should've rang me.'

'He will. I woke him at the crack of dawn. He'd only just got to bed.
He was waiting until a more respectable time to ring you. Don't be too hard on him when he finally gets around to ringing you.'

'Okay. So – what did he say to you?'

'He said that Pertwee died from rodenticide poisoning – exactly as those poor souls in the church. He said that the poison was in the wine he'd been drinking.'

'Exactly the same wine as at the church?'

She nodded. 'And, he concluded the time of death as being *before* the church deaths.'

Simon let out a slow whistle. 'That's interesting.'

'Very.'

'What do you make of it?'

She thought a moment before saying, 'Two possibilities... He poisoned the wine at the church, took a bottle for himself and committed Hari Kari, or - he was the first victim.'

'Or... here's a third option... he stole a bottle of wine from the church, and died by accident?'

'I guess that's also a possibility... accidental death... misadventure.'

'So... he was either the murderer and committed suicide, or he was an intended victim, or he just happened to grab the wrong bottle of wine and died accidentally?'

'That about sums it up.'

'How, on earth, will we suss out which one is correct?' He let his
frustration show.

'I haven't worked that out, yet.'

'It's not for *you* to work out. That's my job.'

'I want to help.'

'Well, you can't... not directly.

She tossed him a thin smile. 'I can be discreet.'

'How discreet?'

'You won't even know I'm doing anything.'

'And, what about Fredrickson and Scully?'

'Leave Fredrickson to me and, as for Scully, he won't have a clue.'

'We can't have parallel investigations running. That would be too messy.'

'I agree. I'll report directly to you. I'll keep you well and truly in the loop.'

'You can't report to me.' He was aghast. 'You're my superior officer.'

'No, I'm not. You're the SIO. You're the boss. I won't do anything
without running it past you first.'

He wasn't convinced. 'I don't know,' he said. 'I'm not sure it'll work.'

'It will, if you give me a couple of officers to help me, and to act as liaison.'

'What two officers? Scully would be onto them in a heartbeat.'

'The two PCs... the ones we spoke to earlier, and who alerted us to Pertwee.'

'Cox and Prince?'

She nodded. 'Scully won't notice two uniformed constables. They're too far below his sight-line, and too near the bottom of the food chain, to interest him. They'd be ideal. Do you think they'd be up to a bit of skulduggery?'

'Are you kidding? You're wonder woman. I'm sure they'd jump off Tower Bridge if you ordered them to.'

'It's settled then? You agree?'

He mulled it over. 'I'd have to bring Lovell into the loop.'

'Fine by me. Lovell won't balk at bending the rules a little.'

'No, but it puts her at risk.' The thought of Lovell getting into trouble bothered him, but – if he agreed to accept Lorrie's help – Lovell would have to know.

'You're taking this better than I thought you would,' she said. 'I
thought you'd argue a little bit more.'

'What would be the point? You always get your own way in the end.'

'I can't sit at my desk twiddling my thumbs, Simon. I'd go mental.'

'I know. I understand where you're coming from, but...'

She raised a hand and shook her head. 'I know the risks. I know I might end up being suspended - or, worse - sacked. But, Scully's in the wrong, and I'll be damned if I'll stand by and allow him to dictate any of my actions.' Her expression was fierce. 'Hell will freeze over before I give in to his harassment.'

Simon thought that she was magnificent when she was all riled up and righteous. 'What is it that you plan to do? We've got all the bases covered.'

'Not all of them,' she returned. 'Something's been niggling at me, and I want to pursue a couple of things that might, just might, pan out.'

'Do you care to explain?'

She nodded. 'Of course.'

She spent the next fifteen minutes explaining what it was that had grabbed her attention and spent the following half an hour outlining what she was going to do. By the end, Simon had relaxed enough to smile and give her his blessing.

Now, all he had to do was tell Lovell.

DAY THREE: AFTERNOON

Sue Prince was enjoying a cup of coffee and playing with her twelve-month old daughter, Lisa, when she received a call from Julie Cox. It was a few minutes after twelve, and she had another hour before she was due in at work, so was somewhat surprised that Julie was ringing her.

'What's up, partner,' she said into the phone.

'I'm not sure,' Julie replied. 'I've just had a call from DI Grant...'

'Acting Superintendent, Grant,' Sue corrected. 'He rang you? He *actually* rang you?'

'A couple of minutes ago. I got the fright of my life when I realised who it was.'

'What did he want?'

'To tell me to report to Superintendent Sullivan as soon as I arrive at work. I'm not to go near the major incident room or speak to anyone.'

'Sounds like you're in trouble, girl.'

'Oh, don't say that, Sue.' Julie's voice cracked. 'I *can't* be in trouble... I haven't done anything wrong.'

'Calm down... I'm pulling your leg. Of course, you're not in any trouble.'

'Then, what do you imagine she wants from me?'

'Beats me, but I wouldn't worry about it.'

'That's easy for you to say – you didn't get the summons.'

'Chill, girl.' The baby, Lisa, squealed in the background and Sue turned to check on her. 'I've got to go,' she said into the phone. 'Lisa is trying to stuff a bit of apple up her nose.'

'Okay... I'll see you later and give you the run-down on what Sullivan wants.'

'I might not see you,' she replied, reaching back to grab the apple from her daughter's sticky hands. 'I'm doing my FLO duty again this afternoon.'

'Well, I'll ring you.'

'Okay, speak later.'

Julie placed her mobile on the table and anxiously chewed on her bottom lip. It was all right for Sue to say that she shouldn't worry, but Sue had more of *a couldn't care less* attitude than she did. To receive a phone call directly from someone of Simon Grant's rank was worthy of worry. At the time, she didn't have the sense to ask him, straight out, what was going on. She wouldn't have quite worded it like that. She wouldn't have said, '*What's going on, sir?*' but she should have, at least, said *something*.

She decided to go into work early – believing it best to get whatever it was out of the way.

It usually took her twenty minutes to drive to New Scotland Yard at Victoria Embankment, and that would make her about forty minutes early. She could live with being early far better than she could live with pacing about the house wondering and worrying, so she grabbed her keys and headed out the door.

*

Sonia Lovell wanted to tell Simon that he was stark, raving mad. She wanted to tell him to start thinking for himself and stop allowing Sullivan to lead him around by the nose. The whole idea of the Superintendent sticking with the case, and working her own angle was – in her opinion – bonkers. Sullivan might not give a shit about her own job and her own career, but she should have more respect for Simon's. She shouldn't have embroiled him in her cooky plan to hoodwink Scully and stay active in the investigation, and it was on the tip of her tongue to tell Simon exactly that. But – and it was a whopper of a 'but' - she would do anything... *anything*... that Simon asked of her, and there he was, asking her to support his decision to allow Sullivan to chase down her hunch, so she really had no choice but to swallow down her objections and hope for the best.

As if thinking about Superintendent Sullivan conjured her up, Sonia saw her approach.

'Afternoon, Lovell.'

'Guv'.' Sonia avoided eye contact. She was afraid about what the
Super' would read in them.

'I'm assuming that Simon filled you in?'

'Yes, Guv'. He told me.'

Lorrie wasn't stupid. She realised that Lovell wasn't completely on board. 'You're not happy,' she said.

Sonia dragged in a breath. 'Can I speak freely?'

Lorrie nodded and braced herself.

'I'm not on with it, Guv'. You're taking too big a risk.'

'I understand…'

'No, Guv', I don't think that you do. DI Grant could get into a great deal of trouble. You're putting his job, his future, in jeopardy.'

'I won't let that happen. I can protect Simon. I'll fall on my sword, rather than see any of you get into trouble.'

Lovell was having none of it. 'Commander Scully will go after him. You know, he will.' She set her jaw and didn't flinch when Lorrie's eyes flashed with irritation. 'You said that I could speak freely. I'm speaking freely, Guv'. I don't agree with any of this.'

Lorrie let out an exasperated sigh. 'You need to have a little more faith in me,' she said. 'Surely, you know that I didn't do anything wrong with Father Young? You must know that I didn't bring about his death?'

Sonia nodded.

'And, you know that Commander Scully is just trying it on?'

Sonia sighed, and nodded once more.

'So… why should this investigation suffer because of his foolishness? All those children… all those families…. Jesus, Lovell, how can I simply walk away and watch you all struggle to find their killer?'

Sonia closed her eyes against the picture that Lorrie's words conjured up, but the images of the dead bodies couldn't be easily erased.

Lorrie pushed her advantage. 'We're nowhere near finding a lead on who did it. Every day that passes, we get further behind. What use am I sat behind a desk?'

The fact that the Super' was making an attempt to pull her onboard, was gratifying to Sonia. She might have been recently, if temporarily, promoted to Acting DI, but – if truth be told – she was an insignificant and lowly DS, and there was no reason for her to expect her opinion to matter so much.

She mulled it all over, and finally nodded her head – just one sharp nod, but it spoke of her acceptance.

'Thank you, Lovell,' Lorrie said on a sigh. 'I promise that I won't get you or Simon into any trouble.'

Sonia didn't necessarily believe that the Super' had the ability, or the power, to protect either Simon or her. Scully had marked her cards and he was cunning enough, and wily enough, to sniff her insubordination out. So, she had to simply trust that Scully would remain in the dark.

Lorrie wasn't as confident as she'd made out. She was under no allusions about the fact that she was not only jeopardising her own career, but Simon and Lovell's as well.

By the time that Lorrie got back to her office, PC Cox was already there, waiting in the corridor.

'You wanted to see me, ma'am?'

Lorrie looked at the young PC, and for a brief moment, she had no idea why, or even *if*, she'd asked to see her. She mentally shook herself, smiled and invited her to follow her into the office.

Cox was obviously anxious, and Lorrie put her at ease by pointing to a chair and asking her if she wanted a cup of coffee.

Flustered, Cox said, 'A cup of coffee, ma'am? I couldn't possibly...'

'Nonsense. I've got my own special machine... one that takes those little pods. There's all kinds of flavours - although I tend to stick with boring black with no sugar.' She walked to the far end of the room and picked up a box full of little plastic coffee pods. 'Let's see what we have... hazelnut, caramel, vanilla. There's even an Irish whisky one, but we won't try that.' She looked expectantly at Cox and raised an eyebrow. 'Well, what's it to be?'

'Em... vanilla, please.'

'Vanilla, it is.' She picked out the required pod and inserted it into the machine then placed a cup in the receptacle to catch the coffee.

'You're not in any trouble, Cox,' she said over her shoulder. 'So, you can take that terrified look off your face.'

'Yes, ma'am.'

'And, for fuck's sake, stop calling me ma'am. If you call me ma'am again, you and I will have a serious falling out.' She handed her the cup of coffee, ejected the used pod and replaced it with one of her choosing.

'I know some senior female police officers love being called ma'am... it makes them feel all superior... but I'm not one of them. My team address me as Guv'... and, you're one of my team now, so *Guv'* it must be.'

Cox sipped nervously at her coffee and nodded her understanding.

Lorrie sat behind her desk and contemplated how best to bring her on board. She didn't simply want her to follow orders. She wanted her to feel the buzz of excitement that comes with really wanting to do something risky, something that blurred the edges of propriety.

She decided that honesty was the best policy.

'I've been taken off the case,' she said. 'I'm supposed to put myself behind this desk until such time as I'm cleared of any wrongdoing in the death of Father Young. You know about Father Young?'

Cox nodded. 'I heard that he had a heart attack in one of the interview rooms.'

'Yes, well, it seems that the Bishop thinks I caused that heart attack, but it's all bullshit and I'm not prepared to just sit on my arse and let everyone else do all the work in figuring out who killed all those people.'

A silence descended between them and Lorrie thought that she was about to lose her. It was obvious that Cox was a straight arrow and was much too new at the game to contemplate bending the rules. She would have to draw her in another way.

'What do you know about me, Cox? What have you heard?'

Cox set her coffee cup on the desk, and Lorrie could see the struggle she was having in finding the right words of response.

'You can speak freely,' she assured her. 'I won't bite, and I won't take offence.'

'I've... I've heard only good things about you,' she said.

Lorrie smiled at that. 'That can't be true. Too many people hate the sight of me for that to be an accurate statement.'

'Not anyone I've spoken to, Guv'. You're well respected.'

Lorrie accepted that with a healthy pinch of salt, but it meant that Cox might trust her enough to be agreeable to working outside the lines.

'I'm ignoring the order to stand down,' she said, 'and I need your help.'

Cox gulped back in her throat. 'My help, with what? What can I do?'

'You can start by relaxing. I won't order you to *do* anything. I'll run a few things past you and, if you're willing, you can choose to help... or not. It will be up to you.'

'Okay.'

'The first thing is simple... just a little bit of research.'

'I can do that, Guv'.'

'And, the second thing...'

Cox shifted forward in her seat and looked at her expectantly.

Lorrie took a deep breath and said, 'I want you to come to France with me.'

*

Sue Prince was uncomfortable. She was alone in the house with Davidson. His mother had taken the baby out – she said for some fresh air, but Prince thought it was more to do with escaping her son's dour mood than for the need of fresh air - and his weird behaviour was making the hairs on the back of her neck stand up.

She couldn't quite put her finger on what it was about the man's demeanour that had red flags flying in her mind. He didn't say much – deciding not to answer her questions with any more than a nod or a grunt – and he feigned indifference whenever she showed sympathy for his loss. He kept himself busy on his laptop and, occasionally, Prince caught him staring at her with wide, dead eyes. What was most unnerving was that, when he saw that she'd noticed his stare, he didn't
look away. She was always the first to break eye contact.

Prince regretted the FLO training she'd volunteered for. She had never been cut out for the liaison role, and she had taken the first opportunity to transfer out. Now, because of that training and her short stint as an FLO, she was lumbered with babysitting Davidson. It was a responsible job – she didn't deny that – but it simply wasn't for her. She didn't mind subtly questioning victims' families, and collecting best evidence from them to help with the chronology of the crimes, but she couldn't resign herself to the responsibility for establishing and maintaining a good relationship with them. Their grief and shock was often too raw and too in your face for her liking and – although she sympathised, and although, at times she cried herself to sleep thinking about what they were going through, - she wasn't a hand-holding kind of girl. She much preferred the cut and thrust of everyday policing to drinking numerous cups of tea and handing out hankies.

She marvelled at the lack of tears in the Davidson household and, if either Davidson or his mother had been shocked by what had happened, it had very quickly worn off. It didn't feel like a house bereaved. It felt like something out of *The Twilight Zone*.

His hysterical grief on the steps at the church now seemed to her to have been fake. As she'd come to know him - albeit briefly - she'd realised that he didn't have an emotional bone in his body. There was nothing behind his eyes and, to her mind, he was an empty vessel.

She was just about to go and put the kettle on – again – when a loud hammering at the front door took them both by surprise.

Davidson made no move from his chair and it was up to Prince to make her way through from the lounge to answer it.

A uniformed PC stood on the doorstep. His face was flushed, and it was obvious that he'd been running.

'I've radioed for an ambulance,' he said. 'I've left PC Sanderson with her, but I knew who she was, so I came straight here.'

'Who? What?' Prince was totally bewildered. 'What are you talking about?'

'The woman. She's his mother.' He nodded over Prince's shoulder, and she turned to see Davidson hovering at her back.

'My mother?' he said. 'What about my mother?'

'She's been stabbed in the street. An ambulance is on its way.'

'Then, what the fuck are you doing here?' Prince snapped. 'You shouldn't have left the crime scene.'

The PC was nonplussed. 'I thought...'

'No, you obviously *didn't* think. You bloody idiot. Get back there... now.'

The hapless PC turned a deeper shade of crimson and turned on his heel to walk back up the path. He was stopped short by Prince's next words.

'What about the baby?' she called after him.

He turned, looked at her and shrugged. 'What baby?' he replied.

DAY THREE: EVENING

Seated around the table in the open-plan major incident room were Fredrickson, Lorrie, Simon, Lovell, Powell and Baxter. Standing in small groups around them was the entire squad, plus all the uniformed add-ons.

There was complete silence, except for a ringing phone somewhere further along the room.

Lorrie had spent the afternoon trying to persuade Fredrickson to allow her to follow-up on her hunch, and to authorise a trip to France for her and Cox. She wanted to interview the aid worker who'd had a fling with Mackie, but, he'd repeatedly refused her request and was on the brink of suspending her - just so he could get her to quit nagging him - when the call had come in.

'What were the two PCs thinking?' Lovell asked, breaking the silence. 'I mean... for fuck's sake.'

Lorrie glanced over to where Prince stood with Cox and said, 'Good job Prince had the sense to go to the scene from Davidson's house, and corral the witnesses to the stabbing, or fuck knows where we'd be. One stupid PC left the scene and the other one did nothing to secure the body, look for the child, or stop people from walking away. What sort of training are officers getting these days?' She didn't expect an answer and didn't get one.

Fredrickson sighed and stood up. He was still in pain from his operation and still a little unsteady on his feet.

'Let's get a move on, shall we?' He moved away from the table, walked towards the media screen and gestured for everyone to gather round.

'Right, everyone.' He paused to take a deep breath. 'We have a twelve-week old baby missing, and granny on a slab in the morgue. Cause of death ... a stab wound to the throat. We have multiple witnesses who, so far, have told us jack shit.' He turned to Simon. 'What else?'

'We're not treating the murder and the baby's abduction as related to what happened in the church.' When he noted the disbelieving glances being thrown around the room, he held up his hands and shook his head. 'I know what you're all thinking - too much of a coincidence - but nothing points to the cases being connected. That said...' he dropped his hands, 'we're going to work it. The murder and the abduction are ours.'

He nodded to Lovell, who reached for the remote and switched on the screen. A CCTV image immediately appeared.

'This is the view from the camera outside the newsagents on the street where the murder took place.' Everyone's eyes were riveted on the screen. 'The two PCs are emerging from the shop, when they notice an altercation taking place a few yards away.'

Maxine Davidson was clearly visible on the screen. The baby was being wheeled away in his buggy by a man in a hoodie, and Maxine was struggling with a second man, trying desperately to break free from his hold to follow the retreating buggy.

'The two PCs are just standing there,' DS Powell commented. 'Can't they see how distressed she is?'

There were head shakes all around. No one could quite believe what they were seeing.

The suddenness of the knife appearing, and the spurt of blood from the woman's throat, caused a wave of shocked gasps.

Lovell pressed the remote a second time, and a second image appeared.

'This camera caught the murderer running up Richmond Street behind the other man and the buggy,' Simon continued. 'No faces, I'm afraid.'

'They look young,' Lorrie said. 'Fit.'

Lovell brought a third image up.

'You'll see we lost them when they entered the park, and CCTV doesn't pick them up again.' Simon looked at Fredrickson. 'Nothing more, Guv'.'

Simon eyed Prince. 'PC Prince?'

Sue Prince felt every eye on her. 'Yes, sir?'

'Well done on your management of the crime scene.'

'Thank you, sir.'

'You spoke to a few people as soon as you arrived?'

'Not immediately, sir. I had to push the crowd back. There were about a dozen or so rubber-neckers at the scene, and I could hear the sirens in the distance. I was worried that the paramedics wouldn't get through, and I was worried about the scene being contaminated. I lost count of the number of people who'd trampled through Maxine... Mrs Davidson's blood.'

'And, the two other PCs?'

Prince was reluctant to make any complaint about her fellow officers, but her anger at their stupidity overruled her feelings of loyalty.

'Nerves got the better of them, sir. I asked one of them to take Mr Davidson back to his house. He'd followed me to the scene and was in rather a hysterical state over his baby being missing.' She paused a beat. 'I asked the other PC to start taking down names and addresses of any witnesses to the attack... just in case people started wandering away.'

'Very good.'

Prince dropped her eyes, embarrassed at the attention. 'I took a few preliminary statements from the witnesses. I waited until the paramedics, and our emergency response team, had arrived, and then I just made myself useful asking people what they'd seen. Then, you arrived, sir.'

'Well, thanks to you, we have four eye-witnesses who saw the whole thing, and two of them gave matching descriptions of the assailant.' He turned his attention back to the room. 'None of the witnesses made any reference to the man running off with the buggy. It was as if he was invisible.'

Lorrie hadn't been listening. She was perturbed. 'Put that first image back up,' she instructed Lovell. 'The image of the stabbing.' She waited the few seconds it took for the screen to once more show Maxine struggling with the assailant and – just as the knife plunged into the woman's throat - Lorrie called out, 'Freeze it just there.'

Everyone's eyes were glued to the screen. Freeze-framed, the image of the knife stabbing into the woman's throat was even more horrific.

'What do you see?' Fredrickson asked, confused.

'It's what I *don't* see,' she replied, smiling. 'I don't see any gloves.'

'So?' Simon looked from the screen to Lorrie and then back to the screen.

'So?' Lorrie sighed with frustration. 'I thought I'd taught you better
than that. What do no gloves mean?' She turned to the room. 'Anyone?'

'Fingerprints,' Cox piped up. 'Fingerprints on the murder weapon, Guv'.'

'But, we don't *have* the knife,' Simon put in. 'We did a fingertip search of the road, the park, the cul-de-sac where they took off in the car, and... no knife.'

Lorrie smiled once more. 'Where did they come from... those two thugs?'

'What are you getting at?' Fredrickson interjected.

'Well, they came from *somewhere*, didn't they?'

'Of course, but...' Realisation dawned, and Simon suddenly returned her smile. 'We need to widen the CCTV search... try and track them *onto* Richmond Street – before the attack.'

'We know where they parked the car, but, we don't know if they went through the park to *get* to Richmond Street... just that they went through it later with the baby. Let's see if we can pick them up from the first camera on...' She thought a moment. 'Okay, there are cameras on Booker and Saltwells, but they would go along Saltwells if they were heading for Richmond. There's CCTV on Puller Street, just off Saltwells and a camera outside the pub on Calswell Street. Let's start there. If we're lucky, we'll spot them heading on foot from Saltwells to Calswell to Richmond and – if we're luckier, still – we might see them deposit some DNA or a fingerprint along the way.'

It was a long-shot, but Lorrie had a good feeling about it. 'Right,' she said, 'On with other business. We've brought

Davidson in. We'll be putting the description and a photo-fit of the assailant to him in a few moments, meantime a picture of the baby is going out across all media platforms. Unfortunately, Mr Davidson can't remember what the baby was wearing, but PC Prince thinks he had on a blue knitted cardigan and a matching hat.'

'I'm not a hundred percent on that,' Prince piped in.

Lorrie acknowledged her admission with a curt nod then continued, 'To re-cap... as you all already know, the search of the park led to us finding the buggy outside one of the rear exits. *That* exit leads on to a small cul-de-sac and, we believe, the baby was transferred to a vehicle in that cul-de-sac. There's no CCTV until Booker Road on the one side and Saltwells Road on the other, so we have no idea of the make, model or colour of the vehicle, and we have no idea what direction they took.'

'Any fingerprints on the buggy?' Powell asked.

'Loads,' Lorrie returned. 'We're working on them, but there are too many smudged prints, and I'm not hopeful.'

'Superintendent Sullivan will be leading on the search for the baby and the two men,' Fredrickson put in. 'As was said... we're not jumping to the conclusion that the two crimes are connected and, although the Super' isn't working the church crime, her familiarity with it will ensure any sudden, unexpected links are seen right away.'

'PC Prince,' Lorrie said. 'You will sit in on my interview with Davidson.' She turned her eyes on Lovell. 'Your promotion to acting DI still stands, but you'll be working with me.'

Lovell looked across to Simon for confirmation and, on his subtle nod, turned back to Lorrie. 'Yes, Guv'. What's your instructions?'

'The CCTV, of course. Put Baxter and one of the techies onto it. Then, liaise with forensics. Re-interview the witnesses and get out to all those shops on the street where the murder took place, and check for any other CCTV sources. Question the shopkeepers, the shoppers, and anyone else, who just happened to be walking up the road.'

'We still have a great deal of work to do on the church murders,' Simon said. 'Those of you who continue to work on that with me need to keep their eyes on *that* ball and not get distracted. 'We're going to follow-up on a French lead.' He gave Fredrickson and then Lorrie a look before continuing, 'DS Powell and PC Cox will be jetting off to France to question an aid worker who knew Father Mackie quite intimately. Meantime, we're trying to source the rodenticide used to poison the congregation, and we're also following up on the histories of all the people who died.'

'That's all,' Fredrickson said. 'Heads down and shoulders to the grindstone... and, good luck.'

*

'What's your take on Davidson?' Lorrie asked Prince. She'd asked
her before, but now her opinion of the man was crucial to how the interview with him would be planned.

'I'm not sure, Guv'. He's a pretty closed book.'

'What does your gut say?'

'My gut?'

Lorrie had to remember that, these days, young officers hadn't much of a clue as to how to work their guts. Their training was more science driven, more structured and depended on observations that had nothing to do with how something or someone made them instinctively feel.

'You must have an opinion of him, Prince.'

'I guess so. To be honest... he gives me the creeps.'

'Oh, how so?'

There was a moment of silence whilst Prince tried to collect her thoughts. She didn't want to say anything that could be construed as unprofessional, and yet, all her thoughts on Davidson could only be expressed in a manner that was, frankly, improper.

'Just spit it out,' Lorrie ordered. 'No need for subtlety.'

'Okay, well... I suppose it's his eyes.'

'What about his eyes?' Lorrie settled herself back in her chair.

'They're dead, Guv'.' Prince blushed at the absurdity of her words. She was going to blow her chance to work with the Super if she wasn't careful. 'I mean – they don't have any expression, not even when he's weeping and wailing. He goes through all the motions of shock and grief, but...'

'His eyes are dead?'

Prince nodded. 'I'd catch him staring at me... when I was in the room with him.' She shuddered involuntarily. 'He wouldn't say anything – just stare – and I swear I could see evil at the back of those eyes.'

Lorrie digested that. 'What was his relationship like with his mother?'

Prince didn't need to think too hard before saying, 'I think he hated her, but he was glad she was there to look after the baby.'

'What was he like with the baby?'

'Cold. That's the only word for it. I don't think I ever saw him even hold him, or feed him... not after that first time at the church. Then, he clung to him and didn't want to let him go. Afterwards, he completely ignored him.'

'What about the dead wife?'

'Maxine didn't like her... Mrs Davidson, I mean. I picked up on that from day one from something she said. I didn't get the opportunity to ask her about it...I meant to.'

'Did you have a chance to have a snoop around the house?'

Prince nodded. 'Nothing out of the ordinary. They were a middle-class couple with nice things. The baby had a beautiful nursery.'

'*Has*, Prince... the baby *has* a beautiful nursery.'

'Of course. Sorry, Guv'.' She blushed once more and dropped her eyes.

Lorrie sighed. She needed something more – something tangible to take into the upcoming interview with Davidson.

'Did the mother usually take the baby out for a walk when you were there?' she asked.

'No, that was the first time. I got the impression that they'd had a falling out - Maxine and Davidson. You could cut the atmosphere with a knife when I got there.'

'Any report from the FLO who'd been there in the morning?'

She shook her head. 'Just a wry smile as she escaped through the door.'

'Any visitors to the house? Anyone calling to give their condolences?'

'Not a single one, Guv'.... Not when I was there.'

'Okay, we'll need to talk to the other FLO, but first... Davidson. Let's get that photo-fit under his nose.'

Lorrie stood and led the way from the office to the interview room. Outside the door, she hesitated and turned to face Prince.

'I want you to take the lead. Show him the photo-fit and ask him whatever questions pop into your head. The questions don't matter... I just want to get a good look at how he responds to you.'

Prince swallowed down on her anxiety and entered the room ahead of Lorrie.

Davidson immediately jumped to his feet, saying, 'Have you found him? Have you found my baby?'

Lorrie realised that Prince was right about his eyes. Although his body language was spot-on - for a worried, anxious father - the expression in his eyes betrayed him. He wasn't worried, and he certainly wasn't terrified at the thought of what could be happening to his infant son. The fact that both his wife and his mother had been murdered didn't seem to have penetrated his psyche, but Lorrie was still inclined to give him the benefit of the doubt.

'Well... have you found him?' he asked once more.

'Not yet, Mr. Davidson, but we're doing everything we can,' Prince replied, taking a seat at the table. 'Why don't you sit down, and I can show you this picture of the man who attacked your mother? We're hoping the face might ring a bell with you.'

Davidson reluctantly re-took his seat. 'I don't know who attacked her,' he said, glancing across to where Lorrie stood just inside the door. 'But, show me the picture.'

Prince opened a folder and extracted an A4 sized piece of paper. She laid it flat on the table and waited until his eyes briefly scanned it.

'Do you recognise him?' she asked kindly. 'I know the image is a bit rough, but do you see the mole on his cheek? It's pretty distinctive, don't you think?'

Davidson's eyes flicked across the picture a second time, and he shook his head. 'I don't know him, and I don't know why you think that I might.'

'We have to ask, sir. If there's even the smallest possibility that you might recognise him...'

'I understand, but – no - I don't know him.'

'Could I ask you to look again... take a longer look at it?' She pushed the paper forward an inch. 'A witness puts him at just under six feet in height, and she caught a glimpse of blonde hair under the hoodie.'

She tapped the picture with her forefinger and the motion brought Davidson's eyes back to it. He obliged her by a five second examination of the picture, and then shook his head and leaned back in his chair.

'Okay, that's perfectly okay.' Prince left the picture where it was and closed the folder. 'Can I get you a cup of tea?' she asked. 'I know you've been here a few hours and are probably gagging for a drink.'

'I've had tea, thanks,' he replied. 'I'd much rather go home and pour myself a stiff whisky.'

'Yes, I can understand that, sir. You've been through a lot… far more than I could ever cope with. A stiff whisky would be welcome, I'm sure.' She thought carefully before asking her next question. She felt the Super's eyes on her and she wanted to do a good job.

'Have you any idea why someone would want to kill your mother and abduct your baby? I mean, it's quite *something*, isn't it … to do such a thing in broad daylight?'

'I don't know *what* to think,' he replied. 'Just as I don't know what to think about my wife being murdered in that church alongside dozens of others.' He threw his head back and glared at Lorrie. 'Just what are you doing about *that*, Superintendent?' He turned back to Prince. 'She should be out looking for my wife's killer, and searching for my baby, instead of skulking in here with you.'

Prince ignored his outburst. 'Your mother didn't like your wife, did she Mr Davidson?'

Lorrie held her breath. Prince had stepped it up a notch, and she hoped that she hadn't blown it by getting to that touchy subject too soon.

'What the fuck is that supposed to mean?' His anger at the question was absurdly dramatic. 'My mother loved her.'

Prince shook her head. 'Not according to what she said to me.'

Davidson frowned, and for the first time, Lorrie saw something in his eyes. It was fear. Prince saw it and decided to gild the lily. 'We had a chat about your wife, and I'll tell you, Mister Davidson, your mother wasn't very complimentary about her.'

It was as if all of his defences suddenly came tumbling down. He began to perspire and both Lorrie and Prince saw the slight tremor in his hands. It was a small victory for Prince and she had to suffocate the smile before it gave her elation away.

'What did she say? What did my mother tell you?' Davidson's voice was shrill with fear. 'Tell me,' he cried.

Prince wasn't ready to answer him. She wasn't experienced in interview techniques, but she'd watched enough cop shows to have picked up enough know-how to reel in the likes of Davidson.

Ignoring his demands, she said, 'You'd been arguing with your mother before I got there. That's why she went out with the baby. What had you been arguing about?'

It took him a few seconds to register the fact that she'd changed the subject. His unchecked emotion was beginning to be his undoing and he began to hyperventilate.

'Take it easy,' Prince soothed. 'Calm down.' She reached out a hand and placed it on top of his. 'I have to ask you these questions. It doesn't mean anything. Just be honest – like you promised – and everything will be okay.'

He nodded and hauled in a breath.

She waited a minute, until he got his breathing under control, then asked again, 'What did you and your mother argue about?' She asked it quietly, kindly, and kept her hand on his.

'We weren't arguing.' The fear was still evident in his eyes, but there was also a look of resignation. 'She was just worried about me... thought I wasn't coping. You know what mothers are like – fuss, fuss, fuss.'

Prince didn't believe him. 'Did you get impatient with her?'

'Who... my mother?' He shook his head. 'Never.'

'Never?' Prince recalled an incident the day before. 'What about yesterday?'

'What about it?'

'The baby was crying, and your mother was busy in the kitchen. She wanted you to go to him and you lost your temper with her.'

'Rubbish. You're making that up. I don't *ever* recall an instance when I lost my temper with my mother. She was a saint.' He huffed in another deep breath. 'We didn't argue, and I never raised my voice to her.'

Prince let it go. She knew that he was lying, but what she didn't know was why.

'Are you sure that you don't know this man?' She moved her hand and picked up the photo-fit. 'Anything, at all, familiar about him?' She held the picture out and urged him to take hold of it.

He accepted it and stared at the image. 'No,' he said, placing it back on the table. 'I wish I could say that I *did* recognise him, but I don't. You're wasting precious time asking me about that bloody picture. How many times do you need to hear the words... *I don't fucking recognise him...* before it sinks in?'

'He killed your mother, Mister Davidson. He, and his accomplice snatched your baby. We're desperate to put a name to this man.' She took the picture from his hand and placed it back in the folder. 'If you can't help us, then we're no further forward in our investigation. I thought that you wanted to help us? Was I wrong in that assumption?'

He shook his head and glared across the table at her.

Prince knew that she had hit a brick wall. She was out of questions, and out of options, and she didn't feel it was appropriate to press him. She felt such a failure. Davidson was a liar, and he was definitely hiding something, but she neither had the skill nor the experience to nail him.

She shifted in her seat and turned her head slightly so as to catch Lorrie's eye.

Lorrie gave a small nod of her head. It was time to end the interview. She'd seen and heard all that she needed to – for the moment.

DAY THREE: NIGHT

It was unusual for Commander Scully to be anywhere but in bed at eleven o'clock at night. For him to be hovering outside the major incident room so late meant that something was up.

Fredrickson spied him, dragged in an impatient breath, and made his way over to where he stood.

'Can I help you with something, sir?' he asked.

Scully cut his eyes at him and pursed his lips. 'That would be a first, Fredrickson,' he said, with more than a hint of sarcasm. 'But, I appreciate the offer.'

Fredrickson waited as Scully contemplated his next words. That he was perturbed, Fredrickson could quite clearly see, but he wasn't about to make it easy for him. If he had something that he wanted to get off his chest, then he wasn't about to offer any encouragement.

Before Fredrickson moved from Manchester to work in London, he'd heard many a tale about the Commander. He had a reputation for being a slimy son-of-a-bitch, but Fredrickson always made his own mind up about people. Gossip neither interested nor titillated him, and – more often than not – the person being gossiped about tended to be a much better human being than people gave them credit for.

Not so, Commander Scully.

Fredrickson neither liked nor respected him. The fact that he made Lorrie's life and job so difficult, was the main reason – but not the only one. He found the fat little fuck an utter disgrace to the uniform. His total disregard for the rules of the game, and his manipulative, power-hungry personality – which bordered on the psychopathic – was what really got up his nose. Lately, his feelings for the man had verged on hatred. Nevertheless, he was his superior officer and – unless he wanted his marching orders – he had to at least feign a tolerance, and an obedient demeanour... regardless of how much it made him want to vomit.

'There's a press conference planned for tomorrow morning,' the Commander finally said. 'I'm only just getting around to mentioning it to you because I've been trying to postpone it... with no luck.'

Fredrickson drew his brows together in confusion. 'Why would you want to postpone it, sir? I'm surprised that the press office hasn't pulled one together before now. We usually get straight on the telly when there's a child missing.'

'Yes... yes, I know that.'

'Then...?'

'Sullivan... Fucking Sullivan, and her hard-on for the priest.'

'One has nothing to do with the other. The dead priest certainly didn't murder Maxine Davidson and snatch the baby.'

'Don't be obtuse, Fredrickson. *You* might think that the church business, and the missing baby aren't connected, and I might agree, but... Sullivan?'

Fredrickson was at a loss. He had no clue what the Commander was going on about. What had the press conference, the priest and the missing baby have to do with whether, or not, the conference was called?

'I don't understand,' he said. 'I don't know your reasoning for wanting to postpone it.'

Scully scowled and sighed. The mixed expression made him appear almost maniacal. 'Because, the AC wants Sullivan to be there to make a statement about the missing baby and – knowing her – she won't be able to help herself from bringing up any links to that other thing, and her stupid, unfounded belief that Father Mackie was somehow involved in the murder of the congregation.' His expression took on a furious look. 'I can't trust her, Fredrickson. She's a loose cannon.'

'There are *no* links. Sullivan knows that and, anyway, she wouldn't mention Mackie without some proof to back up her hunch. She's not stupid... and, she's not a *loose cannon*.'

Scully puffed out his fat cheeks and thought for a moment. If it was anyone else but Sullivan, he knew that he would be able to accept Fredrickson's reassurance that she wouldn't go all rogue on them and divulge her interest in Mackie to the press... links or no links between the cases. He had contemplated simply allowing her to hang herself, but he couldn't calculate the damage she would do - if she started with her wild accusations.

'No, she's not stupid – I agree with you there – but she has a mouth on her that she can't control, and a holier-than-thou attitude that makes her believe she's always in the right. This business with father Young is a perfect example.'

'How so, sir? I believe that the complaint the Bishop made will prove to be unfounded.' He gave Scully a knowing look. 'After all, sir, she was only doing her job and, by all accounts, was doing it by the book.'

'She caused that heart attack, Fredrickson. As usual, she went at him with her typical *I'm right and you're wrong* attitude and tried to ram that home to him in a way that was both aggressive and – as it turned out – dangerous. She could see that he wasn't well, but she just *had* to verbally batter him, until he collapsed dead on the floor.'

'I've seen the tape,' Fredrickson said. 'She was forceful, yes, but I wouldn't say that she was aggressive, and there was no way she could've known that he was ill.'

'Trust you to be in her corner. She always *could* wrap men around her little finger.'

Fredrickson felt his face colour. Scully was well and truly out of order and – superior officer or not – he had a good mind to punch the fat fuck on the nose.

Scully immediately realised that he'd gone too far. 'Look,' he said, 'I didn't mean that the way it sounded. You're loyal to your team, and I respect that. Your loyalty includes trying to protect Sullivan, but you have to realise that she'll end up bringing you down with her.'

'I fail to see...'

Scully flapped a hand in his face. 'Spare me,' he said. 'Spare me your blustering denials. Ever since you got here, you've been protecting her. Okay... Okay,' he conceded. 'I was out of order in implying you've got the hots for her, but – you must admit – she's a fucking liability?'

'I don't see her that way, sir.' Fredrickson was doing a heroic job of keeping his temper in check. 'She's an excellent officer.'

Scully refused to take the bait. He knew that he was flogging a dead horse, and that Fredrickson was too far gone to listen to reason. 'Well, anyway, the press conference is all set.'

Fredrickson waited for him to say more and, when he didn't, asked,

'What is it that you want from me?' He continued to succeed in keeping the anger from his voice. 'If the AC wants the press conference to go ahead, and she insists on Sullivan fronting it... which is the right thing because, after all, she *is* the lead on the Davidson woman's murder and the missing baby... then that's what will happen. Any concerns that you have about her shooting her mouth off about the church murders, and her interest in Mackie are ridiculous... sir.'

Scully's mouth worked. He would like nothing better than to use his tongue to put the upstart in his place, but he knew that he needed him. Sullivan would listen to him, where she wouldn't listen to anyone else, and Scully had to trust that Fredrickson could be used to effectively gag her. The man was a fool, if he thought that his precious Sullivan wouldn't take the opportunity to get her views on Mackie out there for the world to hear and – if she did that – the Bishop would have his guts for garters.

'Your faith in her is commendable,' he said – feigning sincerity – 'but mine is a little tarnished where she is concerned. I need your assurance that you'll speak to her - put her on notice – and get her word that she'll stick to the Davidson woman's, murder and the missing baby, and not deviate from the statement I'm having prepared for her.'

It was obvious that Scully really didn't know Lorrie, Fredrickson mused. The Commander had formed an opinion of her, that painted her as an irresponsible maverick, and the idiot simply didn't realise just how wrong he was. Fredrickson knew that Lorrie's main priority was finding the missing baby and nothing – not even her continued interest in Mackie and her fervent belief that he was somehow involved in his congregation's murders – would detract her from her mission of finding the child. She would know just how important the press conference was, and would never dream of sabotaging her own case, and further endangering the child – just for the pleasure of sticking it to Scully.

'I'll have a word with her and get you the assurance you need,' he said. 'But, for the record, you're wrong about Sullivan, and one day you'll come to regret your treatment of her.'

Scully chose to take that moment to walk away. Although he had plenty more to say, he had enough sense to realise that Fredrickson was too enamoured of the blonde floozy, with *the come to bed eyes*, to listen to him. He was beginning to think that he was the only man immune to her particular brand of wanton manipulation. Well, one day, he would have her... and the thought of that was the only thing concerning her that gave him a hard-on.

Fredrickson watched him waddle up the corridor and felt himself deflate. His defence of Sullivan had certainly made an enemy of the Commander and, although he wasn't worried about it, he silently bemoaned the fact that his allegiance to her was going to cost him. If she would only learn to play the game, then she would have the likes of Scully eating out of the palm of her hand. She was good – damned good – and Scully would like nothing more than to ride on the coattails of her successes, but she didn't have the sense to spread a little honey instead of vinegar and, until she learned the psychology of managing someone with Scully's ego, she would continue to fall foul of his mean temper and his attempts to sabotage her.

He would have to go looking for her and impress on her the importance of sticking to Scully's script. He had to make her realise that she was skating on some very thin ice, and that she couldn't depend on either the AC or himself to save her.

He found her in her office with Lovell. They were going through the witness statements and were too engrossed to notice him standing in the open doorway.

He took the opportunity to study her and felt the now familiar feeling of hopelessness overwhelm him. It was then – at that exact moment – that he decided, when both cases were closed, to go back to Manchester. He needed to distance himself from her – but not for the reasons Scully gave. He had no fear that she would destroy his career, as hers went down in flames, because she would outmanoeuvre Scully. Despite his fears that she would end up losing a long-term battle with the Commander, he realised that she was quite formidable in her own way and would probably survive – even if it was by the skin of her teeth. No, she would outrun and outplay Scully at his own game - just as she always did - and her future at the Met' would remain bright... at least, he hoped so.

No, he had to distance himself from her because he ran the risk of making a complete and absolute fool of himself. His emotions were all over the place. He believed that he was falling in love with her, and that was dangerous as he knew that she would never return that love. She was still mourning Kelly and he could never compete with his memory. Anyway, he told himself, he was the complete antithesis of that big, broad, handsome man, and there was no way Lorrie Sullivan would settle for someone like him.

Lorrie raised her head and caught sight of him. Her smile almost brought him to his knees.

'You need something?' she asked.

He shook his head. 'No, carry on. I'll come back later, when you're not so busy.'

Obviously distracted, she gave him an absent nod and returned to her work with Lovell. Fredrickson looked at her for a few seconds and noted her total obliviousness to his presence. She was busy - and he thought that he really shouldn't read into her dismissal of him that he was invisible to her - but, apart from his role as her superior officer, he *really was* invisible.

Lorrie could see him hovering in her peripheral vision. He wanted something from her – she fully realised that – and she felt heart-sick. Not for the first time, she wished that she had been born ugly. Her looks were nothing more than a red flag to the men that orbited her world, and Fredrickson's puppy-dog eyes put her at a loss.

She liked him. She respected him, and she didn't know how she would've coped without him. He had virtually parachuted into her life when she was at an all-time low, and, over many months, had saved her bacon on more than one occasion. Apart from Simon, he was the only man she trusted and – if it wasn't for the fact that she was terrified out of her wits about losing yet another loved one – she might have contemplated seeing how deep his feelings for her ran. But – being someone who couldn't help but be brutally honest with herself – she knew that she had nothing to offer him. Her heart belonged to Sean Kelly. He might be dead, but her heart still beat to the rhythm of his memory.

She saw him leave and sighed with relief. She knew that she would have to say something to him – put him straight – but, the thought of what she might say, and how he might react, made her feel physically sick.

'He's gone,' Lovell said.

'What?' Lorrie didn't quite understand what Lovell meant.

'The Chief Super'... he's gone.'

'Oh? Yes, I see that.' She lifted her eyes to Lovell and saw the knowing look in their depths.

'I think that he has a thing for you. I think... I think that you could hurt him quite badly.'

Lovell had never overstepped the mark before, and Lorrie was intrigued – rather than angry – at her obvious disregard for protocol. She didn't quite know how to respond and finally said, 'I don't want anyone to get hurt on my account. I don't invite anyone's attention.'

'I know, but I can see that the attention comes, nevertheless. The Chief Super' is different, though.'

'Oh, how so?' Lorrie stopped what she was doing and gave Lovell
her full attention.

Lovell shrugged. 'I'm not sure. Sorry... I shouldn't have said anything.'

'No... No... I want to hear what you have to say.' Lorrie wasn't sure that was true. 'Go on.'

'Well, he kind of wears his heart on his sleeve, and I really think that his feelings aren't simply those of sexual attraction. He's quite soft around the edges and doesn't come across as a man with experience of women.'

'That's...' Lorrie couldn't think of the right words and screwed her eyes up in thought. 'That's either very astute, or very insulting.'

'I don't mean to imply any insult. He reminds me of the DI in lots of ways.'

'Simon? Fredrickson reminds you of Simon?'

'In certain ways, yes. Simon is always getting hurt by women. His ex-wife broke his heart and took him to the cleaners, despite him loving her very much. She wasn't the right woman for him... none of the women he falls for are ever right for him... and I don't think, you're the right woman for Chief Superintendent Fredrickson. He's fallen for you... in much the same way that Simon falls for certain women... and it'll end in tears for the Chief Super'... in the same way that it does for Simon.'

Lorrie smiled to herself. Lovell's feelings for Simon were an open secret. 'Does Fredrickson's feelings for me, and my reticence, mirror you and Simon's relationship? Is that why you're paying so much attention to what – frankly – is none of your business?'

Lovell blushed furiously and dipped her chin to her chest. She wasn't surprised that Lorrie knew about her feelings for Simon. *Everyone bloody-well knew,* and a sudden sense of utter mortification threatened to choke her.

'You feel sorry for Fredrickson, because you see your situation reflected in him.' It was a statement and not a question. 'You think I'll hurt him because that's precisely what Simon is doing to you... hurting you.'

Lovell shrugged, not trusting herself to utter another word.

'Anyway... it's all a load of rubbish. Fredrickson is nothing like Simon. I don't get why you've made such a ridiculous comparison.'

Still, Lovell said nothing. If the Super' wished to ignore the similarities, then that was her prerogative.

'You're comparing apples with oranges.' Lorrie knew that she was beginning to protest too much, but she couldn't help herself. 'You're mistaken. Surely, you know that, Lovell?'

Okay, Lovell thought, time to be honest. 'The worse thing is everyone feeling sorry for me... and Simon pretending that he doesn't know how much I love him.' She lifted her eyes. 'You can't do that to the Chief Super'. He'll dangle like a puppet with loose strings and live in hopeful misery... just as I do... and it's fucking hellish.' She dropped her eyes once more. 'Sorry. I'm sorry. I'm speaking out of turn.'

Lorrie was lost for words. She couldn't ever remember a time when she'd sat with another woman discussing affairs of the heart. It wasn't in her nature to chat about such things and, despite feeling uncomfortable, she couldn't let Lovell's words go without saying anything further. She felt sorry for her. She knew what it was like to live through years of unrequited love. She'd suffered much the same with Sean. He had a wife, of course, so it was a slightly different scenario, but the pain was the same.

'He thinks a great deal of you,' she said. 'Simon... He respects you.'

'That's comforting.' Lovell closed her eyes and dragged in a huge sigh. She didn't know what had possessed her to cleave open her heart and talk to the Super' so candidly. It was seeing Fredrickson's forlorn, dejected, yet achingly hopeful face, that had spurred her on. It was exactly the same expression she imagined was on her own face every time she was with Simon.

'Why do you stick around?' Lorrie asked. 'You could get a transfer out anytime you wanted. Why put yourself through it?'

'I love my job,' she replied. 'I love working with him and...'

'And?'

'He needs me.'

Lorrie thought about that for a moment. 'Yes,' she said. 'I believe that he *does* need you. You make him special.'

'Oh?'

'You know exactly what I mean, Lovell. Don't get me wrong... Simon is quite brilliant, but you elevate him *beyond* brilliance.'

'I wouldn't go that far, Guv'.' She blushed once more – despite her best efforts not to.

'*I would*,' Lorrie returned. 'You bring out the best in him. You're so damned good at your job, and you make him dig deep and surpass himself.'

Lovell accepted her words with a brief nod. She only wished that Simon realised how much more she could do for him. If she elevated him to do miraculous things in the job, just imagine what she could do for him if they were lovers.

'You have to leave him, Lovell. You have to give him a chance to experience life without you. Let him miss you. Let him feel what it's like to not have you. I think you'd be surprised at just how quickly he would run after you.'

She shook her head. 'I couldn't bear to never see him again. I'd much rather have *this* relationship, rather than no relationship at all.'

She turned her attention back to the computer screen. As far as she was concerned, the conversation was at an end. She'd said far too much – given too much of herself – and it was time to move on before she ended up saying something that would expose the true extent of her agony.

Lorrie watched in silence as Lovell tried to concentrate on the CCTV images on the computer screen. She felt for the other woman and, in a moment of complete clarity, she finally saw the pain she would ultimately cause Fredrickson.

'Sorry, what did you say?' Lorrie leaned forward. Lovell had spoken, and she'd been too engrossed in her own thoughts to pick up her words.

'I said that I've got nothing, so far, from the cameras off Saltwells, but I think that I might have found something on the CCTV from the off-licence. It's from two days before Maxine's murder.'

'You went back two days?'

'I went back a week, and I got lucky.' She turned the screen, so Lorrie could see the image. 'Look what I found.'

'That's Davidson,' Lorrie said.

'And, I believe he's talking to the man in the hoodie who stabbed his mother.'

'Jesus.'

'Exactly.'

DAY FOUR: MORNING

As Lorrie climbed from her car, and walked across to New Scotland Yard, the morning sun was warm on her face. Its unforgiving rays exposed her dry, patchy complexion and highlighted the worry lines around her eyes. Sleep had been allusive, and she arrived at work with no more than two hours of rest under her belt.

They had been unable to confirm that the hooded man talking to Davidson on the CCTV was, in fact, the murderer. Everything about the image had screamed that it was, indeed, him, but – without a clear image of the man's face – they were forced to concede that they might be wrong.

There was nothing else to whet either her or Lovell's appetite, or to persuade them to stay at work beyond midnight, so she had gone home and spent the night tossing and turning and praying to a God she no longer believed in to allow her a pitiful four or five hours of sleep.

Fuelled by numerous cups of coffee, she'd gone through everything in her mind and drew blank after blank. The search of the park had elicited no trace evidence and no murder weapon. She had no idea of their identities, or the make and model of their getaway car, and, so far, CCTV was worse than useless.

Was Maxine Davidson a random victim, and the baby simply unlucky, she wondered? Then, why kill her, she asked herself over and over again? She wasn't a threat to them. There was no way that she could have overpowered them or hurt them. There was no real way – without help – for her to save the baby, so, perhaps she recognised them and had to die to maintain their anonymity?

She had wracked her brain trying to come up with a motive that wasn't related to some evil perversion on the part of the abductors and, try as she might, she could not find anything to link the murder and abduction with the horror at the church. That was no surprise. They didn't have the slightest inclination of a motive for the church, and – without that – finding a link was nigh on impossible. The fact that she wasn't supposed to be looking for a link was, to her mind, neither here nor there.

There was nothing else for it – she would have to start bringing in all the perverts on the sex offenders' register and grill them on both sides until they felt well and truly roasted. If one of them had the baby, then, God help the little mite.

She reached the main door and used her fob to gain entry. Her heels clacked on the floor as she made her way across to the lift and the sound made her head bang. A migraine was evidently seeding itself in her brain and – with the morning she was about to have – it was almost the straw that would ultimately – before the day was out - break her back.

Fredrickson had rung her an hour before – just as she'd stepped out of the shower - to warn her about the press conference and, the thought of placing herself in front of the cameras – with the way she looked and felt, and considering the fact that she had little or nothing to tell the press – was enough to make her stomach roil and make her head bang all the more.

The telephone conversation with Fredrickson had been a little on the strange side. He'd hinted that Scully was nervous about her taking the press conference, and she didn't quite understand what it was he was trying to insinuate. Scully was always nervous about one thing or another and – where *she* was concerned – that nervousness tended to turn him into a Rottweiler. She couldn't care less about the Commander's nerves, and she made that clear to Fredrickson, and, in the end – exhaustion making her irritable – she had used a couple of expletives that she wasn't proud of and then hung up the phone.

She used the time it took to ascend to her floor to run through the order of the morning in her mind. She planned to speak to Davidson later. He would be at the press conference to make an appeal to the public and she'd grab him afterwards and question him about his image on the CCTV. If he could identify the man he spoke to, then it would be *something*. Perhaps it would lead nowhere, but *something* was better than *nothing*.

She would get Lovell rounding up the perverts for questioning and she would get Prince hunting down any and all known friends and contacts of Maxine Davidson. Then, there was Davidson's dead wife – the mother of the abducted baby.

There *had* to be a link, she told herself for the thousandth time. *There had to be.*

Lorrie stepped from the lift and was immediately accosted by Lovell. 'Morning, Guv',' she said breathlessly. 'I didn't mean to pounce on you, but Davidson is here.'

'So? He's here for the press conference. No need for excitement, Lovell.'

'The press conference?' Lovell was nonplussed. 'There's a press conference?'

Lorrie marched along the corridor with Lovell trotting behind her. Over her shoulder, she said, 'The Chief Super' rang me about it earlier. Davidson is going to do an appeal to the public.'

'But, he wants to speak to you,' Lovell said. 'He's insisting on it.'

That halted Lorrie in her tracks. 'Where is he?'

'I put him in one of the interview rooms. He's been there an hour.'

Lorrie was distracted for a moment. Davidson's insistence on speaking to her had thrown her and she needed a minute or two to clear her head.

'I'll see him after I've had a cup of coffee,' she said, continuing the journey to her office. 'Is he on his own in the interview room?'

Lovell nodded.

'Is PC Prince about?'

Lovell nodded a second time.

'Well, get her to take him a cup of tea and ask her to sit with him.'

Once seated behind her desk with a coffee cup in her hand, Lorrie contemplated her options. She could go in all confrontational and knock him off balance before he started spouting any lies he might have concocted, or – and she was beginning to favour this second option – she could go easy on him, hang on his every word, and lull him into a false sense of security.

Her thoughts gave her a start and she rocked back in her chair in shock. In her eyes, Davidson was a bit of a weirdo – and she thought that he might have information that he was keeping to himself – but, she had never consciously considered him a suspect in either the church crime, the murder of his mother or the abduction of his son. So, why was she contemplating interviewing him as if he *was* a suspect?

Prince had done a brilliant job on him the day before, and he'd shown that he was guilty of something, but she hadn't seriously considered him a suspect.

She stood up and placed her coffee cup on the desk. The hairs on the back of her neck were standing to attention and, the more she thought about Davidson, the more she became convinced that he was actually guilty of something. *But, what*? There was only one way to find out, and she left her office in pursuit of the answer to that question.

He hadn't touched his cup of tea and Lorrie noticed the skin already forming on its surface.

'Your tea's getting cold,' she said. 'Shall I get PC Prince to fetch you a fresh one?'

He shook his head. 'I can't stomach it. I can't keep anything down.'

'Oh? Is it a recurrence of that problem you had a few days ago?'

'What?' he was genuinely confused by her question.

'Your dicky tummy,' she returned. 'The dicky tummy that kept you from the church on Sunday.'

His eyes seemed to glaze over, and he shook his head. 'I didn't have a *dicky tummy*... as you put it. I lied.' He clasped his hands in front of him on the table and bowed his head over them. 'There was nothing wrong with me.'

Lorrie took her time seating herself opposite him. Her mind was racing and question after question popped into her head, only to be discarded before they reached her lips. She decided on silence and gestured for Prince to remain quiet.

Seconds, and then minutes, passed and the silence wasn't broken until an animal-like wail emanated from deep within Davidson's throat.

Lorrie forced herself not to react. Let him weep and wail, she thought to herself. Let him get it all out, and then she would be ready for him.

It took longer than she'd anticipated but, finally, he lifted his head, wiped the snot from his nose on the sleeve of his jacket, and began to talk.

'I was screwing the neighbour,' he said. 'Georgina Collins... She lives two doors up. She's married. I couldn't say anything. I couldn't tell you.'

Lorrie urged him on with a nod.

'I'm not a church-goer, but my wife insisted I go to the service because Father Mackie was going to speak. I'd already arranged to meet Georgina, so I had to come up with an excuse not to go.'

'Why are you telling us this now, Mister Davidson?' Lorrie kept her tone neutral. 'Why now?'

He shrugged. 'I don't know. If Georgina's husband finds out, he'll knock ten buckets of shit out of her, but I wanted to tell you anyway. I don't want to hide anything from you. I want you to find my son and I don't want to lie to you.'

'Well, we appreciate honesty and, better late than never.' There was now an element of reproof in Lorrie's voice. 'Now, perhaps you can tell us about the man you were speaking to outside the off-licence a couple of days before your mother was murdered.'

His stunned expression was almost comical. 'You... You know about that?' he spluttered. 'How?'

'You were caught on camera. We've been looking at every CCTV image of the road where your mother was killed.' She raised an eyebrow. 'Well, what about it, Mister Davidson?'

He swallowed deep in his throat and said, 'He wasn't anybody... just someone I know.'

'His name?'

'Anthony.'

'Does he have a surname?'

He shrugged. 'I'm not one hundred percent sure.'

Prince could sense the Super's impatience and she threw Davidson a *come-on* look - which he ignored by closing his eyes and leaning back in his chair.

'Open your eyes and look at me,' Lorrie said irritably.

To make a point of not being at her beck and call, Davidson kept his eyes closed for long seconds before opening them and staring up at the ceiling. 'I don't know what his surname is. I just know him as Anthony,' he said.

'Well, this *Anthony* looks a lot like the person who stabbed your mother, so you had better think long and hard about the answer to my next question.'

He lowered his eyes and turned his head slightly to look directly at her. 'I came here to tell you about Georgina. I didn't want to lie any more, but you're treating me as if you think I know something. Well, I know nothing. *I'm* the victim here.'

'Your wife is the victim, Mister Davidson. Your mother is the victim.'

'Anthony didn't stab my mother,' he said. 'Ask all the questions you want, but that fact won't change.'

'You seem so sure. Why is that?'

'I just know.' He set his face. 'You're wasting your time with him.'

Lorrie captured his eyes and held on. 'Where can we find him? Take your time... think about it a moment. Show me that you were serious about not wanting to hide anything.'

He took her up on her offer to think and didn't immediately respond.

Lorrie waited him out and, finally, heard him say, 'The community Centre on Almond Close. He's usually there around lunch time. I can't swear that he'll be there today, but...'

'Thank you.' She let out a relieved breath. 'That wasn't so hard, was it?' She crossed her arms. 'Tell me... how do you know him?'

'I don't... not really.'

'But, you know him well enough to categorically state that he had nothing to do with the stabbing of your mother and the abduction of your baby?' She was incredulous. 'Forgive me, if I find that hard to believe.' She turned to Prince. 'Do you believe him, PC Prince?'

'No, Guv'.'

She turned back to Davidson. 'Even PC Prince doesn't believe you.'

'I can't help that… it's the truth.'

A knock at the door cut off Lorrie's next words and she swore under her breath.

Prince opened the door to DS Baxter.

'The press conference is about to start, Guv'. Everyone's waiting.'

She felt like saying *fuck the press conference*, but Davidson was already on his feet and, anyway, what choice did she have but to jump through the media hoops in an effort to get the public's eyes and ears on the missing baby?

She allowed Davidson to precede her through the door and, with Prince taking up the rear, they walked in single file behind Baxter to the conference room.

The large room was packed with journalists, television cameras and a smattering of uniformed police officers. Scully and Fredrickson were already seated at the long table at the top of the room and Lorrie saw the two seats reserved for her and Davidson.

Seated, she adjusted the table-top microphone and waited until the noise in the room abated.

She waited until the room settled down and then said into the cameras, 'I want to make a brief statement to the public at large and then you will hear an appeal from Mister Davidson. I would appreciate it if the journalists in the room left any questions until the end.' She cleared her throat. 'Yesterday – Tuesday the twenty-second of June, at fourteen-twenty-two, Maxine Davidson, forty-nine years old, was stabbed by an unidentified male on Richmond Street. She was returning home from a walk with her twelve-week old grandson when she was attacked and stabbed in the throat. She died at the scene. A second unidentified man was seen leaving the scene pushing the baby in his buggy and he was soon followed by Maxine's assailant. We have not located the baby and we ask that members of the public keep their eyes and ears peeled for any sightings.'

For the benefit of the cameras, she held up a photograph of the baby and a picture of the identical make and model of the buggy. 'These pictures will be circulated to the press directly. We also have a photo-fit picture of the man who stabbed Mrs. Davidson, as well as CCTV images of the unidentified males. If anyone knows of a baby suddenly appearing in the house next door, or the house across the street – or if anyone believes they may have seen this baby or this buggy – please get in touch. The telephone number is at the bottom of the screen.' She dragged in a breath. 'I must stress that these men are dangerous, and no one should approach them.'

One journalist – ignoring the request to leave questions until after Davidson made his appeal – fired out – 'Has this incident anything to do with the atrocity at the church on Sunday?'

Scully shifted uneasily in his seat and turned anxious eyes on Lorrie.

'No,' she said, 'and, please don't speculate.' She turned to Davidson, adjusted his microphone and nodded for him to speak.'

He looked a pitiful sight beneath the glare of the lights and it looked as if he would be too overcome to speak.

Lights flashed as dozens of cameras grabbed his image and the room fell deathly silent.

Lorrie gave his arm a reassuring squeeze and forced herself to give him a smile of encouragement.

'My baby,' he began, 'he's only twelve weeks old. He's already lost
his mother and his grand-mother, and he can't lose me too. He needs to be with me, so... please, please, please give him back to me.' He paused to wipe a hand across his eyes. 'Please,' he went on, 'please don't hurt him. He's been through enough. If the people who have him are the ones who poisoned everyone in the church... and, I think that's *exactly* who you are...' He ignored the noisy stirring of the crowd and brushed off Lorrie's now restraining hand and stood up. 'You've killed enough of my family. You took my wife and my mother, and I won't let you take my baby.' His voice rose. 'The police haven't a clue. I'm being made the scapegoat. All I want is my baby back. I've done nothing wrong. I just want my baby back.'

Scully jumped to his feet and glowered at Lorrie before turning to the media. 'That's all,' he called out above the barrage of questions being fired at Davidson. 'This press conference is over.'

DAY FOUR: AFTERNOON

Prince couldn't believe that she'd been stuck with babysitting Davidson *again*. The Super' had gone with Lovell to the community centre to find the Anthony character and she had been left with strict instructions to watch Davidson like a hawk and take note of anything he said.

He hadn't said a word. Since being deposited back in the interview room, he had clammed up as tight as a drum. She'd spent the first few moments attempting to get him to chat, but he studiously ignored her. Apparently, Davidson believed that everything that was worth saying had already been said, but Prince knew that not to be true. She was the one person on the team who knew him best – although she had to admit that she could probably list everything she knew about him on the back of a postage stamp – but she was determined to eke at least one new piece of information from between his clamped lips.

She forced herself to relax. Many times, since she had become a police officer, she'd found herself in a situation where nerves of steel and patience were the only tools necessary to get the job done. Faced with violent criminals, distraught victims, and the chaos of a rowdy pub on a Saturday night, she'd learned the hard way not to simply wade in believing she could control the situation or manipulate the people involved into doing what she wanted.

She was proud of her previous questioning of him. A full night's reflection had brought her to the conclusion that she'd actually done a decent job and it had pleased her no end that the Super' found no fault with her method or technique. It made a difference – the Super' looking at her with admiration – and, pumped up with the Super's praise, she decided to do whatever it took to ensure a second helping.

Her tone was pleasant, her manner laidback, as she said, 'I get why you were seeing your neighbour.' He looked at her and she saw a questioning look in his eyes and, emboldened by that look, went on, 'I mean – your wife had just had a baby and sex was probably not her top priority. She would have been tired and grumpy and would have, most certainly, been neglecting you.'

He dropped his eyes and shrugged, but still remained silent.

Prince knew that she was onto a way of cracking his silence. He'd said something earlier. He'd said, *'I'm the victim here'*, and *that* statement gave her an 'in.'

'I know that it didn't mean you didn't love her... your wife. Sex is different from love. You could have sex with your neighbour, and still love your wife.'

She was gratified when she saw him nod. She had laid the foundation, and now she had to build up his trust in her brick by brick.

'Everything would've worked out okay. The baby would have begun to sleep through the night and your wife would have regained her libido. She would've wanted you again, and you would've dumped the neighbour with no harm done. But...' She sighed and shook her head. 'Life's a bitch and she was taken from you before you could make it up to her. You must be in so much pain right now.'

He nodded once more, and she could see that he was really listening to her. She pondered the wisdom of stroking his ego and making the cheating bastard into a saint, but – as far as she was concerned – all was fair in the hunt for his mother's killer and the baby's abductors.

'When I was at home with you, I could see just how much you'd suffered since the church. You found her... found all those bodies... and no one has so much as acknowledged how devastating that was for you. I could see how traumatised you were and, for what it's worth, I'm sorry I wasn't kinder to you.'

He looked up sharply and they stared at one another for long moments. 'Thank you,' he said. 'I know you were just doing your job.'

She nodded her acknowledgement of his words. 'Yesterday, when I interviewed you, my boss was watching me... testing me. I know that I came on a little strong. I wanted to impress her.'

'I'm sure that she was impressed.'

'Not so you'd notice,' she returned. 'She likes to take the credit for everything.'

Davidson appeared to be weighing everything up in his mind. 'Is she off looking for Anthony?'

'I'm not sure. She doesn't confide in me,' she lied. 'But, probably.'

'It was *you* who did the work on me admitting I knew his name... not her. Why aren't you involved in looking for him? That doesn't seem fair.'

She shrugged and dropped her eyes to hide her satisfaction at how well the conversation with him was going.

'I'm just a PC,' she said. 'I'm just the dogsbody.'

'Good enough to be left to babysit me?'

'Yes.' She forced a smile onto her face. 'It's about all she trusts me with.'

He threw her a sly look. 'How would you like to get one over on her?'

'Hell would freeze over before *anyone* got one over on Superintendent Sullivan, but...'

'But, what?'

'*You* managed it... at the press conference. Did you see her face when you came out with all that about you being made a scapegoat?'

He grinned, and, for the first time, Prince saw life in his eyes. Wary that she might go too far and shut him down, she said, 'I feel bad, talking about her like this. Can we change the subject?'

'I like talking about her. Where's the harm?'

No, she thought – *you like talking about yourself.* 'I just wanted you to know that I understand how it feels to be put down, but I'm being disrespectful about my superior officer and – no matter how badly she's treated you – I can't talk about her anymore.'

'What if I tell you something that will knock her socks off?'

Keeping her voce free from any hint of enthusiasm, and repressing any interest in what he said, she replied, 'I've given up trying to impress her, and you shouldn't say any more. I don't want to get you into trouble... not on my account.' Then, on a bright note – 'How about a cup of coffee? I promise to avoid the despicable mud that comes out of the machine in the lobby and make a proper cup for both of us. How about it?'

'Sure.'

He seemed to deflate before her eyes and she thought that she'd blown it. She almost back-tracked – and fed him another line to get him back on the hook – but thought better of it. He wasn't a fool and, if she continued feeding him disgruntled statements about the Super', he would get suspicious.

'I'll be right back,' she said, standing up. 'And, Mister Davidson?'

'Yes?' he looked at her expectantly.

'Try not to worry. Superintendent Sullivan may be many things – and I can't say that I like her very much – but she's good at her job. She'll find your baby.'

Out in the corridor, Prince leaned back against the wall and the full weight of her behaviour made her knees buckle. She thought that she was on the verge of a full-blown panic attack and had to ruthlessly will herself not to pass out.

She had no experience to speak of. She wasn't a detective and had no right playing mind-games with a man who wasn't a suspect, wasn't dangerous and was – first and foremost – a grieving husband and a terrified father. So... *what the fuck*?

'Prince?' PC Cox hurried over to her. 'Are you all right?'

Prince blinked away the black spots dancing across her eyes, dragged herself up the wall, and took several quick breaths.

'You look as if you're ready to faint.'

'No. I'm fine. I just came over a little light-headed.'

Unconvinced, Cox took her arm and led her over to a chair. 'Sit down and catch your breath. I'll fetch you a glass of water.'

Cox returned mere seconds later and Prince sipped at the cool water gratefully.

Cox pulled over a chair and sat down beside her. 'Are you going to tell me what's going on?'

Prince shook her head. 'Nothing. I've been sitting in there with Davidson and it all got a bit claustrophobic.'

Cox gave her a wry smile. 'You expect me to believe that?'

Prince returned her smile. 'I guess not.'

'Did he say something to upset you?'

'No.'

'What, then?'

She contemplated lying. She didn't want to look like a fool in Cox's eyes. Instead, she told her the truth.

'Let me get this straight,' Cox said, after a moment's contemplation. 'You've been attempting to gain Davidson's trust by bad-mouthing the Super' in hopes of getting him to say... what, exactly?'

Prince shrugged. 'Something... anything.'

'You honestly think that he's got *anything* to say? You think that
he's hiding something?'

'I don't know. I really don't know.'

'Well,' Cox stood up. 'What if he *is* hiding something? What if your little game with him succeeds in nothing more than alerting him and interfering with the Super's strategy? What, then?'

'I don't think that I've alerted him to anything,' Prince returned defensively. 'He's beginning to trust me.'

'Well, that's all right, then.'

'No need to be so sarcastic.'

'Sorry.' Cox sat back down. 'Just... Just, be careful.'

*

The community centre was a few bricks away from being wholly dilapidated and stood testament to the local youths' artistic exuberance by being completely covered in graffiti.

'Nice neighbourhood,' Lovell said, wiping her hands down her trouser leg after turning the handle on the door. 'I bet all the good and the great from the criminal fraternity spent their days here, learning their trade.'

Lorrie glanced at her, smiled - acknowledging that she was most probably right - then turned and eyed the group of teenagers morosely watching their entrance into the building. She noted that they were all wearing hoodies. *They should be in school*, she thought, and made a mental note to ask the drug-squad to do a sweep of the place.

The noise blasted them as soon as they entered the building. Music blared, voices squealed, doors banged, and the very walls seemed to reverberate as the hellish din bounced off them.

Lorrie wasn't surprised when – on catching sight of her and Lovell - the occupants of the building – mostly boys and young men - stopped in their tracks and, subsequently, the noise started to abate.

'I like it when I have this effect on people,' Lorrie said, marching up to the only person she spied who looked like he might actually work there.

'You, sir,' she said, heading straight for him. 'I want a word.'

'You talking to me?'

'My God, it's like something from *Goodfellows*,' Lovell said under her breath.

Lorrie sidestepped a suspicious looking puddle on the floor. 'I'm looking for Anthony,' she said.

'I don't know any Anthony,' he returned.

'Really? Everyone knows at least *one* Anthony.'

He cut her a look and shook his head. 'Not me... sorry.'

Lorrie moved close and stood virtually under his chin – invading as much of his personal space as she could get away with. 'And, who might *you* be?'

He took a step back in an attempt to regain his space. 'Who's asking?'

'I asked first.' She matched his step and remained close.

The man shifted his eyes to take in his audience. He knew that she was *filth* and that he would lose face if he accommodated her too readily. Openly co-operating with *the filth* was strictly prohibited in the world he lived and worked in and – if he wanted to maintain his relationship with those he tried to help on a day to day basis – he had to demonstrate his contempt for the police.

Lorrie completely understood his predicament. She had the feeling that – if she allowed him to save face – he might... just might... eventually co-operate and point this Anthony character out to her.

'I could arrest you,' she said. 'On obstructing a police investigation.'

He let out a great bellow of a laugh. 'You could try, but I don't think you'd be stupid enough to attempt it.'

A couple of the hooded onlookers took a threatening step towards Lorrie and Lovell had to step forward to block their progress. They dwarfed her, but she stood her ground and, thankfully, they backed off.

Lorrie contemplated her options. The atmosphere in the corridor was thick with menace and she realised that there was no way she could manipulate the situation to her advantage. It was a *catch-22*. The man would never give up Anthony – not whilst he had so many eyes and ears on him – and Lorrie had no leverage.

Lovell came to her rescue. Removing her mobile phone from her pocket, she brought up a number and allowed her finger to be seen to hover over the connect button. She said, 'Guv', I'm concerned that there are drugs on the premises and I'd like your permission to get the drug squad out here with sniffer dogs.'

A subtle shift occurred in the stance of every one of the people in the corridor. Suddenly, they all discovered somewhere they'd much rather be and, within a matter of seconds, the corridor emptied.

The man let out a sigh of relief. 'Clever,' he said.

Lovell shrugged and put the phone back in her pocket.

'Time to give me your name,' Lorrie insisted.

'John Butler,' he said. 'Sorry about all that posturing, but...'

Lorrie flapped a hand. 'I understand. No need to explain.'

'It takes a lot of effort to get any trust around here,' he put in. 'Best if you leave before I'm dobbed a rat.'

'What about Anthony?'

'I know two. Neither are here today.'

'You know where I might find them?'

He shook his head. 'Your guess would be as good as mine.'

'What about surnames?'

'No, sorry. Surnames aren't usually given.'

'Can you give me anything?'

He shrugged. 'You could try the flats on the Beckingsdale Estate. There's a set of abandoned lock-ups where a few of our regulars hang out.'

'Okay. Thanks.' It was all she was going to get, so she gestured to Lovell to move off and they both left the building – ignoring the surly and hostile stares of the youths - and exited into the fresh air with a sense of exaggerated relief.

*

'I'm afraid that you'll have to repeat that, Mister Davidson.' PC Prince really believed that she had misheard or misunderstood what had just popped out of his mouth.

He nodded keenly – eager to say it again. 'My wife... the wife I loved to distraction... was screwing the priest.' He seemed to revel in the shock his words caused, and added, 'Been going on for weeks. My mother knew... everyone fucking knew... but, I only got to find out after she was dead.'

Prince tried to disguise her shock and hide the realisation that he had just given her the perfect motive for murder.

DAY FOUR: EVENING

The trip to the Beckingsdale Estate was uneventful and a total waste of time. Finding the lock-ups proved to be more difficult than anticipated and, when they eventually stumbled upon them, there was no sign of Anthony or anyone else.

Lorrie climbed into the car, sighed and rubbed her temples. She had a monster of a headache that four painkillers had failed to shift.

'What, now, Guv'?'

'Fucked if I know,' Lorrie replied bluntly, starting the car. 'Stake out this place, I suppose.'

There was silence in the car, the silence only broken by the quiet murmur of the car's engine ticking over. Then, Lorrie said, 'Davidson knows more than he's letting on. He knows who this Anthony character is and I'm going to wring it out of him.' She put the car in gear, released the handbrake, and moved off. 'I'm not convinced by a single fucking word that man says.'

'It's hard to read someone who's grieving and terrified at the same time. Perhaps...'

She was interrupted by Lorrie's mobile going off. Lorrie ignored it and allowed it to go to voicemail.

'You were saying?'

Lovell's eyes had caught the number on the mobile's screen and said, 'That was the Chief Super'. Do you want me to ring him back?'

'No.' Lorrie shook her head. 'Just listen to his message.'

*

Fredrickson threw his phone down and limped from the desk to the door. He was worried that he'd torn his stitches and had hoped to be heading off home before too long. PC Prince's revelation had knocked that notion on the head and he was more than a little pissed that Lorrie hadn't picked up on his call.

He leaned out the door and bellowed down the corridor for Prince, and his bad mood lifted, somewhat, when the young PC came scampering towards him. At least someone had enough respect to come running when he called.

'Yes, sir?' she said breathlessly.

'Get him a lawyer,' he said. 'And, read him his rights. I don't want him uttering another word until we get all our 't's' crossed and 'i's' dotted. He'll be interviewed under caution when the superintendent gets back.'

If she gets back, Fredrickson muttered under his breath. He hadn't a clue where she was, and Lovell was on the missing list as well. There were procedures - rules about not going off without telling anyone where you were headed – and he knew that he was going to have to put his foot down and insist that everyone toed the line in future.

Lorrie should have known better, he ruminated. She'd lost good officers – his niece and Sean Kelly were two perfect examples – to situations where no one had a Scooby where they were. Well, he hoped that the message he'd left on her mobile would be the beginning of her re-education. He was getting sick of her attitude. Or, maybe it was just that he was in pain and utterly exhausted by it? He suddenly wished that he hadn't been quite so derogatory in his message. He usually shied away from direct criticism – especially *angry* criticism, that was neither constructive nor helpful – but, where Lorrie was concerned, he was losing the plot a little.

He hoped that she was on her way back from wherever it was she'd put herself all afternoon. He'd thought about instructing Simon to interview Davidson - because it now seemed likely that he had something to do with the deaths at the church - but the priority was the missing baby. There was nothing to be done for the dead – except to get them justice – but the baby was another matter. Lorrie could use Davidson's admission about his wife's supposed affair to squeeze every drop of information from him before he let Simon loose on him... if she ever got back, of course.

But, he cautioned himself, it could all be rubbish. The wife had only given birth a few months ago and – if she was like almost every other new mother – an affair would be the last thing on her mind, but that didn't mean that Davidson didn't *believe* in the affair, and took steps to punish everyone involved, or who he believed were complicit. From what he'd learned about Father Mackie, an affair with a parishioner wasn't out of the question and, from what little Prince had gleaned from Davidson, his wife suffered a bout of post-natal depression after the birth, so was vulnerable to a predator like Mackie.

It was all such a fucking mess. The days were slipping by far too quickly - without a damned thing to show for hours upon hours of investigation, and, this thing with Davidson, could very well turn out to be a red herring that pulled them completely in the wrong direction. But, they couldn't afford to ignore a single thing. They had absolutely *nothing* and, therefore, any lead – no matter how ridiculous or tenuous – had to be explored.

It didn't help that Scully was being hammered by the press and had been making a nuisance of himself all afternoon. He wanted answers, and he wanted them fast. Dissatisfied with Fredrickson's attempts to reassure him, he'd stomped around, barking insults and putting everyone off their stride, and it had taken a phone call from the Assistant Commissioner before the Commander skulked off to find someone else to verbally abuse.

Fredrickson was forced to sit down. He felt sick to his stomach and the pain around the key-hole surgical sites were sending jolts of sharp pain all the way to his teeth. He was hot, and a thin sheen of perspiration had erupted all over his body. It would be his damned luck to come down with an infection, and maybe even sepsis and, as he closed his eyes against that unhappy thought, Lorrie walked into the office.

'You look like shit,' she said. 'I guess your condition is all the excuse you need for leaving me that insulting voicemail message?'

He opened his eyes and immediately took in her indignant stance and ferocious expression. 'Sorry,' he said.

'Apology accepted.' Her features softened, and she walked over and placed the back of a cool hand on his forehead. 'You're hot.'

'No kidding?' he returned dryly.

'You're also a certifiable imbecile.' She removed a bottle of water from her bag and handed it to him. 'Drink that.'

He accepted the bottle, unscrewed the cap, and chugged at the water. He didn't care that it was warm.

'I noticed Powell and Cox... I thought they'd be on their way to France by now.'

'Change of plans... They're not going.'

'Oh?'

He swallowed the last of the water and aimed the empty plastic bottle at the bin by the door. It missed by a mile.

'The aid worker is on her way to South Sudan,' he said. 'But, Simon managed to speak to her on the phone before she left.'

'And?' Lorrie made an impatient flapping gesture. 'What did she say about Mackie?'

'Nothing good,' he returned. He pulled himself to his feet – meaning to go over and pick up the discarded bottle and place in in the bin – but his legs betrayed him, and he flopped back into the chair with a moan.

Lorrie shook her head and grimaced. 'I'll drive you home and put you to bed. If you're no better after a good night's sleep, I'll fetch the doctor.'

'You can't,' he said. 'You have to interview Davidson under caution. He's been here the whole day, and his solicitor is screaming blue murder.'

'He has a solicitor now?'

'He said some things. You'd know all about it, if you hadn't gone off the grid.'

Lorrie stared for a beat, her eyes firing invisible bullets of indignation, before dropping her gaze and dragging in a calming breath.

Fredrickson kept his eyes locked on her. 'I'm sorry for the unprofessional tone of my voicemail, but I'm not sorry for being pissed at you. No one knew where you were. That's unacceptable.'

Lorrie offered a quiet 'Hm...hm,' then changed the subject back to Davidson. 'What did he say that warranted a solicitor being brought into the mix?'

Fredrickson told her and was not surprised by the subsequent look of shock on her face.

'I'm not sure that I believe him... about the wife and Mackie,' he added. 'Although, according to the aid worker, the good Father – if given half a chance - would fuck anything that moved.'

'You think that gives Davidson a motive?'

Fredrickson shrugged, and the movement elicited a grunt of pain. 'I have reservations. I could accept him killing Mackie... and, even the wife... but everyone in the church?' He gave a small shake of his head. 'I'm not convinced.'

'Well, we'll see.' She took out her mobile and brought up a number.

'Lovell?' she said into the phone. 'I need you to do me a favour.'

*

With Fredrickson bundled into Lovell's car and heading home, and after a quick de-brief with Simon, Lorrie joined PC Prince in the interview room with Davidson and his solicitor.

The aroma of stale sweat, and sour coffee assailed her as she stepped into the room. She was not surprised to see a wrung-out Davidson draped across the table. He'd been in the room for over ten hours and it was no wonder his solicitor had been complaining.

On hearing her enter, Davidson lifted his head and leaned back in his chair. The first words out of his mouth were, 'I didn't kill her. I know how it must seem... but, I didn't kill her.'

DAY FOUR: NIGHT

Lovell walked Fredrickson across to the armchair next to the electric fire and grimaced at his obvious pain. During the car journey, from New Scotland Yard to his apartment, he hadn't uttered a single word to her, and the only sound that he made was the occasional moan when she navigated over a couple of potholes in the road.

She helped him off with his jacket and settled him back against a soft cushion. He closed his eyes and thanked her.

'Do you want me to call a doctor?'

He shook his head. 'I'll be okay when I've sat a moment.'

'Can I take a look?'

'A look?' He opened his eyes and stared up at her.

'At what's causing you so much pain.'

'I don't think that's necessary but... thank you all the same.'

Lovell pursed her lips, annoyed at his attempt at macho nonchalance, and reached down to pull his shirt free of the waistband of his trousers.

'What the hell are you doing?' Fredrickson attempted to slap her hand away. 'Get off.'

She ignored him and yanked up his shirt.

'That looks a little too angry,' she said, eying the bright red colouring around his stiches. 'You've not torn anything, but there might be an infection brewing.'

'Do you have medical training that I'm unaware of?' The pain and embarrassment were making him extremely irritable. 'If not, please keep your opinions to yourself.'

If Lovell had been a tiny bit thin-skinned, or if she wasn't used to people having a pop at her, she would have stepped back, left him to his own devices, and skulked back to her car. But, Lovell was made of sterner stuff than that.

'I'll make you a hot drink. Do you have any paracetamol?'

He wanted to apologise. He wanted to take back his boorish remarks, but he didn't have the energy. Instead, he mustered a quick nod of his head and said, 'In my inside jacket pocket.'

With two painkillers, and a hot cup of sweet tea inside him, he felt better. Lovell had hung around long enough to see him swallow the tablets and drink the tea and, now, she was off back to base, leaving him alone to contemplate how the hell he was going to make it to the bedroom.

He decided to remain in the chair and, exhausted, fell asleep within minutes of Lovell leaving.

*

Conscious of the recent incident of Father Young's heart attack, Lorrie took no chances with Davidson. So, when he began hyperventilating and suffering heart palpitations, she terminated the interview and called the police surgeon.

She instructed Prince and Lovell to go home and retired to her office to think. She couldn't recall a single incidence where she had been so flummoxed by a case. Even the Reaper and the Clown cases hadn't left her feeling so bereft... so devoid of even the slightest notion of where to look for clues.

'Shit,' she hissed under her breath. 'Shit, shit, shit.' Everything was going to hell in a handcart. Every muscle in her body was tense with anxiety and the fear of failure tasted like vomit in the back of her throat.

She glanced up at the door and noticed Simon hovering. Simon wasn't a hoverer, so she was immediately intrigued by his unusual demeanour.

'What?' The word came out sounding like a bark and she immediately regretted her tone. 'Sorry... long night. Come in, Simon.'

He stepped through the door and hesitated before closing it. Lorrie eyed him carefully and noted the slight hunch in his shoulders and the worry lines around his eyes. He looked as if he was carrying the weight of the world on his back.

'You look how I feel,' she said.

'I was just thinking...' he began. 'I was just thinking that maybe the Chief Super' got it wrong.'

'Got *what* wrong?'

He shrugged. 'Me.'

'You? What the fuck, Simon?'

Simon gave her a helpless look. He knew that she would never understand. It would probably be a total waste of time mentioning anything to her, but he *had* to tell her... he simply *had* to.

A lightbulb went off in Lorrie's head and she chewed on her bottom lip in an effort to stave off the words that had rushed to her tongue. She knew that her words could damage him and – to her mind – he looked damaged enough already. She waited for him to speak. She would leave it up to him to lead the conversation.

'Can I sit down?' he asked.

'Yes, of course.'

His body seemed to fold in on itself as he took a seat. He kept his head bent and Lorrie's anxiety increased tenfold when she saw him wrap his arms around his chest, as if to give himself comfort and support.

He took a breath and then let it go slowly. He swallowed hard and raised his head so that he was looking directly across the desk at her.

'I can't do it,' he said. 'You have to tell Fredrickson that I can't do it.'

Lorrie looked around the room, her eyes darting everywhere. She had to give herself a minute to think.

'Please, Guv''... I'm not cut out for this.'

She nodded, obviously uncomfortable, and finally made eye contact with him.

'I can understand why you might think that, Simon. I think that... about myself... every single day.'

'But...'

She held up a hand and stopped him. 'Just listen, for a minute,' she said soothingly. 'I just want you to listen.'

'Okay.'

Her gut instincts told her that Simon was deadly serious. He was undergoing a crisis of confidence and, because the case involved more than a dozen dead children and dozens of murdered adults, he was terrified of cocking up the investigation and she knew that he fervently believed that he would fail in the most humiliating and extraordinary manner. She knew all of that because it wasn't an alien concept to her. She had been honest with him – when she said that she felt like that every day – and, yet, she struggled on, and so must he.

But, how to convince him of that?

'You're an excellent leader,' she said. 'All you're being asked to do is lead a brilliant team towards the clues and towards the exciting moments when all the pieces of the puzzle fall into place. You're an excellent strategist,' she went on – ignoring his attempt to interrupt. 'You think outside of the box and you're creative and instinctual at the same time.'

She allowed him to speak and, he said, 'I'm getting nowhere. I can't think straight, and I *know* that there's someone better to lead on this. *Anyone* would be better than me.'

'Okay,' she said. 'Fine.'

'Okay?' He smiled nervously. 'You'll speak to the Chief Super'?'

'If that's what you want, but...' She stood up and walked around the desk. 'I'll ask to be removed from my case as well.'

'What? Why?' He unfolded and jumped to his feet. 'Are you trying to blackmail me?'

She smiled. 'Of course not. I'm in the same boat as you. I haven't got a fucking clue about where that baby is, and I don't know where to begin looking for Maxine's killer. I'm on the verge of a nervous breakdown and... to boot... I have to undergo an interview tomorrow about the part I supposedly played in the death of Father Young. I don't need this shit, Simon. If you can throw in the towel... and you have less reason to do so than I do... then, so can I.'

'You *are* trying to blackmail me.'

She shrugged and made a grab for her handbag. 'Think what you like. I'm going home. We can both see Fredrickson in the morning and give him the double-whammy of bad news.'

Simon tried to think of something else to say. He'd got what he wanted – an *out* – and he didn't know if he cared enough, about Lorrie's intentions, to back down and carry on, regardless of the misgivings about his abilities.

He stopped her leaving the office by placing a hand on her arm. 'You're not really serious... are you?'

'Are you?' she fired back at him.

A flicker of doubt crossed his eyes and Lorrie suppressed a smile.

'I thought I was,' he said, on a sigh.

She carefully guarded her expression. 'The trouble with you, Simon,' she said, 'is that you have a tendency to think *too* much. It's all well and good to ponder and to muse ... to run things over and over again in your mind... but, you have to be careful not to drown in all those thoughts. Sometimes you have to simply shrug your shoulders, give yourself a shake, and knuckle down. Failure can be self-inflicted, you know?' She dropped her bag and turned to take her chair again. 'I'll give Lovell back to you,' she offered. 'We both know that she's Ying to your Yang.'

Simon blushed, misinterpreting her meaning. 'I don't think...'

'Oh, be quiet,' she admonished. 'I'm not suggesting anything improper in your relationship. God knows, that girl has done everything to make you notice her, but I'm not a fool... you're not interested in her. No, what I meant was – you need her at your back. You're more confident, more capable, when she's working with you.'

'That doesn't, exactly, negate my conclusion that I'm not up to the job,' he stated flatly. 'Anyway – you need her.'

She nodded. 'True, but, you need her more.'

'I didn't think it would be possible, but I actually feel worse about myself than when I stepped into this office.'

'Then, suck it up, Simon. You don't get to quit, and *I don't get to quit*. We'll both simply have to do the best we can and, one more thing...'

He looked at her expectantly.

'No one... and I mean *no one*... will do a better job, so, you had best stop whining and start believing that simple fact or hand in your warrant card and go and find yourself a less stressful job where no one depends on you not to fuck up.'

He crossed his arms and tilted his head. 'You can keep Lovell,' he said. 'I can do this without her help.'

'Good for you.'

'No need for sarcasm.'

'No?' She quirked an eyebrow. 'There's also no need for such high altruism... Unless you believe that I'm not up to the job without Lovell's assistance?'

He blushed once more. 'Of course not.'

'Then, we'll share her. It makes sense to have a liaison between both cases. I have a feeling that they're related.'

'I haven't been able to shake that notion either.'

'Davidson is the key.'

'You've shifted from Mackie as the prime suspect?'

'I'm certainly beginning to believe that his dirty deed with the wife was the catalyst, but I think that he was no more than a mere victim of a cuckolded husband.'

He thought a moment. 'So, what's your thinking on how that relates to Davidson's mother being murdered and his baby abducted?'

'Revenge?'

'That would mean someone had to know he was behind the poisoning.'

'That would make sense.'

'But, why not go after Davidson? Why kill the mother and take the baby?'

'Because, by poisoning the whole congregation, Davidson took *their* mother... *their* child?'

'Wow, that's...'

'Clever?'

He nodded. If she was right, then, at last, he had something to work with... a lead to follow. All of his misgivings suddenly evaporated and his whole body relaxed.

'When did you come up with this hypothesis?'

'Just now... talking to you. I was as lost as you were. I would never have come up with it without you.'

He didn't believe that but accepted it nevertheless. He said, 'Perhaps that Anthony character you're looking for has something to do with it?'

'Perhaps.'

Simon looked troubled.

'What else is on your mind, Simon?'

'I don't want to give up on Mackie,' he said. 'I can see how Davidson might have had a motive, but there's something about Mackie that I can't let go.'

'And, I thought I was the only one who had the hots for him.'

'It's nothing tangible, Guv". I wish I could put my finger on what's bugging me.'

'I heard a little bit about what that French aid worker said… is there anything there? I mean… there's a whole lot of suspicious things surrounding his time at the refugee camp, and with his release from captivity. Did she shed any light on that?'

He shook his head. 'I didn't really have much chance to question her. The phone connection was crap, and she was in a hurry to get off to the airport.'

'Would it be worth trying again? You could set up a video link.'

'That sounds like something worthwhile. You could sit in on it. You know more about the circumstances in Syria than I do.'

She nodded. 'It's a date, then.'

'Meantime, I'll try and find you this Anthony character. We may as well join forces properly.'

DAY FIVE: MORNING

Davidson was back in an interview room at New Scotland Yard. He had been given the *all-clear* and was deemed fit for questioning. Unfortunately, Lorrie couldn't get at him.

'I'd calm down, if I were you,' Fredrickson said. 'Getting all hyped-up, before you face those buggers from the IPCC, will only end up causing you more grief.'

Lorrie's throat constricted as she tried to breathe through her anger. She'd asked for her interview to be postponed, until she'd had the opportunity to question Davidson, but her request had fallen on deaf ears. Now, two jumped-up civil servants from the Independent Police Complaints Commission, were sitting impatiently awaiting her appearance.

'You're going in there without a rep'?'

She nodded. 'It's a preliminary interview. I might need a rep' at a later date.'

'I could sit in. You're within your rights to have a senior officer with you.'

'Thanks, but I'll be all right on my own. I just want it over with. I'll answer their questions and be back out doing my job within half an hour. Anyway…' she eyed him suspiciously. 'I thought you were seeing a doctor this morning? Lovell said that she thought you had an infection.'

'She exaggerated. I'm perfectly fine.'

'You don't look fine.'

'I'm sure that I look better than you. You're as white as a sheet.'

'I didn't have a chance to do up my face this morning. I always look pale without my war paint.' She glanced at her watch. 'I'd better get it over with.' She pressed her lips together, nodded to herself, and marched off to face the music.

Fredrickson watched her go and, when she had disappeared from view, gave in to the pain that was screaming along every nerve in his body. He moaned and clutched at his side. He wasn't sure why he was being such a damned fool. He knew that something was seriously wrong and, yet, he'd refused to do anything about it.

Well, he told himself - as the pain subsided for a moment - if he didn't want to be carted off in an ambulance he'd better man-up and get himself to the hospital.

*

Simon had hit pay dirt. A few hours searching through records had turned up an Anthony Howell – the son of two of the church victims and the brother to a third. Simon had an address for him and went in search of Lorrie to give her the good news.

'She's being interviewed by IPCC,' Lovell said, intercepting him as he headed to Lorrie's office. 'She's only just gone in.'

Deflated, he turned to walk away.

'Can I help?' Lovell asked.

'I don't think so,' he returned. 'I think I might've found Anthony, but I don't want to do anything until I run it past her.'

'He's *our* Anthony,' she said. 'The Guv'' mentioned a possible link between the two cases, so...'

'So?'

'You don't need her permission to bring him in.'

'I guess not.'

'I'll come with you. We'll round up a few uniforms and we can all go get him.'

Simon forced a smile. Trust Lovell to put him on the right path. She was right, of course. He was virtually equal in rank to Lorrie – all be it temporarily - and he didn't need her permission to do anything.

'Okay,' he said. 'Let's bring him in. He can cool his heels until the Super' is ready to question him.'

'Until you are *both* ready to question him.'

This time, his smile wasn't forced. 'Yes, until we're both ready.'

*

Lorrie had watched the video and listened through her interview with father Young. She had to admit to herself that she'd been rather rough on him. Seeing herself on the small screen - and hearing her words and her tone as she fired questions at the priest - made her doubt herself for the first time.

She felt their eyes on her, throughout the duration of the video, and made a concerted effort to appear unconcerned.

'Father Young looked ill from the get-go,' one of them – the young one with the immaculately gelled hair – said. 'I'm surprised that you didn't notice.'

'There was nothing *to* notice,' she said – a little too defensively. 'He didn't complain of feeling unwell. He was obviously stressed... understandably so.'

'Yes, he'd just had his whole congregation murdered,' the other one put in. 'Shouldn't you have been a little more sympathetic?'

It would have taken little effort for Lorrie to wipe the floor with the arrogant prick sitting opposite, but she kept her cool and simply outstared him.

'Please answer the question, Superintendent,' the arrogant prick said.

'What question would that be?'

'I asked... shouldn't you have been a little more sympathetic?'

She shrugged.

'Please... for the tape...'

'In hindsight?' She shrugged once more. 'No.'

'No?'

'I didn't feel sympathetic towards him.'

'Because you thought he was hiding information about Father Mackie? You thought that Father Macke was involved in the murders, is that right?'

'I was pursuing several lines of enquiry at the time,' she replied, dead-pan.

'What other lines of inquiry?'

'I don't believe that's relevant.'

'That's not your call.' The arrogant prick leaned over the table and Lorrie was forced to lean back in her chair to maintain her personal space.

'I ask again... what other lines of inquiry?'

'I'm not at liberty to discuss the details of an ongoing investigation,' she said. 'If you are in any doubt about that, I suggest you contact the Assistant Commissioner for clarification.'

'We don't answer to the Assistant Commissioner,' Hair Gel said.

'But, we'll move on.' He read through a few papers on the table, leaving Lorrie to stew for many more minutes than were absolutely necessary, before he asked, 'When did you first notice that Father Young was ill?'

'When he collapsed, I suppose.'

'Not before?'

'Perhaps, just before.'

'Do you believe that you acted responsibly?'

'Yes.'

'But, a man *died*, Superintendent.'

'So?'

'So?' Hair gel spluttered. 'A man dropped dead, right in front of you – after being on the receiving end of a barrage of questions and accusations - and...'

'I didn't accuse him of anything,' she interjected. 'And, my questions were reasonable.'

'You certainly implied a great deal.'

'I did my job.' Lorrie was fast becoming angry. 'And, sitting here listening to your ridiculous accusations, and far from intelligent questions, is keeping me from that job.' She made to stand.

'You're not excused,' Hair Gel said. 'You can't leave until we say so.'

'Is that right?' Lorrie pushed back her chair and completed her move from seating to standing. 'Just watch me.'

*

'Are you mad?' Fredrickson was on the verge of apoplexy. He was just about to take Lovell up on her offer of a lift to the hospital, when he spied Lorrie stomping from her interview with the IPPC.

'Yes, I'm mad,' she bit back. I'm so fucking mad, I could take a machine gun to those two fucking idiots in there.'

'Those *two fucking idiots* can get you suspended.'

'Let them try. They have absolutely no evidence of any wrongdoing on my part and I'll be damned if I'll pander to their jumped-up sense of self-importance by answering another one of their inane questions.'

He gave a heavy sigh and shook his head – her words doing nothing to alleviate his growing impatience and anger. He said, 'Do what you want. I'm sick of trying to talk sense into that thick head of yours.'

He made to limp away and was brought up short by a hand on his arm. Turning, he glowered down at her and reached to remove the offending hand.

'Sorry,' she said, snatching her hand back. 'I didn't realise that I wasn't allowed to touch you.'

'What do you want, Lorrie? I've somewhere I need to be.'

To say that she was taken aback by his changed demeanour was a vast understatement. The look on his face and the expression in his eyes almost floored her.

'Nothing,' she said, abashed. 'You go to where you need to be. I won't hold you up.'

'Thank you.' He turned once more and left her standing gaping at his back.

'Guv"?'

Lorrie turned to see Simon approach.

'You ready to interview Davidson?'

She nodded. 'As ready as I'll ever be.'

'How did it go with IPPC?'

'Just peachy,' she replied.

She made to walk off towards the interview room and turned when Simon spoke to her once more.

'About Anthony,' he said. 'I've identified him, and I went with Lovell to his home address... with the intention of bringing him in, but...'

'He wasn't there?'

Simon shook his head. 'The neighbours said he scarpered yesterday. No one reported seeing a baby with him.'

'You're sure it's *our* Anthony?'

'As sure as I can be. He had family members at the church on Sunday.'

Lorrie let out a slow breath. 'You need to scour the city looking for him.'

He nodded. 'Already happening.'

'Well done, Simon. You've found us our best lead on finding the baby. Now... let's get at Davidson.'

'He's with his solicitor and raising merry hell,' Simon said, as they approached the interview room. 'Don't be surprised if there's another official complaint logged.'

'Yeah, well... who gives a shit?' Lorrie pushed open the door and entered the room.

'About time,' the solicitor said. 'Do you know how many hours my client has spent in custody? I think you've well and truly broken PACE regulations, Superintendent.'

'Is that right?' Lorrie was in no mood to verbally parry with the lawyer. 'Put your concerns in writing and we'll look into it.'

Simon turned on the video camera and the voice recorder, introduced everyone for the record and then stood back as Lorrie got to work.

'Now...' She said, as she faced Davidson. 'Let's hear all about this affair your wife had with Father Mackie.'

'On the advice of my solicitor, I have nothing to say,' Davidson returned, his face not quite masked and the anxiety seeping from his features.

'Really?' Lorrie threw the solicitor a withering look. 'No matter... PC Prince had the good sense to record your conversation with her.'

'Inadmissible,' the solicitor spouted. 'She had no right questioning him without my being there. It's a complete breach of...'

'Yes, yes.' Lorrie flapped a hand in his face. 'I know what you think, but, you're quite wrong.'

'I'm *not* wrong.' The solicitor was indignant. 'She should *not* have questioned him, and – anything he happened to say, under those circumstances – cannot be used against him.'

Lorrie's face was a picture of pure innocence. 'Oh, don't tell me that Mister Davidson told you that PC Prince questioned him? Surely, he didn't mislead you?'

The solicitor glanced at his client and raised an eyebrow.

Davidson shifted uncomfortably in his chair. 'I didn't say that... I didn't say that she *actually* questioned me. I didn't say that... not exactly.' He dropped his eyes from the scathing look of his solicitor and clamped his mouth shut.

Lorrie bit back a smile and settled herself back in her seat

For a brief moment, the solicitor was stuck for words. If the PC hadn't questioned him, and his client had simply offered up information, then he didn't have a leg to stand on. But, he wasn't going to go down without a fight.

'This recording,' he said. 'It was done without my client's consent.'

'It was,' Lorrie conceded.

'Then, you can't use it.'

She nodded her agreement and shrugged. 'I have no intention of using it. I merely mentioned it so that your client is under no allusions about the fact that I know *exactly* what he said to PC Prince.'

Lorrie knew that a clever solicitor could scupper her whole plan of attack, but she was betting on this particular solicitor not quite having the nous to take her on.

'This is highly irregular and prejudicial. You have to take into account the anxious state of my client when he spoke to your PC.'

Lorrie could see that he was struggling to form a coherent argument – one that would see Davidson walk out of the interview room without answering a single question.

She said, 'He's fit to be questioned.'

'Then, my advice to him stand. He will make no comment.'

'Despite the fact that he can help find his wife's killer? Despite the fact that he can help us locate his baby?'

'Okay... Can I have a moment alone with my client?' he asked, clearing his throat anxiously. 'We need a moment.'

'No,' Lorrie returned sharply. 'You've had hours to confer with him.' She made a point of relaxing further back in the chair. 'He can make all the *no comments* he wants, but, regardless, I *will* ask the questions.'

A silence of stalemate dropped between them, before being broken when Davidson said, 'It was entrapment. She tricked me.'

Progress, Lorrie said to herself. He was talking and talking led to questions being answered.

'How did she do that? How did she trick you?'

Davidson was more than willing to respond. 'She was bad-mouthing you and lulling me into a false sense of security. All those things she said about you... they were all lies. She ran you down and slated you, so I would trust her.'

'Oh, I think most of what she said was perfectly true, Mister Davidson. I'm not well-liked around here.'

'I can perfectly well understand that,' the solicitor said under his breath.

Lorrie ignored the solicitor's chuntering.

'You volunteered the information about your wife and the priest. In fact, you were tripping over yourself to spill the beans. You wanted to give PC Prince the goods on both of them, and you hoped that – the fact that you didn't want to tell me... telling Prince instead... would put my nose out of joint.'

Lorrie was completely accurate in her assessment of Davidson's motives, but - despite his obvious wish to get one up on her - she still fully believed the truth of his words. His wife *did* have an affair with Mackie, and Davidson was now trying to back-peddle and deny the whole thing. She didn't imagine, for one moment, that he had the sense to realise the trouble his admission to Prince could cause him, but the solicitor would know that the wife's affair could, very well, put his client in the frame for all the church murders – hence his advice to keep his trap shut.

Davidson chanced opening his eyes and glancing from his solicitor to Lorrie. He wasn't sure what he hoped to read on either of their faces – sympathy, understanding, indifference – but, what he saw caused him to drop his eyes again, and say, 'Well, I want to retract what I said to PC Prince. I was lying to her, and I take it all back.' He risked another glance at his solicitor. 'I *can* take it back, can't I?'

The solicitor pursed his lips and sighed. He knew that a retraction wouldn't immediately help. It was obvious that Sullivan had the bit well and truly between her teeth and she certainly wasn't about to allow a mere retraction to stop her from going after his client. Truth be told, he couldn't really blame her. Davidson was, at best, an idiot and, at worst, complicit in some serious crimes. That, however, was beside the point. It was his job to protect his client from himself and stop him from digging a hole that he would never climb back out of.

'I suggest you keep quiet, Mister Davidson,' he said. 'A *no comment* to any of DS Sullivan's questions will suffice.'

Davidson chose to ignore his solicitor's sage advice. 'Look,' he said to Lorrie. 'I know I can get into trouble for lying. I apologise for all the trouble I've caused, but I won't repeat what I said to your PC. I didn't mean to say all those things to her about my wife and the priest. I'm sorry that I said anything, and I take it all back.'

'It's not that simple,' Simon said – getting in on the act. 'You surely understand that?'

'It was stupid... *I was stupid*. Can't you just forget it?'

'We will, if you convince us that it was all a lie,' Simon returned. 'Can you convince us of that?'

'I... I don't know.'

'Okay... Let's start by you explaining your wife's relationship with Father Mackie.' A look of alarm passed over Davidson's face and Simon had to give his arm a reassuring pat. 'No need to panic,' he said. 'I'm not trying to trick you. I just want to know if they knew each other very well.'

Davidson visibly relaxed. He wasn't aware that the look of acute cunning, that flit across his eyes, was seen and registered by both Simon and Lorrie. He said, 'They knew each other... yes, but they weren't close. Father Mackie came to the house a few times.'

'He did?'

Davidson nodded. 'I was there when he visited. My wife was a staunch supporter of the church, and one priest or another crossed our threshold many times over the years. There was nothing special about Mackie's visits.'

'But, he was a stranger to the parish and he didn't have any official role in your church. Why would he visit your wife?'

'My wife was a friendly person. She probably saw that he was in need of some company, and she invited him.'

'Did she invite him over when she knew that you were going to be out?'

'No.' His reply was hesitant.

'No?' Lorrie sounded incredulous. 'Why don't I believe you?'

'Believe what you like.' Davidson looked to the more sympathetic Simon to rescue him.

Simon continued to play the part of good cop. He was flabbergasted that Davidson – after being taken in by Prince – should trust that any one of them was on his side. He said, 'I believe you, Mister Davidson.' He ignored the, not so subtle, clearing of the solicitor's throat at his words and added, 'Of course, you *have* lied to us, so I hope you can understand DS Sullivan's reticence?'

'She doesn't like me.'

'I've yet to meet a liar that I *did* like,' Lorrie said.

'I've apologised for lying. Why can't you let it go?'

'Because, I wasn't born yesterday. Because, I don't believe a word that's currently coming out of your mouth. Because I know that you told the truth to Prince.'

Davidson attempted to laugh off her words, but it came out sounding more like a cat being strangled. Something shifted in his demeanour, and a haunted expression settled behind his eyes. Everyone in the room was shocked when he said, 'My wife was no better than a whore.'

Lorrie licked her lips and willed everyone to remain silent. The last thing she wanted was anyone cutting Davidson's change of heart off at the knees.

'I lost count of the men she fucked behind my back, but not the priest... No, definitely not Mackie.'

'Mister Davidson...' the solicitor interjected.

Davidson flapped a hand in his face. 'They want the truth, so I'm giving it to them. I want this over with. I want to go home.'

'I strongly advise...'

'Oh, shut the fuck up. I'm not listening to you.'

'You were saying?' Lorrie prompted.

'I was saying...' he ground out through clenched teeth. 'I was saying that my wife didn't screw the priest. She screwed everything else in trousers, but not him.'

'How can you be so sure?' Simon asked.

'I just am,' he shrugged.

'Did you confront her about her lovers?'

Davidson glared across at Lorrie. 'I loved her. She was a whore, but I loved her. I didn't want to lose her by accusing her, so I kept quiet.'

'But, the priest was different? Did you think she was falling in love with him?'

'No!' he roared. 'No fucking way.'

Lorrie remained completely still on the other end of his anger. She'd hit a nerve – quite by accident – and now she wanted to milk it.

'That's it, isn't it? The priest made a habit of visiting her at home, paid her some attention, flattered her and they made love... no screwing around this time, eh? It was a love job, wasn't it?'

'No.' The word was uttered quietly and painfully.

'Just so we're clear,' Lorrie said, leaning forward. 'You are being interviewed under caution, and you were read your rights earlier. You understand that, by continuing to lie to me, it will cause you untold grief later?'

The solicitor tried again. 'My client has no further comment. I don't appreciate this fishing expedition, Superintendent, and I want this interview stopped.'

Lorrie ignored him. She spoke directly to Davidson. 'It must have

hurt? I mean – a priest, for fuck's sake. But, let's put aside your wife's affair for the moment and talk about Anthony.'

Davidson frowned. 'Anthony?'

'The man we suspect killed your mother and snatched your baby. You know... the man we saw you speaking to on CCTV... that Anthony?'

'What about him?'

'You know that we've got a lead on him? We know who he is and where he lives, and the hunt is on to locate his whereabouts. Unfortunately, he's scarpered from his home address, but we'll catch up with him soon enough. I wonder what he'll have to say about your little chat with him in the street before he killed your mother?'

'He didn't kill my mother,' Davidson insisted.

'We know that he lost family members in the church. Was that why he killed your mother and took your son?'

'You're being ridiculous. Why would he do that? My mother had nothing to do with what happened at the church.'

Lorrie pounced. 'Did *you* have something to do with it? Did *you* take revenge on your wife and the priest by putting poison in the communion wine?'

'What?' His shock was very real and caused Lorrie a moment's pause.

'Are you going to charge my client with multiple counts of murder, Superintendent?' The solicitor seemed as shocked as his client.

'We'll see,' she replied nonchalantly.

'I didn't kill anyone. This is insane.' Davidson hauled himself to his feet and threw himself towards the door. 'I've got to get out of here.'

Simon stepped in front of him and put a restraining hand on his arm.

'Do I have to handcuff you, or are you going to sit back down and behave yourself?'

All the air seemed to leave Davidson's body and, before his knees buckled, Simon had propelled him back across the floor and deposited him back into his seat.

'Why should we believe you?' Lorrie asked. 'You had motive enough to see your wife and her lover dead. What I don't understand is why you murdered eighty other people? Why the others, and why the children? They'd not harmed you in any way. They were simply attending church, minding their own business, and didn't deserve such horrible, agonising deaths.'

'I didn't kill anyone.' Davidson's voice was so low that it was difficult to make him out. 'You've got it all wrong.'

'Convince me of that,' Lorrie said. 'Stop pissing about, and start being honest with me,'

'I must insist on conferring with my client,' the solicitor demanded. 'You have no right springing this on him and expecting me to sit quietly by and allow you to brow-beat him. He needs the opportunity to hear my counsel.'

Lorrie allowed a few seconds to pass before she said. 'Do you want a moment with your solicitor, Mister Davidson, or do you want to get this over with? Remember... we still have to find your baby and can't afford to waste any more time with lies and protestations of innocence.'

'I just want you to leave me alone,' he said.

Lorrie sighed. She had to be scrupulous in her dealings with Davidson and, allowing him time with his solicitor was probably the wisest course of action. She'd rattled his cage, and there was always the danger that the solicitor would succeed in shutting him up, but it was a chance she had to take. Denying him a few moments alone with his solicitor could very well come back to bite her on the bum, so she acquiesced.

'Very well,' she said. 'You've got twenty minutes and then I'll be back. If I don't hear anything to convince me that I'm barking up the wrong tree, I'll be seeking permission from the CPS to charge you.'

Out in the corridor, they were immediately approached by DS Baxter, who said to Simon, 'There's some French woman on the phone insisting on speaking to you.'

'Frenchwoman?' Simon was momentarily confused, then his face was cut by a huge grin. 'It must be Francine Galliard.'

'The aid worker?' Lorrie frowned.

Simon nodded. 'I wonder why she's calling?'

'Only one way to find out. Let's go talk to her.'

DAY FIVE: AFTERNOON

Everyone seemed to have someone – everyone except him. The hustle and bustle of the busy A and E department did nothing to alleviate his feelings of utter dejection and sense of being completely alone. He had no one to sit with him, no one to talk to and no one to tell him that - despite his pain, and in spite of his raging temperature – he was going to be all right.

Chief Superintendent Fredrickson lay back on the trolley and watched the comings and goings through a fog of pain. Lovell had dropped him off and waited long enough for him to be booked in and then, understandably, left him to go back to work. With a missing baby, a multitude of dead bodies awaiting justice, and at least one murderer on the loose, he couldn't blame her for breaking her neck to leave.

He was alone, and he just had to suck it up.

He was waiting on a bed to become available on one of the medical wards. He had an IV line running from one arm - pumping antibiotics into his bloodstream - and he had never felt so ill or so exhausted in the whole of his life. Sepsis had been confirmed and there was the risk of his organs shutting down as a consequence. After he had withstood the severe rollicking from the A and E doctor for being such a prick – the doctor had actually used the word *prick* when he told him off - for not coming to the hospital sooner, he'd had no choice but to settle back and contemplate his stupidity.

He had no one to call and no one he could ask to be at his side. His sister had enough to contend with – following the murder of her daughter – without him bothering her with the simple fact that he was knocking on death's door, so – if he was *actually* about to die – he was going to have to do it alone.

A nurse approached. She threw a smile at him and it angered him no end. She was young, and he knew that he really should be more tolerant, but her cheery demeanour – in the face of his impending demise – infuriated him so much that it added a wave of sharp pain to his existing hurt.

Oblivious to his black mood, and ignorant of his growing anger, she said, 'Well now, Mister Fredrickson, how are we doing? Are we in any pain?' She didn't await a response and blatantly ignored - and talked over - his sudden scowl. 'You'll be pleased to know that we've found a bed for you and you'll soon be on your way to the ward. I've sent for a porter, and you'll be tucked up, nice and comfortable, in a matter of minutes.'

Fredrickson eyed her with a mixture of disdain and resignation. He wanted to swat her – and her inane, cheery face – away, but, instead, said, 'You've found me a bed? How very clever of you. Why don't you simply wheel me straight to the morgue and save the bed for someone who'll benefit from it?'

The nurse couldn't tell if he was joking, and her smile wavered for a second.

'You're a good few years away from a place in our morgue,' she returned brightly – if rather hesitantly - 'and, with the state you've got yourself into, you're in need of one of our beds far more than most.'

'I didn't give myself sepsis,' he returned sourly.

'No, but you certainly didn't help yourself by suffering in silence. You've been a very silly boy. You're very lucky we caught it in time.'

'I'm not a boy. I'm old enough to be your father.' His hand itched to slap the silly mare. 'Haven't you got other patients you need to attend to?' He turned his face to the wall, hoping that – if he ignored her – she would go away.

'Is there anyone I can call… To let them know what ward you'll be on?'

'No.'

'No one? Surely, there's someone?'

'I said… no. Now, can you please leave me alone?'

The nurse inhaled deeply, then exhaled slowly before shaking her head, turning, and walking away. She hadn't failed to take into con-sideration that he was grumpy because he was afraid, alone and vulnerable, but she wasn't in the mood for bad-tempered patients and, anyway, she was run off her feet and there were plenty of patients who would be more receptive to a cheery smile and a word or two of conversation.

During the three hours he'd been lying on the trolley, Fredrickson had found out more about himself than he cared to admit. He'd always thought himself as a pragmatic realist, and someone who could take a knock to the floor and always come back fighting. This news of the sepsis was one knock he had neither the strength nor the inclination to clamber up from and, considering his usual stoicism, it was remarkable that he was prepared to simply accept his fate.

He took a moment to assess his frame of mind. He'd been rude to the nurse - and, he was never rude to anyone if he could avoid it – and he was wallowing in a level of self-pity that should have been embarrassing. So, just what the fuck was wrong with him? It wasn't the sepsis - and it wasn't that he was afraid of dying – so *what the fuck*?

He found himself trying to reason through his current thinking and his present state of belligerence. He blamed himself for the predicament he found himself in. His pig-headedness - in not seeing a doctor or taking himself to the hospital earlier - was the sole reason for the seriousness of his condition and, for that, he had no one but himself to blame. But, he didn't believe that was why he was so frustrated and so miserable and so despondent. It was because he was alone. It was because he didn't have the balls to admit to Lorrie Sullivan that he was falling in love with her. It was because he was going to die a damned coward.

They'd told him that the infection had caused his immune system to go into overdrive and made his body ripe for sepsis. In reality, that meant his organs were vulnerable. His kidneys were already affected - and he couldn't piss to save himself – but he'd been assured that the broad-spectrum antibiotics and the intra-venous fluids would work their magic and he would be fine in a day or two.

He didn't believe them.

He didn't consider himself a hypochondriac. He wasn't in the habit of worrying about every sniffle and every ache or pain, but he felt so ill that he was sure they'd failed to realise the seriousness of his condition. His blood results weren't back, so they hadn't identified the bacteria causing the sepsis, and they even questioned if it was a virus – in which case the antibiotics would be utterly useless – and, yet, here he was on a trolley waiting on a porter with no one to give a damn.

Just as the porter arrived, the vital signs monitor he was attached to by a rubber bung on his forefinger went ape-shit.

By the time the nurse arrived back in the cubicle, Fredrickson had relapsed into full-blown septic shock.

*

Lorrie was stunned into complete silence. She had no words to express the utter shock she felt at the aid worker's confession.

Simon, too, was stunned, but he was vocal about it.

'Holy shit! Do you believe what she just admitted to? I don't fucking well believe it. It's... it's just so God-damned incredible.'

Lorrie stared across at him. She felt the anger coming off him in waves, and she thought that he was about to burst a blood vessel.

'Calm the fuck down, Simon. At least she told us, and better late than never.'

'Bullshit. She should never have lied. If I have anything to do with it, I'll make sure that she ends up in a whole bucket of shit.'

'We can't exactly haul her back from the Sudan and clap her in irons.'

'Why the fuck not? Look at what she did.'

'I know what she did.'

'Can you believe it? Can you believe Mackie... the lying bastard?'

'I think I *can* believe it of him.'

'The lying fuck. This is going to cause ructions.'

Lorrie nodded. 'I'll have to talk to Fredrickson. He can get in touch with his contacts... the ones who did the debrief with Mackie.'

'What good would that do?'

'Who knows?' She shrugged. 'But, it really doesn't have anything to do with our cases.'

'It *could* have. This could've followed him from Syria.'

'Perhaps, but we can't worry about that scenario. We just have to pass the information on and continue with our own investigations.'

'It's your call, I suppose.'

'Yes.' She scrubbed at her eyes with the back of her hands. 'Jesus, I'm knackered, and we've still got Davidson to contend with. We'll get back to him as soon as I speak to Fredrickson. Where is he, anyway?'

'Lovell took him to hospital this morning?'

'Oh?' Lorrie felt her heart lurch in her chest. 'Is he okay?'

'I've not heard.'

'He *was* pretty fucked-up.'

Simon raised a brow. 'You look worried.'

'I'm not worried,' she lied.

'Do you want me to track him down and find out how he is?'

'No.' She shook her head. 'Our priority is still to find the whereabouts of Anthony Howell. You concentrate on finding him and the baby, and I'll track down Fredrickson and brief him on what we learned about Mackie.'

'What about Davidson? You only gave the solicitor twenty minutes. If we don't charge him, we'll have to let him go.'

'We don't have enough to charge him.'

'So, we let him go?'

She nodded. 'But, I want him left on the hook. Between him and Mackie, I don't know who the biggest liar is. Get Lovell to dig into every aspect of his life. I want to know when he last shit and how often he takes a piss. Get her to track his every move over the past couple of months and interview the neighbour he was screwing. And,' she finished up, 'put surveillance on him.'

*

PC Sue Prince finally managed to grab a coffee and take a five-minute breather from the tedious list of tasks assigned to her by DS Baxter. Sitting in front of a computer screen and working her way through every known contact of Anthony Howell, and then collecting every inconsequential titbit of information on all his known associates, had been slowly corroding her brain. She was goggle-eyed, fed up and frustrated by her obvious lack of progress.

Thankfully, it was time to go out and do some actual police work - no more numbing her arse sitting at a desk – and, after she swallowed her coffee, she was going to join Acting Super' Grant, DS Baxter and PC Cox on an outing to apprehend Howell.

Although *she* had failed to find a single lead on Howell's whereabouts, Cox had succeeded where she had flopped. Cox had stumbled across a property Howell's parents had rented in Essex and discovering it had caused a few ripples of excitement amongst the team.

Julie Cox approached at a trot. 'You ready? DS Baxter said to meet him and Grant in the car park.'

Prince drained her cup and nodded. 'I suppose so,' she said. 'Although, why I'm being allowed to tag along beats me.'

'Why shouldn't you? You've worked hard on this.'

'But, you found the place in Essex. I came up with a big, fat nothing'

'Essex might come to nothing. I might have found jack-shit.'

'You've played a blinder, Julie. Whatever happens, I'm so proud of you.'

Cox eyed her friend and smiled. 'We've both done well. You got that information from Davidson about his wife and the priest. Not bad for a couple of rookie uniforms.'

Prince returned her smile and, linking arms with her friend, they both left to go on the hunt for Howell and, hopefully, the baby.

*

'Intensive care? Are you sure? For fuck's sake, he only had his appendix out. Why should that result in a stint in intensive care?' Lorrie listened for a few seconds and then slammed her phone down on her desk. She ran agitated hands through her hair and sank down into a chair. *Septic shock... Septic fucking shock. Unbelievable.*

Simon popped his head around the office door. 'We're off, Guv'.'

Dazed, she said, 'Off?'

'To Essex... To find Howell.'

'Oh, right.'

He frowned. 'You okay?'

'Yes, I'm fine.'

'Did you track down Fredrickson?'

'I did.'

'Is he okay?'

Lorrie shook her head and blinked back tears. 'He's in intensive care.'

'Holy shit. What happened?'

'The silly bastard went into septic shock. He could die.'

'No.'

She nodded. 'It's *that* bad.'

Simon had no words. He gaped at her and swallowed back hard.

'I'm going to the hospital. He doesn't have any family nearby.'

'There's his sister in Manchester.'

'Yeah. I think the hospital rang her, but she's still grieving. She never got over the death of her daughter.'

'Friel.'

'Yes, DS Friel. I'll have her death on my conscience for the rest of my life.'

'It wasn't…'

'I know, but she was my responsibility and I let my maniac husband and his side-kick murder her.' The tears came. They were silent and heartfelt.

'I need to go.' Simon was reluctant to leave her, but he had no choice.

'I know. You get off and find Howell and find that baby. I'll be okay.'

'Let me know how he is. If he's awake…'

'He won't be awake.'

'Well, on the off chance, tell him…'

'I'll tell him, don't worry.'

*

'Ricky? Oh, thank God you're here. They won't let me in to see him.' Lorrie embraced the forensic pathologist. '*Family only*, they said, but he doesn't have any fucking family here. You have to do something. He's all alone in there.'

Ricky took a step back and surveyed the wreck of a woman in front of him. Gone was her poise and her calm. She looked as if she'd been crying and, to all intents and purposes, she was acting like Fredrickson's bereft wife, and not merely his colleague.

'I'll get you in,' he said. 'I'll cash in one of my favours with his consultant.'

Lorrie curled a hand around his arm and leaned into him. 'Thank you,' she whispered.

He gave her a slow smile and patted her gently on the back. 'You know that you have to get a grip, don't you? If he wakes and sees the mess you're in, he'll have a heart attack.'

'*If*, he wakes,' she sniffed. 'By all accounts, he only has about a fifty percent chance of surviving this.'

'He's got better odds than that,' Ricky returned. 'He was started on IV antibiotics in A and E and he began fighting the infection well before the shock grabbed him.'

'He could still die.'

'Yes.' Ricky wasn't about to lie. 'He could still die.'

'We can't let him, Ricky. I can't lose anyone else.' Her brain refused to accept such a terrible thing. 'I *won't* let him die.'

*

They headed towards Asheldham Dengi, drove through, and wound their way along the B1021 towards Tillingham. Cox and Prince were in the forward vehicle, with Simon and Baxter, and they were followed closely by the armed response vehicle.

The target was a cottage on the outskirts of the small village. They'd been travelling for close to two hours and the afternoon was quickly moving towards evening, but the light was good, and everyone was hopeful of a quick and clean extraction of Howell and the baby. No one wanted to contemplate a hostage scenario and, as Prince drove, Simon and Baxter were poring over maps and getting a clear picture of the terrain up to and surrounding the cottage.

They planned to stop half a mile from the target and synchronise their plan of action with armed response. Thankfully, the cottage sat back from the road behind a small wooded area and the cover that the trees would provide meant that they could approach undetected.

There were no plans to storm the cottage. They weren't even sure if Howell was there but, if he was – and he had the baby – storm trooper tactics would only result in failure and, perhaps, the death of the innocent child.

'We'll hold back and let the armed response team do their thing. They won't want us in the way.'

'I can't see Howell being armed,' Baxter said. 'He doesn't have any form with guns and doesn't move in those circles.'

'We'll proceed as if he *is* armed,' Simon returned. 'He's killed once – albeit with a knife – but, who the fuck knows what he's capable of?'

Prince slowed the car and pulled to the side of the road. 'We're half a mile out, Guv',' she said.

'Good. Cut the engine and pass me the binoculars from the glove compartment.'

Simon climbed from the car and put the binoculars to his eyes. He adjusted the focus and searched for the cottage.

He saw a small, squat building at the head of a small driveway. There were no cars parked in front and no obvious signs of any occupants.

'The curtains are closed,' he said to Baxter. 'There's no way of telling if anyone is inside.'

DI, Greg Peters approached from the armed response vehicle. 'We'll move closer on foot,' he said. 'Two officers will take the back, and two will take the front. Let's determine what we're dealing with.' He made to move off, waving his colleagues on in front, and turned to give a final nod to Simon. 'I'll radio you if, and when, we secure the building.'

Simon returned his nod and put the binoculars back to his eyes.

'What do you want us to do?' Prince asked.

'Keep your heads down and your eyes peeled,' Baxter said. 'We need the road watched in both directions. Warn us of any traffic heading our way.'

They knew the drill. Prince moved off to the left and Cox to the right, and both hunkered down and took up positions where they had the best views of the road. Neither of them needed to be told that Howell may approach in a vehicle and both were relieved to find that two of the armed response team had remained on the scene to provide vital cover.

The minutes ticked past in total silence. Simon remained focussed on the cottage, whilst Baxter did several revolutions, eyeing up the horizon in every direction.

Sound carried extremely well on the quiet late afternoon air so, when the cottage door was kicked in, the noise sounded like a crack of thunder.

No shots were fired, but everyone on the road heard shouting.

'DI Grant has gone in,' Simon said. Then, seconds later, 'They've all gone in, now.'

One of the remaining armed response officer's radio crackled and all eyes turned to him.

'All clear,' the cracked voice said through the radio.

'Roger that,' the officer responded.

Simon's relief was palpable, but it wasn't over yet. He spoke into his own radio. 'Is Howell there?' he asked. 'Is the baby there?'

'That's a negative,' DI Peters replied.

Simon closed his eyes and swore under his breath. Just as he raised the radio to his mouth once more, a vehicle was heard approaching.

'Eyes on it,' Simon screamed.

Cox was the first to see it – a red transit van with blacked-out windows – and she immediately memorised the number plate.

The driver of the van spotted the police vehicles and screeched to an immediate stop. The engine idled and, when Simon took a step towards it, the driver gunned it – causing the van to leap forward. Simon jumped out of its path, and – his legs buckling – fell at the side of the road.

Without being told, Cox radioed dispatch and gave the van's number plate with a request for immediate road and aerial back-up. She described the van and confirmed that they would be in pursuit in a matter of seconds.

'Go! Go! Go!' Simon screamed, and all four-clambered back into their car and sped off after the van. Simon radioed Peters, and, within a couple of minutes, the armed response vehicle was close on their tail.

DAY FIVE: EVENING

Fredrickson opened his eyes and blinked against the glare of the lights. He could see the outline of someone sitting to his right, but he didn't have the strength to turn his head.

He tried to speak, but his tongue was glued to the roof of his mouth. He wondered where the hell he was, and it took a few seconds to unscramble his brain before it all came slowly back to him.

A nurse approached the bed and smiled down at him.

'Welcome back, Mister Fredrickson. I bet you feel like shit.'

He tried to smile.

'Do you know where you are?'

He managed a brief nod.

'And, do you know who this is?' She gestured for Lorrie to stand so that she was in his line of vision.

He finally managed a smile.

'Hello, sir,' Lorrie said thickly. 'I hope you feel better than you look?'

He closed his eyes and willed his tongue to work.

'You, too,' he finally got out.

Lorrie ran a hand self-consciously through her hair. 'Neither one of us will be winning any beauty contests, that's for sure.' Her voice broke and she choked back a sob. 'You silly bastard. You scared the life out of me.'

He reached out an arm and clutched her hand. 'Sorry,' he croaked.

'That's enough talking, for now,' the nurse admonished. 'You're not out of the woods yet, so reserve what little strength you have. The doctor's on his way, so lie back and relax. Plenty of time to get re-acquainted when you've had the once over.' She drew Lorrie a warning look and left the room.

'What... happened?'

Lorrie placed a finger on his lips and shook her head. 'You heard what the nurse said... lie back and shut up.'

He forced another smile. It was worth almost dying to have her at his side.

'Septic shock,' she said. 'You were knocking on death's door for a while, there.'

He nodded and dragged in a sigh.

'You've been *so* lucky. I'm surprised that skinny body of yours had the strength to fight the infection.'

It was gallows humour and Fredrickson was grateful for it.

The door opened, and the doctor made an appearance.

'Well, now,' he said. 'This is a pleasant surprise. We weren't expecting you to come around quite so soon. Well done.'

'It was a different doctor – not the one who'd called him a prick in A and E – and Fredrickson was relieved. He couldn't cope with further reminders of how stupid he'd been.

Lorrie squeezed his hand and said, 'I'm stepping out for a minute. Everyone will be keen to hear that you're awake.'

He panicked and refused to let go of her hand.

She understood and summoned up the widest, brightest smile she could muster and gave him a reassuring nod. 'I'll be back. Just give me a minute.'

He let go of her hand and watched until she disappeared from view.

'She's been here for hours,' the doctor said. 'Wouldn't leave your side for a second. It's not usually allowed, but she has a powerful and persuasive friend in Ricky Burton.'

'Thank you.'

'No need to thank me. I just do as I'm told.'

'What happened?' Fredrickson asked again. 'I don't remember anything.'

'Well, you took us all by surprise by diving head first into septic shock. Your condition was much more serious than originally thought.'

'That's a bummer.'

'Yes, you could say that. Thankfully, we'd already started treatment, or...'

'I'd be dead?'

'Perhaps.' The doctor tinkered with his IV. 'Let's put it this way... you've been very lucky.'

'I don't feel lucky. I feel stupid.'

'Yes... well... lesson learned, I think. Perhaps, next time...'

'I won't be so pig-headed.'

The doctor smiled, and said, 'You'll be in hospital for a couple of weeks. Your kidneys and heart took a bit of a battering, and we'll have to be satisfied of no lasting damage before you regain your freedom.'

'I'll suck it up.'

'Good man.'

*

They had lost sight of the van.

'Where the hell is aerial support?'

Cox was back on her radio, demanding answers. 'On its way, Guv',' she said. 'Two minutes out.'

'Tell them to head towards Southend-on-Sea. He's heading that way.'

Simon's mobile phone chirruped. and he answered it with a bark. 'What? I'm busy.' He swallowed. 'Sorry, Guv'. It's a bit mad here. We're chasing down Howell but lost him a few minutes ago.' He listened for a few moments, then said, 'Glad to hear it. Relief all round. Yes, I'll update you as soon as we nab the bastard.'

Lorrie disconnected the call and made her way back to the room. She was torn between needing to stay with Fredrickson and being with her team as they hunted Howell and the baby. Being with Fredrickson won out and she made herself comfortable back in her chair and waited as the doctor finished his examination.

Alone, once more, Fredrickson turned his head to face her. It hurt – it hurt like hell – but he simply had to see her.

'What's happening?' he asked.

'Nothing for you to worry about. I'm not talking shop with you.'

'Please.'

'Nope.' She shook her head. 'My lips are sealed.'

'Not fair.'

'Nothing is fair… Live with it.'

'Still… still so bloody bitchy.' He tempered his words with a watery smile.

'You wouldn't have me any other way.'

'I'm not so sure about that. You make my head hurt sometimes.'

'Sorry.'

He laughed and doubled up in pain. 'Jesus,' he moaned. 'I'm in Hell.'

Lorrie leaned over and pushed him back against the pillows. 'No, you're slowly climbing your way back out of Hell. Just know…' She drew in a breath. 'Just know that I've been in Hell alongside you.'

'I didn't know you cared.'

'Who said I cared?' She leaned back and grinned. 'I just don't want to have to train up another Chief Super'.'

'Ouch… that hurt.'

'Stop being such a pussy and take it as a compliment. I don't want another boss. I want you to get better and get back to work. No one covers my arse quite as thoroughly as you.'

'So, you owe me.'

'For covering my arse? Isn't that your job?'

'It's not my *only* job.'

'You're on sick leave. Technically, at the moment, you don't have a job to do.'

'Bullshit.' A wave of nausea overtook him, and he gagged.

'Fuck, Fredrickson… You need to rest.' Even as she said it, Lorrie knew that he wouldn't rest until she gave up everything on the case. Fredrickson was definitely bone-headed enough to risk his health for the sake of the job and – if she was being entirely honest with herself – to help her.

He leaned his head back and swallowed down the bile at the back of his throat. He looked at her through lowered lids and let a silence fall between them. His head was splitting, his abdomen felt like he'd been punched numerous times, and his whole body was on the verge of shutting down, but he would be damned if he would simply lie in bed and watch her struggle.

'I was all alone,' he said. 'I didn't have a single person I could reach out to. My sister is a head-case, and spends her time popping pills and drowning her grief in booze. Did you know that her husband left her... after?'

Lorrie shook her head. 'I can understand the booze part. After Ollie and Sean were killed, the only relief I got was when I was roaring drunk. It's a shame about her husband, but most men are arseholes.'

'*He* certainly is.'

'You could've called me. Why didn't you call me?'

'The point I'm trying to make,' he said, ignoring her question, 'is that I didn't like it... being alone. When you think that you're going to die, all you want is a hand to hold and someone to give you a little bit of courage. I don't want you to be alone, Lorrie. I want you to know that I'll always be there for you.'

The conversation was taking an unwelcome turn, and Lorrie found that she could no longer meet his eye.

'I'm making you uncomfortable.'

'No. No,' she protested. 'It's just that...'

He flapped his hand – despite the pain raising it caused him. 'No need to explain. I understand. All men are arseholes and, I guess, that includes me.'

'I don't think that about you?'

'No?'

'Certainly not. If I could...'

'I know.'

Lorrie took a deep breath and let it go slowly. She wondered where their conversation would leave them? Continuing to work together – now that Fredrickson had all but admitted his feelings for her – would be nigh on impossible.

'You have to give me the consolation prize,' he said.

'What?'

'You have to give me something to think about... to mull over... something other than thinking about how pathetic I am.'

'You're not...'

'Yeah. Yeah. Save it for someone who deserves it.'

'Okay.' Lorrie felt herself relax. She'd tried to keep it from him. She'd tried to protect what little strength he had – so he could work on his recovery - but she was relieved at his insistence. She needed him to know everything, because – without him – she didn't think she was up to figuring anything out.

'Okay, what? You'll share?'

She nodded. 'I'll share, and I'll begin with a phone call Simon received from the French aid worker.'

*

'Brilliant. Just fucking brilliant.' Simon slammed the car door and kicked ferociously at the dirt at his feet. 'How could we lose him? I mean... we had a fucking helicopter following him.'

Everyone had the sense to remain silent. The desperate chase, and the fruitless effort to catch Howell, tore chunks from everyone's insides and there was no response adequate enough to counter Simon's anger. In the circumstances, silence seemed the best policy.

'I want a forensic team at the cottage. I want the whole place turned upside down. If there's a clue as to where he might go to ground, I want it found.'

Baxter nodded and walked off to relay the message to the crime scene investigation lot.

'I suppose I'd better give the bad news to the Guv",' Simon said. 'You two get off home.'

Prince and Cox nodded and turned on their heels – glad to be leaving the whole debacle behind them. They heard the sound of Simon punching the car as they walked away.

*

'She'd been having it off with Mackie for months, but he ran cold on her and began disappearing from the camp on a regular basis.'

'We know that he crossed the border into Syria almost every day.'

She nodded. 'But, no one knew why.'

'The aid worker knew?'

'Not at first, but she was angry and felt bitter about his rejection, so she made it her business to find out.' Now for the whammy... 'He was meeting up with a fifteen-year-old Muslim girl. He was screwing her, and her family found out.'

'You're kidding me?'

'Nope.'

'And, the kidnap?'

'Her family… apparently.'

'Holy mother of God.'

'He was freed after a bomb blasted the girl, and most of her family, to Kingdom Come.'

'They kept him a prisoner all that time?'

'Not exactly. They forced him to marry her. She was pregnant when she was killed.'

'How…?' Fredrickson was finding it difficult to digest the story. 'How did the aid worker find all this out?'

'She had friends across the border. She asked the right people the right questions and got the whole sordid tale explained to her.'

'But, why did they free him?'

'Honour was satisfied, and the remaining family didn't want him anymore.'

'I can't believe that the aid worker didn't rat him out.'

'She said that she loved him. She made excuses for him and was happy enough to go along with the assumption that terrorists had nabbed him. Anyway… she didn't want her relationship with a priest to be made public.'

'Does this change things?' he asked. 'Do you think it had anything to do with what happened at the church?'

'I don't know. I don't think so.'

'Perhaps, indirectly?'

She shrugged. 'Only Mackie knows the answer to that, and he's brown bread.'

'But, there's a pattern. Mackie had no scruples, and goodness knows how many enemies he had because of his behaviour. He had no qualms about taking advantage of a young girl, and he certainly didn't hold true to his vow of celibacy.'

'And, that brings me to Davidson.'

'Davidson?'

'He admitted that his wife was having an affair with Mackie.'

The information was overloading his severely restricted thinking processes, and Fredrickson had to take a minute to digest Lorrie's latest bombshell. None of it made sense. None of it brought him any closer to understanding what had gone on at the church.

'Didn't she have a three-month old baby?'

'She did,' Lorrie said, nodding. 'Mackie didn't let that stop him, though.'

'So… you're putting two and two together, and now making the husband your number one suspect for the church?' He could see how that made sense. 'But, where does his mother's murder and the abduction of the baby come into it?'

'Well, we've identified an Anthony Howell as Maxine Davidson's killer. Howell had family who were church victims. We think the murder of Maxine, and the abduction of the baby, was revenge.'

'Howell blames Davidson?'

'Perhaps, with good reason.'

'So, Davidson took out the whole church, and Howell retaliated by killing his mother and taking his child? Is that what you're saying?'

She nodded.

'Fuck me, Sullivan… that's a stretch.'

'Can you think of a better motive for the church, or a better explanation for Maxine and the baby?'

'No,' he admitted.

'Then, it's what we're running with.'

Lorrie's phone rang. She glanced at the screen. 'It's Simon. He found Howell and I'm hoping he has him in custody.' She put the phone to her ear. 'Simon?'

She listened with increasing frustration to Simon's voice on the other end of the phone.

She heard him say, 'Sorry, Guv'… we lost him.'

'You lost him?' She threw a look at Fredrickson that spoke volumes. '*Where* did you lose him?'

'Around Southend-on-Sea. The helicopter is still circling, but there's no sign of him.'

Lorrie hung up without uttering another word and dropped her head to her knees. She couldn't think. Her heart pounded in her chest and she felt herself floating.

'Pour yourself a glass of water,' Fredrickson said. 'I'd do it for you, but I'm afraid the effort would finish me off.'

'I'm okay,' she managed to force out. 'I just need a minute.'

'Think positive, Sullivan. You know who you're looking for, and you can run him down.'

'Before he hurts the baby?' She lifted her head and the look she threw him was murderous. 'He's a fugitive with a baby, and he knows that having that baby, stacks the odds against him.'

'*If* he still has him.'

'Yes, there's *that*. He could've killed him already.'

'What if he hasn't? What if he has no intention of harming him? That
could give you your best hope of finding him.'

'I don't follow.'

'Think about it. He'll need food and nappies and all sorts of shit. Start there.'

'Well, he was holed up in a cottage and he probably left everything behind. He'll need to do a supply run at some point.'

'Now, you're getting it.'

'It's a long-shot.'

'Better than nothing.'

She nodded. 'It's somewhere to start.

'And, find out if he has any female friends. He'll probably need a woman to help with such a small child.'

She hauled herself to her feet. 'I'm going to have to leave you alone again.'

'That's okay.'

'Will you be all right?'

'I'll be fine.'

'You look a bit better.'

He didn't feel better. In fact, he felt close to fainting, but, he replied, 'I feel much better. You get off and find the bastard. Don't worry about me.'

'Thanks,' she said. 'I'm glad I've got you.'

'Always.'

She chewed on her lip. It was hard, leaving him, but he was no longer her top priority.

'Go,' he said, and, she went.

DAY FIVE: NIGHT

Neither Cox nor Prince went home, and neither were surprised to see the full team present and correct when they returned to base. When the Super' arrived, it was all hands-on-deck, and both PCs felt a sense of wonder at the dedication and selflessness of every member of the squad. Everyone had been working since early that morning and – tired, or not, dejected, or not - no one was prepared to give up or give in.

'I've got a job for you both,' Lovell said. 'You found Howell once,' she stared directly at Cox, 'and, I'm sure you can find him again.' She turned to Prince, saying, 'I want you to canvas every shop and every store across Essex and find me someone who saw Howell buying baby items.' To Cox – 'You find me a woman... *any and all* women... known to Howell.'

Lovell strode off and Cox and Prince stared after her with mouths hanging open.

'*Every* shop and *every* store?' Prince muttered. 'Is she mad?'

'I must admit that you drew the short straw,' Cox said, smiling. 'Good luck.'

Prince's voice dropped to a hoarse whisper. 'How am I supposed to do it? There must be thousands of shops and stores.'

'Not all of them sell baby products. Whittle them down, and then check what ones have CCTV.'

'That will *still* be hundreds, at least. Then... then there will be finding the solitary needle in a multitude of haystacks.'

Cox cleared her throat, then said, 'Get yourself some help. Lovell tasked you with getting the job done and left it up to you how you did it. There's probably a couple of uniforms floating about with little, or nothing to do... grab them, sit them down with a computer and a phone, and use them.'

'I can't do that. I can't order other officers around.'

'Who says that you can't? You've got authority through Lovell. If any uniform gives you any shit about toeing the line...'

'I know,' Prince gave a watery smile. 'Threaten to sic Lovell on them.' She drew her brows together. 'You're beginning to resemble the mouse that roared. Where's the Cox, I know and love?'

'Right here,' Cox returned with a smile.

'You seem different... more confident.'

'I'm loving it, Sue. I don't mean that I'm loving all the terrible bits, but I'm enjoying using my brain and being part of something this big. We've both showed the plain-clothes that we can contribute and they're trusting us with actual, important tasks. Do you see any other uniforms welcomed into the fold the way we've been?'

Prince shook her head. 'No.'

'That's super confidence building, don't you think?'

'I suppose so.'

'You suppose so? Get a grip, girl... this is career building stuff. If we carry on doing a good job... if we find Howell... we could have opportunities.'

'As long as they don't include family liaison,' Prince joked. 'Okay, point me in the direction of some uniforms. I've a few orders to bark at them.'

*

'I've brought in Davidson's floozie,' Lovell told Simon. 'She was being a cheeky mare, and refusing to co-operate, so I dragged her fat arse in.'

'Your timing could've been better. We're up to our necks in it, Lovell.'

'I can leave her picking her nails for a couple of hours'

'No. Question her and then toss her. I'm not sure that she has much to offer but have a go.'

'Okay, sir. Give me an hour with her. Before I'm through, I'll know all there is to know about her lover's exploits. The Guv' still has Davidson marked as a person of interest, and who else but a fuck-buddy can give us the full low-down?'

Within five minutes of sitting opposite the floozy, Lovell realised
that an hour probably wasn't going to be long enough.

*

Anthony Howell didn't have female friends... or none that Cox could find. He was a man's man and – apart from numerous one-night stands – there was no woman in his life. He no longer had a mother – she being one of the church victims – and he had no other female relatives. If there was a woman in tow – one who was tasked with looking after the baby – she was invisible.

Howell's social media accounts were a revelation, but pretty useless in tracking down any girl or woman he could rely on to help him. She was about to give up, admit defeat, and own up to her failure, when she had an idea.

There was no rule that said it *had* to be a woman. Anyone with experience of being around young children and babies would be able to put on a nappy and make up a bottle, and she turned her search to male friends with young siblings.

She thought that she'd hit the jackpot with Jeremy Swan. He was a close friend of Howell, and he was big brother to twin baby girls. And - most exciting of all – he fit the scant description of the other person caught on CCTV when Maxine Davidson was murdered.

She went in search of Lovell. There was no way that she was going to share her findings with either Sullivan or Grant – not before she bounced it off Lovell – but Lovell was tied up interviewing Georgina Collins. She considered interrupting the interview but wasn't sure of protocol and chickened out. It took a few stern words from Prince to convince her that she had to put her money where her mouth was and believe in herself and the importance of her information.

'Get the fuck over to Grant and tell him what you found,' Prince had almost barked at her.

'But, I might be completely wrong, Sue. I was told to find a woman, and I'm taking a man to the DI.'

'So, what if you're wrong? Neither the DI, nor the Super' will blame you. But, what if you're right and don't say anything? How do you think that would pan out for you?'

Julie Cox shrugged, but was already contemplating the severe reprimand she would be on the receiving end of should she continue acting the chicken.

'You don't believe that you're wrong,' Prince stated. 'You believe
that you've found Howell's accomplice.'

Cox nodded. 'I'm *almost* sure of it,' she said.

'*Almost* sure is good enough. Get over there and tell him.'

*

Georgina Collins was a right piece of work. She had a mouth like a sewer and wasn't backwards at coming forwards when discussing her exploits with Davidson. She had a cheek to come off as haughty and ill-done to, because she was a blousy, bottle-dyed blonde without even a semblance of sophistication, and Lovell had her card marked even before she opened her mouth.

At first, she'd refused to even admit that an affair had been going on but, when Lovell prised it out of her, she sang like the preverbal canary.

Lovell considered herself a woman of the world, and she wasn't easily shocked, but she had to admit to never-before having encountered a woman like Collins. What Davidson ever saw in her was beyond her comprehension. Despite his weird manner, lack of apparent empathy, and obvious underlying deviousness, Davidson was still a perfectly groomed, middle-class snob who shouldn't – by any account – have been attracted to the rather smudged, coarse neighbour.

Apparently, the affair began as soon as Davidson's wife fell pregnant and had carried on right up until the day of her death.

'He wasn't getting it at home,' she said to Lovell. 'He was a poor soul who needed some genuine attention from a woman.'

'And, he ended up with you?' Lovell couldn't hide her shock.

'And, why not?' Collins sniffed, obviously offended. 'What's wrong with me?'

'Nothing... if you were what floated his boat.'

'Oh, I *more* than floated it... I can assure you of that. He's highly sexed, you know?'

'No, I didn't know that.'

Collins warmed to her theme. 'He couldn't get enough of me. I know that you didn't get to meet his wife, but – if you had – you would understand why he was mad for me.'

It was obvious that Davidson had found an easy conquest in Collins. Lovell had to endure a blow by blow account of where they did it, how often they did it, and in what positions they did it, before Collins settled down to answer the more important questions such as - did Davidson ever make threats to hurt his wife? Did he confide in her about his wife's affairs? Was he ever violent? Did she know if he ever visited the church outside of normal services? What did he think of Father Mackie?

'Look,' she concluded, 'I was never in any doubt that he loved his wife. I never knew that she was screwing around... so... who knows if he was jealous enough to kill her? Neither of us was looking for any more than a quick fuck a couple of times a week and, if his wife had been doing it with every Tom, Dick and Harry, then he couldn't very well complain, could he?'

Two hours into the interview, Lovell gave up and sent the woman home.

'I need a shower after that,' she said to Simon. 'I feel dirty just by being in the same room as that woman.'

'Never mind that,' he said shortly. 'Come and hear what PC Cox has to say.'

Cox sat on the very edge of a chair in Lorrie's office. She was terrified that she was wasting everyone's time and worried that Lovell would berate her for not sticking to the brief she'd been given.

When she explained that Howell had no female friends, and that Jeremy Swan was the most likely character to have been sucked into Howell's plan of murder and child abduction, she half expected to be laughed out of the room.

Surprisingly, no one laughed, and Lovell actually smiled at her.

'Okay,' Lorrie said to Cox. 'You have my attention. What do we know about him?'

Cox pulled in a breath, and said, 'Well, he's nineteen years old and lives with his mother and stepfather in a flat on the Roxdale Estate. His mother and father are divorced, and she recently took up with, and married, an Errol White. She had twin daughters with White, and they're eight months old.'

'And, he's friends with Howell?'

'Best friends, I would say, Guv''. They went to school together and they're plastered all over another's Facebook.'

'I need more, Cox. What more do you have?'

Cox wasn't sure that she had any more. Her fingering of Swan as Howell's accomplice was more gut than reason, but she searched her brain for something else of significance. Finally, she said, 'There was a slew of Facebook messages between them that was highly suggestive.'

'How so?' Simon was hanging on her every word. 'What were the messages?'

'Swan mentioned how cute his little sisters were, and Howell took the piss out of him.' Cox noticed Lorrie's frown, and hurried on. 'Then... well, Howell started to take an interest. He wanted to know what it was like to babysit them. He wondered if they cried a lot.'

'Hardly significant, Cox.' Lorrie was beginning to lose interest. 'Clutching at straws at this stage runs the risk of us losing valuable time.'

'Hear me out, please, Guv'. There's more.'

Lorrie nodded and gestured for her to get a move on.

'Howell went into great detail... wanting to know everything about how the twins were looked after, and Swan boasted that it was a piece of cake. He said that looking after a baby wasn't as difficult as most people made out. He said that - as long as they were fed, watered and not left with a shitty bum - then they were happy. He began to wonder, though, why his friend was taking such an interest, and the last message Howell posted was a request for Swan to private message him, as he wanted his help with something.'

'Okay,' Lorrie conceded. 'Let us say – for argument's sake – that Swan is with Howell.' She turned to Simon. 'Any fingerprints found at that cottage Howell was holed up in?'

'Hundreds, Guv'.'

'Do we have Swan's on file?'

'We'll need to check that,' he replied.

'I've already checked, Guv',' Cox put in. 'And, we do. He was arrested on two occasions for breaking and entering. We have fingerprints *and* DNA.'

Cox blushed under the hard stares of all three of her superiors. She couldn't make out if they were pleased or offended at the use of her own initiative.

'Fast track it, Simon,' Lorrie instructed. 'If we get a hit on Swan at the cottage, then we're in business. It will be easier to track two men with a baby, rather than one.' It was still a long-shot – and Lorrie wasn't completely convinced – but, she conceded that it could end up being the break that they so desperately needed.

'Well done, Cox. You're a star. Even if this doesn't pan out, you've impressed me.'

Cox blushed again and struggled to speak. She wanted to thank the Super' for her kind words, but only succeeded in opening and shutting her mouth like a demented fish.

*

'Anything, Prince?' Lovell hovered over Prince's shoulder and scrutinised the computer screen on the desk.

'A couple of dozen possibilities,' Prince replied over her shoulder. 'But, we've only managed to troll through about fifty shops and stores. I've narrowed them down, somewhat, but I'm being cautious. I don't want to inadvertently disregard somewhere that – on paper – wouldn't be the sort of place to sell baby products. Even petrol stations sell nappies these days.'

'It's a shitty job,' Lovell said. 'It's a bit of a hail Mary, but...'

'I know, and I don't mind. It's good to be doing something.'

'I see that you've roped in a couple of uniforms to help you.' She eyed the two PCs opposite. 'They don't look very happy.'

Prince shrugged. 'As you said, Guv'... it's a shitty job.'

Lovell smiled in sympathy. 'Run through what you're doing.'

Prince tapped a couple of keys and a fresh screen came up. It was a spreadsheet and she talked her way through it.

'On the left are the shops and stores within ten miles of the cottage and the one's I've highlighted are those that definitely sell nappies etc. I've added phone numbers and made a record of the preliminary calls we made to them. I've then identified those stores that have CCTV and asked them to check for any images matching Howell's description.'

'What about stores heading out towards Southend-on-Sea?'

Prince brought up a second spreadsheet. 'About twenty shops and petrol stations identified,' she said. 'Same procedure with the phone calls and checking of CCTV. We've had a few callbacks and there's a couple that warrant a visit.'

'Because of what they saw on their CCTV?'

Prince nodded. 'We've got eleven or twelve, in total, that sound promising, but I thought it best to concentrate on the ones towards where we think he's headed. If he doesn't have supplies... if he left everything back at the cottage... then he'll need to do a shop.'

'He'll also need to bunk down and hide out somewhere. I wonder...'

Lovell thought for a moment. 'Expand your search to include those large, anonymous hotels... Premier, Travelodge, Holiday Inns... close to where you get potential hits on the stores' CCTV. Chase up those stores that haven't called back and forward me a list of those you deem worth a visit... along with any hotels he might have sneaked into.'

'Won't the receptionist in the hotel be suspicious? I mean, pictures of the missing baby are plastered over every newspaper and is on every news channel.'

'I know plenty of hotels where you don't have to go through reception to get to your room. He'll choose one of them. He'll sneak the baby in... I'm sure of it.'

'What if...?' Prince could barely bring herself to ask. 'What if the baby has become too much of a liability?'

'Then, we're fucked,' Lovell returned. 'And, I'm not going to admit to being fucked until it's rammed home to me.'

*

As midnight approached, the team were gratified by the amount of progress they'd made. Swan's fingerprints and DNA – as well as Howells's - were confirmed to be at the cottage, and signs were good that the baby had been there and had been well cared for. Tubs of baby milk, nappies, and even soft toys, were in evidence, and – judging by the numerous empty bottles – the baby had been feeding well. They had an idea of why Howell and Swan had left the cottage with the baby – and why they'd been returning when their van was spotted – but it certainly hadn't been to stock up on baby supplies. The lack of grown-up food in the cupboards and in the fridge, was proof enough that they'd gone shopping for themselves.

The van had, indeed, been heading for Southend-on-Sea. It had been spotted two miles from the coastal town before it slipped away, once more, into the ether. Patrol cars were running up and down the coastal roads and aerial support had maintained a tight search pattern. Road blocks had been put up as far as Felixstow and – just in case Howell had doubled back – road blocks were being put in place as far back as Croydon.

Swan's mother's flat had been raided and searched and items that had been removed were being picked apart and pored over for clues. His mother and step-father were being questioned, and known associates were being hunted down and brought in.

Meantime, Prince had identified two potential hotels, and four likely stores, that were worth a visit, and she had accompanied Lovel, Baxter and Simon to the locations, whilst the two unlucky PCs were left to
man, the phones and continue with the on-line search.

Cox found herself side-lined across to the work being done to map Father Mackie's known movements up to and including the day of his death. Lorrie still had a bee in her bonnet about the priest and wanted information to tie him romantically to Davidson's wife. There was still no real evidence that the church murders were tied to Maxine Davidson's murder and the abduction of the baby, but Lorrie refused to let it slide. She knew that she couldn't afford to ignore the possibility that there was, in fact, no link.

DAY SIX: MORNING

Howell's relationship with Swan had begun to deteriorate shortly after their near capture at the cottage. Their friendship – of a long-standing ten years – had been sorely tested by the murder of Maxine Davidson, and the abduction of the baby, but it was the sight of the police at the cottage that had really rammed home to Swan the seriousness and pointless nature of their predicament. For Swan – what had started out as an exciting, if somewhat dangerous, escapade - had degenerated into a mess of hellish proportions. He'd had no actual hand in the killing and, if truth be told, he had no idea what the extent of Howell's plan had been. Although he understood the motive behind killing the woman, and taking the baby, he couldn't reconcile with the consequences. If caught, he expected to spend the best years of his life in prison, and that thought – and the hardship of being on the run – was slowly taking its toll on his sanity.

It had been a long night and, although it was the height of summer, it had been cold and damp. The baby was restless, and Swan feared for its health. They had no food and no water, and he knew that they would soon have to dump the van – thus losing their only means of transport and shelter.

Howell, on the other hand, seemed to be revelling in the whole experience. Swan believed that his friend thought it was all just one big game, and that worried him no end. He wished that he could instil in him the need for caution – the need for a real plan – but Howell seemed oblivious to the danger that they were in, and he certainly didn't understand the threat to the baby.

'Can't you shut the brat up?' Howell barked through a cough. 'That incessant crying is doing my head in.'

Swan gave him a scathing look and stuck his thumb in the baby's mouth. 'He needs milk,' he said. 'He's starving.'

'*I'm* fucking starving, but you don't hear me squalling at the top of my lungs.'

Swan shook his head, anger building inside his chest. 'You need to take us somewhere to buy some milk. Sod the risk – this baby needs to be fed.'

'He can wait a while longer. Look – he's shut up – he'll be fine.'

Swan removed his thumb from the baby's mouth, and it came out with a wet plop. The baby immediately began screaming.

'All right, is he?' Swan said, putting his thumb back. 'If you don't drive us to somewhere that sells baby milk, then I'm phoning the police to come and fetch him. I won't be responsible for killing a fucking baby, Anthony.'

Howell reined in his anger and nodded. 'All fucking right, but on your head be it.' He started the van and pulled onto the road. 'We were well hidden here,' he said. 'But, now, we're a moving target.'

'That can't be helped. What did you expect, Anthony? Did you think they wouldn't track us to the cottage? Did you think they wouldn't put every resource into finding us? We'd be better off leaving the baby where he can be found and getting the hell out of here.'

'No!' The word exploded from Howell's mouth. 'Fuck that. We're keeping him with us.'

Swan chewed his lip and began to feel a surprising shock of antagonism towards his friend. If he wasn't going to do the sensible thing, and if he wasn't going to think and plan his way out of the mess they were drowning in, then he would have to do the thinking for both of them.

'Pull over,' he said. 'Get in between those hedgerows. I'll walk to the nearest town and find a shop. They won't be looking for a man on his own and, perhaps, I'll get away with it.'

'We're miles from anywhere,' Howell returned. 'You could be gone for hours.'

'I'll be as long as it takes.' He fumbled in a pocket and drew out a pacifier. 'Pass me those sachets of ketchup from that McDonald's bag.'

Howell drew him a curious look, and obliged.

Swan tore open one of the sachets with his teeth and squeezed a drop of ketchup on the pacifier before inserting it in the baby's mouth.

'Feed him the ketchup a drop at a time on his dummy. It won't calm him for long, but it should keep him quiet for an hour or two.'

'Good thinking, Batman,' Howell grinned. 'You'll make a wonderful mother, one day.'

'Fuck you, Anthony.'

'Fuck you, Swan.'

*

Lorrie scrunched her eyes shut and groaned with exhaustion. She was so comfortable and warm under the quilt that the thought of getting out of bed was actually painful. It was six A.M. and she was absolutely shattered. She didn't think that she would be able to function without, at least, another couple of hours sleep, but, the alarm clock was chirruping away mercilessly on the bedside table, and bright morning sunlight was piercing her eyelids. She knew she had no choice but to get up and get on with it.

Pain slammed into her head like a two-ton wrecking ball when she pulled herself up from the pillows. She moaned and rubbed at her temples with trembling hands.

'Fuck this,' she said. 'Too much fucking coffee.'

The shower revitalised her somewhat and, by the time she was dressed, she had begun to feel almost human again.

Her last words to Simon – before they'd left to go home, a mere three hours earlier – were instructions for him to sleep until noon and not show his face until at least two o'clock in the afternoon. She wasn't surprised, however, to see him in her office when she arrived a little before eight o'clock.

'Is the early bird going to catch the worm?' she asked with a painful smile.

Simon looked up from the computer screen and returned her smile – although his was more of a grimace. 'I couldn't sleep. I'm knackered, but my brain refused to shut down. I thought I'd be better off here than tossing and turning in my bed. You look like shit, by the way.'

'Thanks, I think.' She shooed him from her chair and collapsed into it. 'You got anything?' she asked.

He shook his head. 'Not a damned thing. No sightings on any roads, and nothing from CCTV in any shops or petrol stations.'

'So, they've gone to ground?'

'It looks that way.'

'But, where?'

'They could be anywhere. They could've slipped past before the roadblocks were set up, or they could have found another bolt-hole in Essex.' Simon looked at her as he spoke. 'It's too much ground for us to cover and...' he frowned, 'there's Epping forest to consider.'

'They wouldn't be stupid enough to take a baby into the forest.'

'I think they would,' a voice said from the doorway.

Both Lorrie and Simon turned towards the door.

'PC Prince? Do you have something?' Lorrie pulled herself to her feet and felt her features form an expectant expression.

'I think so,' Prince said, stepping into the office. 'I've just had two phone calls – one from a Boots pharmacy, and one from a camping goods store – saying that a man had been in and purchased ready-made bottles of formula, nappies, wipes, jars of baby food and a full basket of ready-made sandwiches, water and chocolate... that was in Boots... and a pop-up tent, two sleeping bags, a portable gas stove, etc from the other shop.'

'Fuck,' Lorrie and Simon said in unison.

'I took the liberty of sending a panda to the shops and requested a sweep of the roads in and out of the town.'

'Was it Howell?' Lorrie asked.

Prince shook her head. 'The description was a dead ringer for Swan.'

'When was this?'

'About three hours ago. No-one in either shop thought much about it until both saw the eight o'clock news bulletin. Swan's face was plastered over the screen and, luckily, both shop managers put two and two together and rang it in.'

'Three hours? Jesus.'

'Both shops were open that early?'

'It's the height of summer, Guv',' Prince returned. 'Anyway, the Boots is open twenty-four hours, and the camping shop opens its doors at six to catch the early morning campers.'

'Where?'

'Harlow.'

'They didn't go far, then?' Simon noted.

'And, you think they're heading for the forest?' Lorrie eyed Prince.

'Seems likely, Guv'... given the camping gear.'

'And, they have a three-hour head start on us.' Lorrie groaned and placed her forehead on the desk. 'God help us.'

*

In fact, Howell and Swan had much less of a head start. By the time Swan struggled back to the van with the supplies and the camping gear, they had an hour's grace before both the Boots' manager and the camping shop manager saw Swan's face on television and contacted the police.

'Camping?' Howell said without humour. 'Are you kidding me?'

'You have a better idea?' Swan bit back. 'It's either that, or turn ourselves in.'

'But, fucking camping? I don't know *how* to camp.'

'How hard can it be?'

'Hard enough, with a baby in tow, I would imagine.'

'At least we can feed him,' Swan said, putting a teat on a bottle and ramming it into the baby's squalling mouth. 'I suggest we ditch the van, at least a mile from where we go into the forest, and head for the thickest, densest bit of woodland we can find. It's a big place... the forest... and it will take more than a stroke of good luck for them to find us. It'll give us some breathing space and give us time to think.'

Howell didn't have a better idea, so he reluctantly agreed. Anything was better than being caught on the road with the van.

They set off right away and – unbeknown to them – missed being seen by the panda car dispatched to Harlow by a short ten minutes.

*

They found the van abandoned on the side of the road an hour later and wheels were immediately put in motion to begin the painstaking search of the forest.

Epping forest covered nearly six thousand acres of grassland, woodland, rivers and areas of bog. It stretched twelve miles on the border between London and Essex and was notorious for the dumping of murdered bodies from the sixties up until present day. It wasn't an easy area to navigate or search and Lorrie desperately needed somewhere to start.

Simon was optimistic. He said, 'They're not as clever as they think they are. I'm sure that they have no idea how to cover their tracks, and they don't have that much of a head start. We'll find them.'

Lorrie wasn't so sure. 'I'm not convinced they went in anywhere near
where the van was dumped,' she said. 'That would've been a very stupid thing to do and, so far, these pair of reprobates have displayed a certain lack of stupidity when it matters.'

Simon leaned back on the bonnet of his car and surveyed the horizon. He said, 'They could've gone in either direction. There's cover for miles to the front and to the back of us.'

Lorrie let that sink in and followed Simon's gaze to take in the miles of road, bordered by hedges and trees, that would have given Howell and Swan the cover they needed to enter the forest at a place of their choosing.

'I still don't get it,' Simon said. 'I mean... killing Maxine Davidson and taking the baby.'

'Howell lost his family and he blames Davidson,' Lorrie replied. 'Of course, it might be something else, but my money is on Howell exacting the best revenge that his tiny little mind could muster.'

'Still...'

'I know... I know... I'm stretching it, somewhat.'

'No, it's not that.' Simon pulled himself up from the bonnet. 'There's just too many deaths for it to be Davidson. Why kill everyone in the church simply because his wife was screwing Mackie? And, how the hell would Howell know it was Davidson? And, then there's Mackie and his colourful sex life and lies.'

'It's either Mackie or Davidson. I'm convinced of that.'

'It still doesn't answer the question as to why Howell honed-in on Davidson. What does he know that we don't?'

'Let's find him and ask him.'

'Easier said than done.' Simon sighed and shook his head. His earlier optimism was ebbing. 'I have a feeling that Howell will outsmart us.'

'You're giving him more credit than he deserves. He's not entirely stupid, but he's up against us... and we're the bee's knees.'

'I guess.'

Lorrie had no time for Simon's introspective pessimism. 'A minute or so ago, you were telling *me* that we'd find them. Now, you're going all pansy on me.'

'Sorry. I'm just tired.'

'Join the club.'

He gave her a watery smile. 'They'll be tired, too.'

She nodded. 'And, getting more tired by the second. They'll make a
mistake. In fact, they've already made a big one.'

'Oh?'

'By going into Epping. It might buy them some time, but the forest is no haven for them... not in the long run.'

'I guess.'

'For fuck's sake... chin up, Simon.' Lorrie walked off towards the van. 'Has the van been searched, yet? There's bound to be something in there for the dogs to sniff.'

Simon nodded and followed at her heels. 'Dirty nappies, food wrappers, a hoodie... plenty for the dogs to get at.' Simon thought that there was probably *too much* for the dogs to make sense of, but he kept that thought to himself.

It was as if Lorrie read his mind. 'We can't let the dogs loose with all those scents. Give them something of the baby's. The baby is the priority. If they dump him, I want the dogs to find him.'

'At least the baby is still alive,' he said. 'I'll admit to being shit scared that he'd be harmed, or killed. Do you really think that they might dump him?'

'Who knows?' she shrugged, 'But, if it was Howell's intention to harm him, the baby would already be toast.'

*

Lorrie drove back to London and headed for the hospital. Her intention was to make a flying visit to check on Fredrickson and to update him on events.

The sun was shining, and it promised to be a warm and beautiful day. She shuddered to think how the baby would have fared in the forest if the day had been wet and cold. Thank goodness for small mercies, she thought, as she pulled into the hospital car park.

She found Fredrickson well rested and eager for news.

'Take that guilty look off your face, Sullivan,' he said. 'I'm fine, and I want to stay involved… even from a hospital bed.'

'I must admit… you *do* look a lot better than yesterday.'

'Pain pills, good looking nurses, and plenty of sleep, are the cure-alls for everything.'

'Still…'

'I'm fine,' he insisted. 'Tell me everything.'

When she got to the part of the story that covered Howell and Swan's escape into Epping, he said, 'The dogs will find them. They really
don't stand a chance of hiding out for long.'

'Finding them is the least of my worries,' she said. 'It's *what* I'll find that scares me.'

'If Howell wanted the baby dead…'

'I know.' She nodded and tried to smile. 'He'd already be dead. I've already said as much to Simon.'

'Then…'

'What I *say*, and what I *think*, are two different things.'

'You're close. Have some faith.'

'Am I close, though?'

They knew that Howell and Swan were probably in the forest with the baby. They thought that because of Swan purchasing the camping gear, but a little voice whispered in her ear that she could be sending her troops on a wild goose chase. What if it was a double bluff?

'You *are* close,' he reiterated.

She pushed her doubt away and nodded. Fredrickson was just what she needed. Her reliance on his quiet strength, good sense and support was almost intoxicating.

'You're blushing,' he said, surprised. 'What are you thinking?'

'Nothing,' she denied. 'It's just hot in here.'

'You're just not used to seeing me with no clothes on.' He yanked the sheet up and covered his chest. 'I'm not exactly decent enough for visitors.' If he was capable of blushing, he, too, would be red-faced.

It was a moment when anything could have been said – a moment when feelings could have been allowed to rise to the surface – but it passed in an uncomfortable silence, broken only when Fredrickson asked, 'Has the press got wind of it?'

'No, thank God. They'd turn it into a circus and screw everything up.' Lorrie was relieved to be back to matters of the case. 'We've got radio silence, and a phones-only communication arrangement. The press bastards listen in on our radio chatter, and cutting it was one of the first things I did.'

He nodded his approval. 'Have you updated Scully?'

'Not yet.'

'You have to tell him, Lorrie. Don't give him any reason to have a go at you.'

'I'll tell him, but I want to wait until I'm sure they've gone into Epping.'

'You shouldn't doubt it.'

She shrugged. 'I guess not. I don't think that either of them is clever enough to bluff us, but, who knows?'

Her phone rang, cutting their conversation short, and she checked the screen before answering. Then, after a brief discussion, with whoever was on the other end, she disconnected the call and swore under her breath.

'I've been called back. Apparently, I've to go and answer a few more questions about the death of Father Young. It's fucking ridiculous.' She threw her phone down onto the bed. 'Don't they know what I'm up against? Have they no fucking sense?'

Fredrickson grimaced – more from thoughts of what she'd do to further antagonise the hapless investigators, than from physical pain.

'I was going to head straight back to Epping and, now, I've got to go and defend myself to those pair of wankers.'

'Well, try to behave yourself this time. No more walking out in a strop.'

'I'm not making any promises,' she returned. 'I'll give them ten minutes. If they don't get what they want from me in that time, then fuck them.'

Fredrickson watched her go from the relative discomfort of his hospital bed and marvelled at her stamina and, yet, despaired at her complete lack of political nous. She'd never learned to play the game, and he doubted that she ever would. He wondered if he would truly have her any other way?

*

Simon was convinced that the dumping of the van wasn't a red herring. He was also convinced that – with a baby in tow – they wouldn't have made much headway into the heart of the forest.

Two hundred officers had been drafted in to help with the search and six dogs swelled the ranks.

Simon instructed the officers to avoid the grassland and heathland and to concentrate their efforts on the woodland areas. Unfortunately, because many of the trees in Epping hadn't been cut since the nineteenth century – and since their heavy branches had shed tons of dead wood – the going was precarious in places and didn't make for the ideal search pattern. However, the dogs had a better time of it and, within an hour, one of them had picked up a scent.

DAY SIX: AFTERNOON

PC Julie Cox had now spent a total of fourteen hours delving into every aspect of Father Mackie's movements since his return from Syria. Her focus had been on the time he spent living with Father Young, but she'd also tracked him, as best she could, from the moment he arrived back in the UK, and had also investigated the new job he had secured in Birmingham.

Her first surprise – or, shock more like – was the fact that he had actually turned down the job in the Birmingham parish. She didn't dwell too long on the fact that no one from the church had divulged that little piece of information – leaving that conversation for either the Super' or the DI to have with the Bishop – and, instead, concentrated on finding just what it was that he planned to do as an alternative.

Telephoning, and attempting to ask questions of the Arch Diocese, ended up being a total waste of time, and she had to revert to subterfuge to get any answers at all.

Pushing all thoughts of digging a hole for herself – and running the risk of being severely reprimanded – she pretended to be the personal assistant of a Bishop she had chosen at random from the episcopal rolls and registers. She was amazed at how easy it was to get information when the other person at the end of the phone was in awe of who she supposedly worked for.

Apparently, Father Mackie turned down the job a full week before his death. He gave no explanation and no alternative job was offered. Cox had a feeling in her gut that Mackie planned on leaving the church altogether, and she wracked her brain to find a way of proving her hypothesis.

She acknowledged that he Super' was adamant that Davidson had been telling the truth when he told Prince that his wife was having it off with the priest, so Cox went with that, and surmised that he had made a life-changing decision to leave the church so that he could run off with her.

It was a long-shot, but Cox kept returning to that notion every time she veered off to follow a different line of enquiry.

CCTV had turned out to be a Godsend. In tracking his movements from Young's house, Cox focussed on the camera two hundred yards away from Young's manse and quickly searched through hundreds of hours of footage, and then compared the date and time stamps with images of him on or around the Davidson's home. In the end, she found that she could quite safely say that Mackie had visited Mrs. Davidson at home thirteen times over a three- week period.

When her eyes lost focus, and when her coffee-fuelled body gave up the ghost, she found a quiet corner. She was past the point of caring whether she got into trouble for sleeping on the job. She rationalised that everyone would appreciate that she'd not been home to sleep for more hours than she could count and, exhausted, she immediately dropped into death-like unconsciousness.

Prince woke her at four o'clock to inform her that a dead body had been discovered in Epping forest.

*

Lorrie had been true to her word and gave the officers interviewing her no more than ten minutes before she upped and left. As far as she was concerned, she had better things to do than to sit and attempt to justify herself to a pair of nincompoops who'd probably never been on the sharp end of a murder enquiry. Luckily, Scully wasn't around to reprimand or suspend her.

The questions they asked her were, more or less, a repeat of those asked on the previous occasion although, this time, they were more aggressive in their approach. It was as if they had carte-blanche to treat her as roughly and as unprofessionally as they liked.

Well, Lorrie was having none of it and – fools that they were – the investigators thought that she would be a pushover. In their eyes, she was a light-weight, and a woman who had allowed the power of the job to go to her head. They believed that she had bullied and aggressively treated the priest because she was a woman in a male dominated profession who had a point to prove and – despite the fact that she had walked out on them previously – they thought that they could browbeat her into admitting that she'd acted outside of professional boundaries when she had interviewed Father Young. Ironically, neither saw that – how they attempted to treat her – was exactly the what they were accusing her of.

This time, when she stood up to leave, they were flabbergasted and realised that they had bit off more than they could chew. She was no pushover, and they had to admit that they'd met their match. They realised that they would now have to escalate the matter up the chain of command.

Lorrie had then arrived at Epping forest a little after one o'clock and joined the search just as the dogs were honing-in on a scent that had them pulling their handlers almost off their feet. Now, at a little after three o'clock, forensics were already erecting a tent around a scene that could only be described as horrific.

*

Howell had been slowly losing patience with his constantly moaning friend. They'd been walking for hours – sometimes around in circles – and had, yet, to find anywhere safe and secure enough to hide out.

Contrary, to what Swan had originally stated – when persuading Howell to enter Epping forest - the forest had turned out *not* to be their friend. At every turn, it seemed to conspire against them. It put obstacles in the way, thrust boggy areas beneath their feet and played games with their senses, so that – when they thought they were moving straight ahead – they had discovered that they'd actually gone full circle.

Howell bitterly regretted entering the forest and, he was sure that - if Swan didn't shut up anytime soon - he would feel obliged to punch him in the throat.

He liked Swan. His friend had always been someone he could rely on, and he never would have believed that the day would come when he began to hate the very sight and sound of him. But, that day was almost upon them. A seething sense of umbrage, at his friend's continual sniping and complaining, was slowly taking over Howell's fragile state of mind, and he had to grit his teeth against the words that could potentially set off a war between them. He knew that, if he spoke his mind... *really spoke his mind...* all hell would break loose.

Although they had avoided the marked trails, it was impossible to stay totally under the radar, and – once or twice – they had heard voices in the distance, and footsteps close by, as ramblers made their way through the trees. In those brief moments – where discovery was almost inevitable - it was sheer luck that the baby hadn't cried and alerted anyone nearby.

They'd come across a break in the trees, that Howell immediately recognised as somewhere they'd passed through an hour before and, if it hadn't been dangerous to do so, Howell would have screamed his frustration at the top of his lungs. Instead, he dropped to his knees, moaned, and placed his forehead on the grass.

Swan's response to recognising that, yet again, they'd miscalculated their journey through the forest, was to say, 'This is no good. We'd be better off taking our chances on the road.'

His words brought Howell rearing back and up on his feet once more. Instinctively – and with an anger bordering on a violent eruption – he made a grab for his friend's throat.

'*You* brought us fucking well in here,' he screamed. '*You* wanted to dump the van. *You* wanted to drag us through this hell-hole of a place.'

Howell squeezed tighter, oblivious to everything but the black rage that engulfed him, and Swan – unable to defend himself because he had the baby in his arms - staggered backwards, and almost lost his footing.

'*You* did this... you fucking moron,' Howell spat out viciously, before dropping his hand and freeing Swan's throat. 'Just where you imagined we would pitch a tent is beyond me, and now... now that you see what a monumental cock-up you made... you want to go back on the road? Fucking unbelievable.' He turned his back and took a few steps towards the tree-line. 'I don't even know where we are,' he went on. 'You want to go back on the road?' He turned to glance over his shoulder. '*I have no fucking clue* how far we are from the nearest road. Jesus Christ...you've well and truly fucked us.'

Swan gasped for air but, otherwise, sensibly, remained silent.

Howell slowly regained his composure. He was pragmatic by nature and realised that they had two choices – head back to the road... if they could find it... as Swan suggested, or simply plod on and try to find somewhere to rest and hide out.

Swan took the decision away from him. He staggered forward, thrust
the baby into Howell's arms, and then immediately walked off. The trees immediately swallowed him up.

Howell stood for a moment, his anger fully dissipated, to be replaced by uncertainty, and he then followed Swan deeper into the forest.

Swan walked quickly, and Howell feared that he would lose him.

'Where are you going?' he called after him. 'Stop and get your arse back here.' His voice held more bravado than he felt.

Swan ignored him, and Howell was forced to continue to follow, in what he hoped, was his footsteps.

Walking was difficult with the child. Howell often stumbled over dead branches and, because the baby was wriggling and squirming in his arms, he found it impossible to reach out his hands to steady himself.

Swan got further away from him and, soon, Howell had no idea where his friend was. Hampered by the baby, and struggling to remain on his feet, he came to realise that they were in a part of the forest that was so dense than even the sunlight was unable to find them.

'This is great,' he called out. 'They won't find us here. We can rest up.' He listened intently for a sound – any sound – from Swan. Hearing nothing but silence, he tried again. 'Come on... I'm sorry I grabbed you. Let's just take a breather and work out what to do.'

Still, no sound from Swan, then, 'You touch me again, and I'll knife you.'

Howell spun around and found Swan at his back. 'Jesus, mate,' he gasped. 'You scared the shit out of me.'

'I mean it,' Swan said, grabbing the baby. 'I'll fucking knife you.'

'Yeah. Yeah... I get it,' Howell said, somewhat chastened. 'I was out of order.'

'You can say that again, you fucking maniac.' Swan was not appeased by his friend's obvious regret at nearly choking him to death. 'You're a headcase... a nutjob,' he said. 'I must have been certifiable to get caught up in any of this.'

Howell kept his expression neutral. 'I know... I'm sorry.'

'Sorry doesn't cut it. From now on, we do things my way with no argument.'

Howell nodded. 'Sure. I'm down with that.'

'Good, because we're giving the baby back.'

'What?' Howell's shock was all too evident. 'The whole idea... the whole fucking thing was so I could get the baby. It will have all been for nothing, if I give him back.'

'Yes, but it's not working.' Swan wasn't wholly unsympathetic. 'You need to see that, mate. We need to get him somewhere safe and call the cops to come pick him up. They'll be cock-a-hoop at getting him back and we can use that time... when they're all wrapped up with getting him to the hospital, and shit... to slip away.

Howell's expression remained unchanged, but his mind was working overtime. His temper was beginning to get jacked right up and he was beginning to realise that Swan wasn't truly his friend. No true friend would spout such shit.

Oblivious to Howell's mounting anger, Swan relaxed his guard. 'I can get us some money and we can get the fuck right out of here,' he said. 'Go abroad, maybe.'

'Abroad?' Howell was momentarily stunned by the ridiculousness of Swan's suggestion. There was no going abroad for either of them.

'Yes... somewhere they won't look for us.'

'That's not what I want,' he said in a low, threatening tone. 'I'm going nowhere without the baby.' He moderated his voice. 'You *do* see how that's impossible, don't you?'

The canopy of trees that blocked the light ensured that Swan was oblivious to the dark spark of menace in Howell's eyes and, it was only when he saw Howell reach into his trouser pocket and pull out his switchblade, that he realised his goose was about to be cooked.

'Okay... Okay,' he said, stepping back. 'We'll keep the baby.' He stretched out his arms to hand the baby back to Howell.

Howell ignored the wriggling infant and took the opportunity to lunge forward. He bent his knees, put the full force of his body behind the thrust, and plunged the blade deep into Swan's ribs.

Swan jerked back and the knife, still in Howell's hand, slipped out with a wet sucking sound. Instinctively, Swan dropped the baby and reached up to the gaping wound with a trembling hand.

*

Ricky had to wait until the area was floodlit before he could examine the body. Three small, battery powered lights had been erected inside the tent, and a further two had been set up directly outside so as to allow a search of the ground. They were looking for the murder weapon and were also painstakingly searching for, what they hoped, didn't turn out to be the body of the baby. Thankfully, the dogs didn't need light to continue their search and, so far, neither the knife nor the baby had been discovered.

'There's been a sighting of Howell at Epsom tube station,' Simon said.

Lorrie looked at him expectantly.

'He didn't have the baby,' he said. 'We have to assume that the little mite is somewhere in the forest.'

Lorrie felt as if her heart was about to burst out of her chest. Panic almost set in and she had to dig deep to prevent herself from screaming.

'Guv'?' Simon was worried about her. The news he'd imparted was bad enough, but her reaction to it was much worse. 'What do you want us to do?'

'Do?' Her voice was thick with shock. 'Do? Find the fucking baby... *that's* what I want you to do. Is it too much to ask? Is it too far beyond your capabilities to find a three- month old baby?' It was cruel, it was unfair, and it was wholly unnecessary, and Lorrie realised that as soon as the words were spewed from her mouth, but she couldn't apologise. She couldn't take them back. She was too shocked, too angry, and too frustrated to even consider the effect her words would have on everyone within earshot.

Simon was, technically, the same rank as her. He was acting Super' and didn't have to accept her angry words, nor her unveiled criticism, but he had the sense to know that she wasn't really lashing out at him. He knew that her words were meant for herself. He knew that she was feeling such a profound sense of failure, that her only redress – her only way of coping – was to hit out with words. It wasn't one of her most endearing qualities – this habit she had of lashing out with a vicious tongue – but, it was something he was used to, and something he was always willing to forgive.

'Okay,' he nodded. 'We'll continue the search, but the little light that we have is going to be lost pretty soon. We may have to leave it until full light tomorrow.

'No.' Lorrie shook her head. 'There's never going to be full light in this part of the forest. We'll search by flashlight. He could be close, and nobody moves from here until that baby is found.'

'He could already be dead.' Simon hated saying the words, but they *did* need to be said.'

'Don't you think that I know that?' She dropped her gaze to her feet. 'It's all I can think about.'

'Okay. Perhaps the dogs will sniff him out. We'll keep looking.'

Simon gestured to the dog handlers and they moved off to work their way across the unsearched ground and out beyond the immediate perimeter of the crime scene. After a few minutes – when no new scent of the baby was picked-up on by the dogs – he turned once more to Lorrie.

'It could be a positive thing,' he said, gesturing over his shoulder at the dogs. 'It could mean that Howell carried him away. He could still have him.'

'Not according to CCTV at the tube station,' Lorrie returned.

'We need to check that out. He would know how important it was to hide him.'

'How the fuck do you hide a baby?'

Simon shrugged. 'Beats me, but I wouldn't want to assume that he *couldn't* do it.'

'Put a call through to the office and get it checked out.'

'They're already trying to track him, and new images are being scrutinised as we speak.'

'We might see something, then?'

'Well, I've not heard what train he took... if he took a train at all... and, so far, there's been nothing from any stations on that line. There's nothing for me to do here, so I'm heading back to co-ordinate the search for him. Are you staying here?'

'Yes. I can't leave until I'm sure the baby's not here. Anyway... I want to hear what Ricky has to say about the body.'

'Fair enough.'

She nodded, once more, and watched mutely as Simon walked off.

Ricky Burton had, of course, heard her cruel words to Simon and – when he emerged from the tent and watched as Simon left – he wandered over to where Lorrie stood, alone and dejected.

His first words to her were - 'You can be a right bitch at times, Sullivan. Thankfully, that man respects you, or you would find yourself the victim of another internal investigation.'

'Fuck off, Ricky.' She pressed her lips together, preventing any further profanity from escaping.

'Nice,' he said, sarcastically. 'You really are the epitome of propriety.'

'Sorry.'

He nodded, satisfied with the apology.

She said, 'Look... I know that I'm a bitch. Simon knows that I'm a bitch. I don't understand why he finds excuses for me.'

'He's a good man to have in your corner. None better.'

'I know.' She sighed and nodded towards the tent. 'Well?'

'Stab wound to the chest. Nicked the heart.'

'How long ago?'

'Less than an hour.'

'Anything else?'

'Well, he's covered in baby sick... regurgitated milk... so, I guess he had care of the baby most of the time.'

'We don't know where the baby is,' she almost sobbed.

'With Howell?'

She shook her head. 'Doesn't seem likely.'

'But, you're not sure?'

'No.'

'Then, there's still hope.'

*

Lorrie drove back to New Scotland Yard in a daze. PC Cox tried to grab her attention as soon as she walked from the lift, but Lorrie brushed her off. Whatever she wanted could wait. Lorrie had more urgent things to attend to.

Seeing Scully in her office, seated like a fat pig behind her desk, momentarily infuriated her. She knew why he was there – and it had nothing to do with a missing baby or a slew of unsolved murders.

He didn't know it, but Commander Scully was on thin ice with her. One wrong word from him and – in her current frame of mind – she would go off like a nuclear bomb, right in his face.

'Ah, Superintendent Sullivan,' he said, a smirk on his fleshy mouth. 'You've deigned to show your face, at last.'

'I've been busy,' she returned sharply. 'What do you want?'

'Now, there's a question you should know the answer to. You are, after all, a detective and there's plenty of clues to go on.'

Yes, she knew the answer to her own question, but she wasn't in the mood to humour him. She simply wanted to get on with her job without having to suffer his infuriating presence.

They hadn't found any sign of the baby and – with evening fast approaching - she'd had no choice but to call off the search. That fact alone should have warned the Commander to tread carefully.

'I said... I'm busy. In case you've forgotten – I'm in the midst of a manhunt and I have a missing baby to find.' She hovered in the doorway, urging him with her eyes to leave her alone.

He ignored her silent request to fuck off. 'You're also in the midst of an internal inquiry, Superintendent. Don't let us forget that.'

'It's the furthest thing from my mind,' she returned

'Well, it shouldn't be. Your actions in walking out – not once, but twice – from your interview has repercussions.'

'I'm sure it does.'

'Do you care to know what one of those repercussions is?'

She shrugged. 'Not really.'

He laughed, obviously enjoying the moment. 'Suspension... Suspension from duty is one of the repercussions,' he said. 'I could order you from the premises and send you packing in a heartbeat.'

'But, you won't.'

He was taken aback by her blunt statement and he lost the smirk. 'It's my prerogative. Give me one good reason why I shouldn't boot your arse out of here.'

'Because it's all bullshit. You know it's bullshit, and I know it's bullshit. If you interrupt my investigation at this crucial point, the AC would have your job. If you booted my arse out of here, she'd make mincemeat out of you and your career. I think that you'll have to wait a while longer to wank off on my demise.'

Lorrie was shocked at her words, and her self-destructive bravado, but was even more shocked at her feeling of not giving a damn what he did to her. Her job... her career... no longer meant anything. All she could think about was the baby and what he might be suffering at the hands of a monster. Scully, the internal investigation, and her precarious position, were neither here nor there.

She knew that – once the investigation was over – Scully would get his way and she would be finished, but she honestly didn't care.

Scully gathered himself together. 'You have one more chance to meet with IPCC. I suggest you take it,' he said. 'Only one more chance, Sullivan... I mean it.'

She mulled over his words. 'It'll have to wait. I'm not being pulled away again.'

Scully had two choices – he could insist that she drop everything and present herself to IPCC immediately, or he could do the sensible thing and give her some time to do her job. For once, he did the sensible thing.

'I'm prepared to give you forty-eight hours,' he said. 'If you don't co-operate fully with the internal investigation, at that point, I *will* suspend you, and bugger what the AC has to say about it. Now, fill me in on where you are with this complete fuck-up of a case.'

DAY SIX: EVENING

PC Cox finally managed to attract the Super's attention, and she wasted no time in filling her in on what she'd discovered, via CCTV, about Mackie and Mrs. Davidson.

'So,' Lorrie said, 'we can, pretty much say, that he was fucking her?'

Cox nodded. 'But, I don't think that he was the only one, Guv'.'

'Well, according to her husband, she never had her legs closed, so that's not exactly news, Cox.'

'No, Guv', I guess not.'

'But, well done for confirming their affair. It puts Davidson well and truly in the frame.'

'Should we bring him back in?'

Lorrie nodded. 'Right away.'

Cox remained standing in front of Lorrie. It was obvious that she had something else on her mind.

'What is it, Cox? Spit it out.'

'Well, Guv'...' She didn't quite know how to make the suggestion.

'Jesus, Cox. I've no time for dithering. If you have something to say, then just say it.'

Cox dragged in a breath and went for it. 'What if it was someone else? What if it was a jealous lover... someone else who she did the dirty on?'

'I'm listening.'

'What if it wasn't the husband? Suppose – by taking up with Mackie – she angered someone else?'

'That's a possibility, I suppose, but Davidson seems most likely.'

'I know that, Guv', but, what if we're wrong? I'd like to pursue this line of enquiry. I'd like to carry on checking up on what she got up to, and with whom. Perhaps I can find out who her other lovers were... before Mackie?'

Lorrie thought about it for all of three seconds before she shook her head. 'No. I need you to help out in the search for Howell. He might still have the baby, and I can't spare you on a wild goose chase.'

Cox understood, but she was bitterly disappointed. She believed that the Super' was making a terrible mistake, but she had no option but to shelve her hunch and do as she was told.

Having two high-profile cases was beginning to take its toll on the team. Lorrie tried to keep both separate, and allocate resources according to what was the priority, but everyone – herself included – couldn't help but waste time and energy flitting between both. She knew that she had to interview Davidson again, but she found it difficult to concentrate on that one task.

Simon – the lead on the church case – found that the majority of his time was spent on trying to find Howell and, as that was technically Lorrie's case, everything started to get rather messy.

Thankfully, Lovell was strong enough, and smart enough, to keep all the balls in the air, and her liaison role – between both cases – was enough to prevent a meltdown... at least for the moment. However, everyone missed Fredrickson's calming influence and skill at steering a steady ship. Without him, there was a very real danger of neither case being solved.

'He's got the baby,' Prince called from behind her computer screen.

Everyone's eyes immediately swivelled towards where she was seated.

'He's in the ruck-sack,' Prince said. 'Would you believe it... He's got him in the bloody rucksack.'

*

Howell stood on the corner of Hopewell and Dalton Street and watched as two police cars drove past. The baby was wriggling and mewling in the ruck-sack on his back and he knew that he would need to find somewhere soon to feed and change him. It was early evening and the rush-hour traffic masked the sounds the baby made, but Howell realised that someone was bound to notice both him and the baby pretty soon and – although he had done his best to avoid the many traffic and CCTV cameras – he was in no doubt that he was a mere hair's breadth away from being caught.

He glanced to his right and saw a lone woman drop her car keys. She was weighed down with several bags of shopping and was obviously struggling to hold onto them whilst trying to unlock her car.

Thinking better of it, she placed the bags on the pavement and bent to retrieve the keys. Howell took a chance and rushed over.

The woman straightened up and looked at him as if he was mad. There was no fear on her face. She was in the middle of a busy street, with dozens of people walking past, and had no real reason to believe that anyone would do her harm in such an obviously busy place.

'What?' she said irritably.

Howell ignored her question and snatched the keys from her hand. 'Get in the car,' he said, pressing the fob to unlock it, and pulling open the driver's door.

It was then that she felt the knife press into her side and, for the first time, fear and adrenalin coursed through her body.

'Please,' she said. 'Don't hurt me.'

'Get in the fucking car. I won't tell you again.'

She did as she was told and almost fell into the seat. Howell pulled open the rear passenger's door and clambered inside. With the knife at her neck, he handed her the keys and ordered her to move.

Howell licked dry lips and urged her to get a move on. 'Drive,' he said. 'Get me the fuck out of here.'

'Where?' she asked, terrified.

Howell glanced out of the rear window and then anxiously searched both sides of the road and the pavement for any sign that his car-jacking had been noticed, but everyone was too busy with their own thoughts and their own little lives to have seen anything.

The woman's hand reached out for the horn, and she was just about to press down on it when she felt the blade of the knife prick her skin.

'I'll stick you with this knife,' he said. 'I won't hesitate to cut you from ear to ear. Start the car and move.'

'My... my shopping,' she wailed. 'I need my shopping.'

'Your fucking shopping?' Howell was dumbfounded. 'You're worried about your bloody shopping?' He saw that the bags were still sitting on the pavement and was suddenly absurdly pleased that she'd mentioned it. The stupid fucking woman had just saved him. There was no way he could allow her to drive off and leave those bags behind. God knows what was in them... perhaps something that could identify her? And, anyway, bags of abandoned shopping would draw unnecessary attention.

He used one hand to slip off the ruck-sack, whilst keeping the other hand with the knife against her neck and contemplated the many scenarios where everything could now go tit's up.

'Open the door and lean out of the car,' he said. 'Grab the bags and throw them on the seat next to you.' He grabbed a handful of her hair and yanked her head back. 'Don't try anything funny, because, I *will* kill you.'

It was at that moment that she heard the baby cry and she immediately knew who he was. He'd been all over the news and had been described as armed and dangerous. Instead of the knowledge spurring her onto try and escape his clutches, it served to enrage her. He'd kidnapped a baby and that baby was now rammed inside a ruck-sack. That made her angry and, fuelled by that anger, she managed to twist her head forward and then sharply backwards until it connected with his face.

She heard more than felt his nose pop and, as he reared back and threw his hands to his face, she scrambled over the seat and attempted to grab hold of the bag. There was no way she was leaving the car without that bag, but she failed to take into consideration Howell's own level of adrenalin and, before she could snatch the bag, the knife was back at her throat.

*

'I take it that we've no further sightings of him?' Simon asked Prince.

She shook her head. 'Nothing, sir, but we'll keep looking.'

'You do that, and amazing work, Prince. Nobody else noticed that movement in the bag.'

Lovell patted Prince on the shoulder and gestured for Simon to step to the side, out of earshot.

'The Guv' is just about to go in with Davidson,' she said. 'I think you should join her.'

'It doesn't take two of us, Lovell. I'm needed out here.'

Lovell shook her head. 'She's wound up tighter than a spring and needs you at her side.'

'You go,' he returned. 'I'm too busy.'

He made to move away, but Lovell made a grab for his arm, 'No,' she hissed. 'I'm sorry, sir, but you're needed in that interview room with her. She's hell-bent on pinning the church murders on Davidson, and I'm not sure that she's right.'

'What do you mean? Everything points to him.'

'Yes,' she agreed. 'But, he's not the only one with a motive.'

'Who? Who else has a motive? What don't I know?'

'Nothing. There isn't anything to know... not exactly.'

'Then, what the hell, Lovell?'

'It's just something I overheard PC Cox say to her. It got me thinking, and I've told Cox to pursue it... much against the Super's orders, I might add.'

'You have to do better than that,' he said. 'I can't simply walk into that interview room and babysit her. Give me a reason or get out of my way.'

'Okay... Okay...' Lovell dragged in a breath. 'The wife may have had another lover before she hooked up with Mackie. She probably dumped him in favour of screwing the priest. Cox thinks... *We both* think that gives this other man a motive.'

'Jesus, Lovell... she was pregnant before hooking up with Mackie. I don't think she was screwing around with womb full of arms and legs.'

'That's as maybe, but...'

'No.' He held up a hand. 'This isn't the time for wild speculation. Davidson is our man and it's up to the Guv' to get him to admit it. If you're so worried... you sit in on the interview.'

*

She lived alone at the quiet end of a cul-de-sac. Howell made her drive straight into the attached garage and, once the internal door was closed, he frog-marched her through to the house and tied her to a chair.

She was around thirty years of age, not pretty but not ugly either, and she had a certain arrogance about her that annoyed the hell out of him. Once she'd stopped weeping and wailing in the car, and became somewhat resigned to her fate, she drove home without so much as a squeak and, when she was incapacitated and secured tight, she put on a brave face as she awaited whatever punishment her captor was about to lay out.

She thought that his nose was broken and, despite the fact that she would pay dearly for her actions, she was more than pleased with her handiwork. She hadn't rescued the baby, and she was in a dangerous predicament herself, but she was alive, and she was nothing if not hopeful about her chances of escape.

The baby squealed his displeasure at being squashed and manhandled but was, otherwise, unharmed by the adventure. With a tummy replenished with warm milk, he slept soundly and, for the first time in days, Howell felt he could relax.

In his haste to get away – and after the woman's stupid attempt to grab the baby and escape - he had to leave the shopping behind on the pavement. That meant that there was little to eat in the house. There was bread and cheese and a couple of squishy tomatoes – enough for a sandwich – and he made do with that. There was also coffee, but no milk, but he didn't mind taking it black.

He offered her nothing. He was neither concerned about her hunger nor her comfort. She was a means to an end and, anyway, he had a score to settle with her and filling her with bread and cheese would simply be a waste of good food.

His nose throbbed, and his head hurt, and it was all her fault. It was also her fault that there was nothing decent to eat in the house.

Howell didn't consider himself an unnecessarily cruel man, but he knew that he *could* be cruel when pushed too far. The woman had, very nearly, pushed him towards abject cruelty, but he let her off with a matching broken nose, a few bruised ribs and a well-slapped face.

She cried out only once during the beating and he couldn't help but feel a delayed sense of respect for her. Not many grown men

– never mind a woman – would have been able to sustain those blows without making a hell of a lot of noise and, perhaps it was because of that, that he stopped short of mashing her face to a pulp.

He hadn't uttered a single word to her during the duration of her punishment. He didn't need to speak. She knew exactly why he was beating on her, and no explanation was necessary. He was glad that she didn't beg. Apart from that one time – when he accosted her at her car – she hadn't begged him not to hurt her. He hated people who begged. People who begged were stupid. If he was beating on someone, and they begged, he ended up giving them a few extra blows for the trouble. Yes, he admitted to having a grudging respect for her and he decided to make her a cup of coffee as a reward for her bravery.

He turned on the television and was gratified to discover that Swan's body had been found, and yet, was pleased to note that the police still had no clue as to his whereabouts.

He knew that she was watching the news with him and he swelled with pride to know that she was learning just how much of a bad-ass he was. He didn't know why it was so important to him for her to know who and what he was. He never gave such things much thought. He knew that he never liked to look small and insignificant in anyone's eyes, and he knew that he didn't appreciate being disrespected.

He wished that he'd thought of car-jacking a lone woman, and hiding out in her house, well before the debacle of escaping into Epping forest had transpired. The fact that neither he nor Swan had considered such a brilliant ruse was disconcerting, and he was wholly disgruntled at their complete lack of foresight. It wasn't lost on him that Swan would still be alive if they'd planned better, and if one of them had come up with the car-jacking idea. But, he realised, there was no point fretting over spilled milk

'Do you work?' he asked her.

She nodded.

'Are you due in at work anytime soon?'

'Tomorrow morning,' she replied with a thick tongue.

'So, if you don't turn up, you'll be missed?'

'Yes.'

He thought about that. He wondered if she was lying. If she was expected at work that evening, or that night, someone might stick their nose in and try and ring her or – God forbid – come to the house looking for her.

He made a show of examining his fingernails. He took his time with the next question. 'You screwing anyone? Anyone in particular?'

If she was embarrassed by the question, she made no sign. 'No,' she said. 'I'm single.'

'Anyone sniffing around you?'

She shook her head. 'Not that I'm aware of.'

'Well, you're not all that good looking, so it's no surprise to me that no one's showing an interest in you. If you were prettier, we might have had a problem. You see... I wouldn't have believed you. I would've thought that some man would probably be popping round for a quick fuck... if you'd been prettier, that is.'

She drew him a look of utter contempt and, despite her bruised and battered face, the look was incredibly powerful.

'Don't you look at me like that, you bitch. Don't you go disrespecting me.' He pulled himself up from the chair and loomed over her menacingly. 'I could still cut you. I could still kill you.'

She dropped her eyes, frightened.

He sat back down and put his hands behind his head. His nose had stopped bleeding, but he'd made no attempt to clean himself up, and that was frightening in itself.

'I guess you're wondering what all this is about?'

She shook her head and kept her eyes averted. 'It's none of my business.'

'No, it's *my* business and I won't tolerate you wondering why I've got that baby with me. That baby is no one's business, but mine. You tried to take him from me earlier. If you try to take him again, I'll gut you like a fish.'

'I understand. I won't try to take him from you. He's being well looked after... I can see that.'

'You bet he is. He's well fed, and I don't leave him with a shitty nappy.'

'Yes, I see that.'

'Do you have any children?'

The change of subject, and his conversational tone, startled her. 'No. I can't have children.' Her admission startled her even more.

'No? Why not?' He was intrigued. 'Why can't you have children?'

'I had cancer a few years back,' she said. 'They had to take my womb.'

'So, you're not a proper woman, anymore?'

His ignorance wounded her. She'd often thought that about herself but hearing it from him was like a punch to the stomach.

'Sorry, was that very rude of me?'

She lifted her face and stared him straight in the eye. 'No, not rude... fucking cruel... It was a fucking cruel thing to say.'

His laughter infuriated her. He was an obvious dickhead, yet she was just as angry at herself for allowing his words to hurt so much. They had hurt far more than the slaps and punches he'd inflicted on her face and body.

'You're a prick,' she spat across the room at him.

Her insult cut his laughter short and he contemplated rising from the chair and ramming his fist down her throat. But, he was tired, and he was actually beginning to quite like her. She was spunky, and he respected spunky.

DAY SIX: NIGHT

Lorrie ceased her anxious pacing and, on a deep breath, shouldered open the door to the interview room and stepped through. Lovell was already seated at the table, across from Davidson and his solicitor, and Lorrie acknowledged her with a curt nod.

'About time, Superintendent,' the solicitor said. 'We've been waiting well over an hour.'

'Oh, sorry,' she returned. 'I thought it was much longer.' She took a seat opposite Davidson and leaned forward on her elbows.

Davidson avoided looking at her. This time, he was determined to heed his solicitor's advice, and planned on keeping his mouth shut, as well as his eyes averted.

'Why are we back here?' the solicitor enquired. 'This is bordering on harassment.'

Lorrie ignored him. She wasn't going to be distracted by the whining of a tin-pot little lawyer.

Lovell started the recorder, and, after several long bleeps, Lorrie said, 'Mister Davidson, I would like to remind you of your rights and to confirm that you are being interviewed under caution. You do not have to say anything, but it may harm your defence, if you do not mention when questioned something which you later rely on in court. Anything you *do* say may be given in evidence.' She waited a beat. 'Do you understand, Mister Davidson?'

He nodded without lifting his head.

'For the benefit of the tape... Mister Davidson has nodded his head.' Lorrie took in his appearance and had to admit that he looked as if he'd already been put through the wringer. 'You look shattered,' she said.

'Is it all getting too much for you?'

He looked up in surprise. 'What do you think?'

'I think that it is, indeed, getting too much for you. I think that you'd fare much better if you got a few things off your chest.'

'Like what?' He silently admonished himself for being led into speaking and clamped his lips closed. He didn't plan on saying another word.

'Like... oh, I don't know.' She turned to Lovell. 'What do *you* think he should get off his chest, Acting DI Lovell?'

'Perhaps he should own up to putting the poison in the communion wine, Guv', or own up to knowing why Anthony Howell murdered his mother and abducted his baby. I'm sure he'd sleep better if he rid himself of those secrets.'

'This is highly irregular,' the solicitor interjected. 'My client has already been asked... and has already responded to... those questions. If you have nothing new to ask, and if you have no intentions of charging him, then we're leaving.' He looked expectantly from Lorrie to Lovell and then back to Lorrie.

'We've got proof that your wife was, in fact, screwing the priest,' Lorrie stated. She knew that, what they had, didn't constitute actual proof, but Davidson wasn't going to know that, and she was well within her rights to embellish the truth just a little. 'What do you have to say about that?'

'What proof?' Davidson broke his vow of silence once more. 'I don't believe you have any proof.'

Lorrie smiled and shook her head. 'I don't know whether to feel sorry for you or laugh at your stupidity. Did you know that Father Mackie visited your wife at home on more than a dozen occasions over a two- week period?'

'No, of course not... because, he *didn't*.'

'Would you like to see the images ... time-stamped and dated.... from the CCTV footage?' She came up off her elbows and settled back in her seat. 'Goodness knows what we'd do without CCTV. We've captured you and Howell talking. We've captured your mother's murder, and now we've captured many, many images of Mackie visiting your home.' She watched his eyes for a reaction to her words and was not surprised to see a flicker of fear. 'I'll be quite happy to show you, Mister Davidson.'

'No. I don't want to see them.'

'Would you like to see the post-mortem photographs of the children you murdered in the church?'

He reared back in horror. 'Don't you dare,' he cried. 'Don't you dare show me those photos.'

'I can understand your horror,' she said sympathetically. 'I've seen them, and I've not slept a wink since.'

'I didn't kill them,' he protested. 'I would never...'

'You have a perfectly good motive for killing your wife and her lover, and – perhaps – the others were simply an unfortunate accident?'

'No. No. I didn't poison anyone. Why won't you believe me?'

'Superintendent, is this mere supposition? Do you have any *actual* evidence that my client killed anyone?'

'Was she going to leave you... take the baby, and leave? Did she choose Mackie over you? Is that why you did it?'

'Superintendent.' The solicitor got to his feet. 'I must insist that you cease and desist. You have no evidence, and you're being deliberately cruel.'

'Sit down, sir,' Lorrie said. 'I have more to say and more questions to ask. I don't require your permission, so sit down and shut up.'

'How dare you.' The solicitor was mortified. 'Do you think that I'm here as mere window dressing?'

'If the shoe fits...'

Lovell cleared her throat and threw Lorrie a look of alarm. She was skating on very thin ice and could very well scupper the whole investigation if she carried on baiting the solicitor.

Lorrie reigned herself in. 'I apologise,' she said. 'I meant no disrespect, but *I will* continue with this interview, sir.' She turned back to Davidson. 'Why don't you simply tell us the truth? You asked me why I didn't believe you, and it's because you've already told me several lies. It's hard to believe anything a liar says'

'I've not lied about the poison. I didn't kill my wife, and I didn't kill all those people. I'm not a monster.'

'What are you, then?'

'Not a very nice person. There... I admit it. I'm not a nice person. I probably drove my wife into having those affairs. But, I loved her... I loved her.

'And, you learned that she was just about to leave you. Mackie had already made plans to leave the church for her. They were going off together.'

'No. I don't believe that. She wouldn't have left me for him.'

'It must have infuriated you. After all – you'd stuck by her through all her affairs. How dare she make plans to leave with your baby. How dare a man of the cloth betray everything that he stood for and drag your wife down with him.'

'No. it wasn't like that. She wouldn't have left me.'

'You told yourself that you would see them both dead before you let that happen. You poisoned the wine and you were in such a state that you didn't care who else died.'

'No.' he shook his head emphatically. 'Someone else did it.'

'Who, Mister Davidson? Who else had motive?'

'I don't know. All I know is – it wasn't me.'

Lorrie was losing patience. 'Who, then? Who poisoned them? Who murdered your wife and her lover... and all those innocents?'

All Davidson could do was shake his head in miserable denial.

'Okay, let's move on.' Lorrie leaned forward once more. 'When was the last time you were in the church?'

'What?'

'The church, Mister Davidson... when was the last time you were there?'

'When... when I found them. Sunday... it was Sunday.'

'And, before Sunday?'

'I... I don't know. I can't remember.'

'Did you attend the services on a regular basis?'

He shook his head. 'No. The church was more my wife's thing.'

She persevered. 'So, before Sunday just gone, when was the last time you were there?'

He worked through his cotton-wool stuffed brain to come up with the answer. Thinking was difficult. Remembering was difficult. Then, it came to him and, with some relief, he said, 'A few weeks ago. We went to arrange the christening. We saw Father Young.'

Lorrie noted his relief. 'You didn't see Father Mackie?'
'No.'
'Did you ever go to the church without your wife?'
His response was an emphatic, 'No, never.'
She is not surprised by his answer. In fact, she is not surprised by *any* of his answers. A flicker of doubt had sparked in her brain and she found that she was beginning to believe him. She was neither angry nor disappointed in herself. The fact that, before entering the room, she had been absolutely sure of his guilt – and now that she doubted the wisdom of her assumptions – in no way affected her. She wasn't one to flog a dead horse. She wasn't one to manipulate the situation to prove herself right. If Davidson wasn't guilty of the church murders – and the jury was still out on that - then so be it.
'Okay, Mister Davidson, let's move on to Anthony Howell.'
'You think that, perhaps, he could have done it?'
The thought hadn't entered her head. 'Why would you ask that?'
He shrugged. 'It wasn't me... I know *that* much... so, perhaps it was Howell?'
She wasn't quite ready to make the giant leap to Howell as a suspect for the poisoning, but she was prepared to explore the notion.
'Tell me about him,' she said. 'And, this time... be honest with me.'
She saw fear flare in his eyes and knew - absolutely *knew* – that there was something terrible behind that fear. It was time to throw him a lifeline.
'Can I be frank with you, Mister Davidson?' She eyed him speculatively. 'Can I be honest with you?'
He nodded, intrigued.
'I fervently believed that you killed all those people. If I was a betting woman, I'd have put my life savings on you being the killer. I can't say that I like you very much.' She smiled to lessen the insult. 'I can't say that I find you anything other than weird, but...' She smiled once more. 'But, I don't believe that you're capable of such a heinous crime.'
'Thank God.' Tears of relief formed in his eyes and he absently blinked them away.

'Don't thank God, quite yet, Mister Davidson. Thank him when I'm satisfied that your innocent of *everything*.'

'I've done nothing wrong. Yes… I had an affair, I admit that I've lied, and I've been an absolute prick, but that's all I've done wrong.'

'Yes… you've lied, and I think that there's one or two lies still lurking there, waiting to be exposed. Now,' she went on. 'I've been honest with you. I've admitted my mistake of thinking you were the killer. I've fessed up to that - even though it exposes me as a fool for believing it in the first place – so, now it's your turn. Regardless of how much of a fool it makes you and, regardless of whatever it is that's frightening you, you have to fess up.'

Davidson looked to his solicitor. The man gave a brief nod, and Davidson sighed and, shoulders and head slumped, confessed everything.

*

PC Cox had been relieved when Sonia Lovell gave her permission to continue with her attempts to identify all the previous lovers. She only hoped that she'd discover someone of interest, and that she wouldn't get into trouble with the Super' for disobeying her order to leave it alone.

CCTV had been a special friend to Cox. It had shown her a great deal, but it was a difficult, time-consuming and frustrating friend. It threw up red herrings, confused her with blurry images, and often failed to be in the right place at the right time. She knew that, depending solely on CCTV, was a mistake, so she widened the parameters of her search to include financial records, computer records, and even a search through all of the rubbish found in the Davidson's bins.

Prince offered to help, but Cox didn't want to run the risk of her friend sharing the Super's wrath, so she had declined – and then wished that she hadn't. The sheer amount of information was mind-boggling. The financial records alone took her three hours to simply speed-read, and the numerous emails, text messages and electronic diary entries took her a further two hours – and that wasn't including the hours spent goggle-eyed in front of the CCTV images.

In the end, it was all worth it.

*

He asked her what her name was.

'Lucy,' she replied. 'Lucy Matthews.'

'What do you do, Lucy?'

'Work, you mean?'

He nodded. 'I can see you as a nurse, or a teacher.'

'I'm neither,' she said. 'I work for a department store. I'm a buyer.'

'What's that, then... a *buyer*?'

'I go to fashion shows and decide what lines to buy. I chose what I believe our customers will want to wear.'

'Does it pay a lot?'

She shook her head. 'Put it this way... It won't make me rich.'

'You can afford a nice house and a nice car.'

'Yes,' she agreed. 'I earn enough for that.'

'I don't have a job,' he said. 'I had something lined up in Scotland but...' His face darkened. 'It fell through. I was going to start a new life, but I got kicked in the nuts.'

'I'm sorry to hear that.' She wasn't, but she felt it was important to humour him. Over the past few hours, she'd seen him begin to relax and to lose the hostility in his expression and stance, and she did her best to keep him on an even keel.

He seemed to like talking to her and she milked it for all it was worth.

'You can stay here for as long as you need to,' she said. 'No one will disturb us. I can ring up work and say that I'm sick... the flu, or something... and you'll be safe here with me.'

He thought about it. He wanted to trust her, but he knew that trust often came back to knee you where it hurts.

'Just let's get through the night, and then we'll see,' he said.

'It's just a thought,' she returned. 'I just wanted to make the offer.'

'Thank you.' He squirmed in his chair and threw her a sheepish look. 'I'm sorry I hurt you. I was angry. You tried to take the baby.'

'It's all right. I understand. It doesn't matter.'

'No one is going to take that baby away from me.'

'No, of course not. That would be a terrible thing.'

'I love him, you know?'

'I can see that. He's a beautiful little boy.'

'Yes.' His eyes misted over. 'He's beautiful, all right. He takes after his mother.'

'I heard...' She was wary of mentioning anything about the baby's mother, but she felt she had to test his boundaries. 'I heard that the mother died.'

He nodded, unperturbed by her words. 'Yes. He's motherless, now.'

'And, you want to keep him safe?'

'Always.'

'You'll both be safe here... I promise.'

He wanted to believe her, but trusting another woman was very difficult for him. He'd trusted *her*, and she'd betrayed him. Who was to say that *this* woman wouldn't also betray him?

*

No one went home that night. There was too much to think about, too much to do, and everyone volunteered to stay.

Everything came together all at once – Davidson's confession and Cox's findings being the main ingredients in forming the conclusion to both cases – and there was a real sense of relief in everyone's minds, and a renewed vigour that had them all walking with a spring in their step.

At last, everything made sense. Finally, everything fit.

DAY SEVEN: MORNING

Simon woke her with a gentle touch on the shoulder. Lorrie's eyes sprang open at his touch and she jumped up from the sofa in fright.

'Sorry, Guv'. It's gone eight, and you wanted me to wake you.'

'Yes. Thanks.' She scrubbed at her face with her hands and dropped back down onto the sofa. 'I think I managed a couple of hours, how about you?'

'An hour, maybe,' he said. 'We all got at least an hour.' He handed her a mug of coffee. 'Scully's on his way, I'm afraid.'

'It's early for him.' She sipped at the hot coffee gratefully. 'What's rattled his cage?'

'Someone must've rung him.'

'He has a spy in the camp, after all?'

'Seems that way, but you can't say that it surprises you.'

'No.' She shook her head and took a huge gulp of coffee. 'I'd better go and make myself presentable.'

As she exited the office she caught sight of PC Prince and PC Cox running full pelt towards the lift.

'What's all that about?' she asked Simon.

He frowned. 'Both of their husbands turned up unexpectedly at the front desk. Neither of them knows why.'

'That sounds ominous.'

'Prince has a young daughter... Lisa... I hope nothing's happened to her.'

'Follow them down, Simon. Make sure everything is okay.'

In the toilet, Lorrie washed the smudged make-up from her face and reapplied it. She brushed out her hair and pulled her fringe down in an attempt to cover her puffy eyes. She'd lied, when she'd told Simon that she'd managed two hours sleep. She estimated that it was more like ten minutes, and the truth of it stared out at her from the mirror.

'Looking good, Sullivan,' she said to her reflection. 'Good enough to put in a coffin and bury, anyway.'

She turned from the mirror and headed back out the door. She was immediately assailed by the wonderful aroma of bacon.

Simon sauntered over with a bacon sandwich in each hand.

'What's this?' she asked, reaching out and snatching one of the sandwiches.

'Robert Prince and Richard Cox,' he said. 'They turned up with two hundred bacon sarnies and a breadboard full of Danish pastries.'

'Really?'

He nodded. 'Did it off their own bats. Prince and Cox are mortified.'

'You mentioned Danish pastries?'

'A full breadboard of them.'

'Lead the way. I could murder an apple Danish.'

*

Scully did, indeed, have a spy in Sullivan's camp. He was always the last to know anything – when he should always be one of the first – and, to remedy that matter, he'd installed a young PC who was eager for his approval and eager for some early promotion. The PC had rung him around six and filled him in on the night's events. The news was good, and bad, and Scully was anxious to hear it from the horse's mouth, so he had hot-footed it over and was searching the corridors for the Superintendent.

No one offered him one of their delicious sandwiches, so he'd swiped one when no one was looking and then wrapped two pastries in a napkin for his elevenses.

It was obvious that Sullivan was avoiding him, and he had to settle for Simon Grant.

'Where is she?' he demanded. 'I want to know why she didn't have the good grace to ring me and update me on developments.'

'It's been a busy night, sir,' Simon returned. 'I'm sure a call to you was top of her agenda this morning.'

'Don't bullshit me, Grant. I didn't come up the Thames on a fig leaf.'

'A fig leaf, sir?' Simon couldn't keep the smirk from teasing at the corners of his mouth.

'You know what I mean, Grant. Where the fuck is she?'

'I think she's popped over to the hospital to see the Chief Super'. Things are a bit quiet here at the moment... waiting on the uniforms on the street to report back... so, she thought it was okay to take an hour off.'

'What's she seeing Fredrickson for? Is he at death's door, or something?'

'Not any more, sir. I understand that he's well on the mend.'

'Then, she should be here. She's no right abandoning her post to gossip with him.'

'She's been here all night, sir. We all have. I'd hardly accuse her of abandoning her post.'

'No? Well, you would say that. She's trained you well, DI Grant. Has you wrapped round her little finger.'

Simon bit back a retort and set his face.

'I guess I'll have to settle for the monkey, and not the organ grinder, then. Come on, make me a coffee and fill me in.'

*

They refused to allow her onto the ward until she threatened them with obstructing a police enquiry. She told them that she was visiting Fredrickson on police business, and not – as they had assumed – visiting for personal reasons.

He looked pale and tired and Lorrie's first thought was that he'd relapsed.

'Just a rough night,' he explained, seeing her horrified expression. 'Nothing to worry about. You look as if you've had a rough night as well.'

'You could say that,' she said, taking a seat at the bedside. 'But, we've made very real progress on both cases.'

'Glad to hear it. I was beginning to think that these cases would flummox you.'

'Oh, I was well and truly flummoxed. It took a confession from Davidson, and a PC disobeying my orders, to get the truth out.'

'Davidson confessed?'

She shook her head. 'Not to any of the murders.'

'What did he confess to?'

'Knowing Howell.'

'But...' He was confused. 'You already guessed that he knew Howell.'

'But, not how he'd *come* to know him and...' she gave him a knowing smile. 'What he was so frightened of admitting.'

'Are you going to tell me anytime soon, or are you going to continue to dangle the juicy bits? Stop waffling and spill.'

'Okay.' She made herself comfortable. 'I'll start with Cox.'

'Cox?'

'The PC who went behind my back and made all sorts of enquiries.'

'About Davidson?'

'No. Are you going to shut up and let me tell you?'

He gave her a sheepish smile. 'Sorry. You carry on.'

'Well, Cox had this bee in her bonnet about Davidson not being guilty, and one of his wife's other lovers being the killer. I told her not to waste time on her theory, and to knuckle down with helping with all of the approved lines of enquiry. Lovell countermanded my instruction, and Cox went about her merry way. I must give that girl a hefty amount of credit. She worked solidly for hours and finally hit pay dirt.'

'I'm all aquiver.'

'Meantime,' she went on, 'Davidson was busy telling us one hell of a story. His wife, apparently, had it off with Anthony Howell and Howell was convinced that he was the father of her baby. Davidson was terrified of losing the child and decided to keep his mouth shut about the affair, and the fact that he knew Howell.'

'What did Cox discover?'

'That Mrs. Davidson ended her affair with Howell and took up with Mackie.'

'How, on earth...?

'Text messages, mostly... and emails. We'd not got around to going through all of the victims' phones and computers... my bad... but Cox did. She also came across a blurry CCTV image of – who she thought was – Howell approaching the Davidson's house a few weeks ago.'

'So, he thought that he was taking his own baby?'

Lorrie nodded. 'We think he killed Maxine Davidson – not out of revenge – but because he knew she wouldn't give up the child without a fight, and he couldn't risk her following him.'

'And, the poisoning of the congregation? Wasn't Howell's family victims?'

'Yes, but – in some of the text messages – Howell was ranting on about his family not understanding or supporting his decision to run off to Scotland with his lover and the child.'

'And, she dumped him for Mackie?' He let out a slow whistle. 'I bet that pissed him off, big time.'

'We know what he's capable of. He killed Maxine, and then he killed his friend. I think he's also responsible for putting the poison in the Communion wine.'

'I can see why you might think that.'

'You're not convinced?'

He shrugged. 'He's a violent man... Volatile. He likes to use a knife. That's a far cry from planning and executing the scenario at the church.'

'It all fits,' she insisted. 'He wanted revenge on his lover and the priest. He wanted his baby all to himself. He knew that his family wouldn't support him... Hell, they might even shop him to the police... so, he killed the lot of them. The others were simply collateral damage.'

*

The subject of Lorrie and Fredrickson's conversation was having breakfast of toast and marmalade with his new friend, Lucy. He had untied her, and allowed her to join him at the table, and they were both relaxed and enjoying the food... scant though it was.

True to her word, Lucy had called work and feigned illness, and that act had caused Howell to begin to trust her.

Lucy, on the other hand, didn't trust him an inch.

'We'll need to get some food in,' she said. 'We left my shopping behind, remember?'

He thought about that for a moment. 'The baby has plenty of milk left, and we can survive until tonight.'

'What's happening tonight?'

'We're ordering pizza.'

'What about tomorrow?'

'Chinese.'

'Oh, okay. I can live with that.'

'Meantime, I need to catch up on some sleep. I'll have to tie you up again, I'm afraid.'

It was on the tip of her tongue to protest, but she had already decided that her best course of action was to play the long game, so, she merely smiled and nodded.

*

'Can you believe that pair?' Prince said to Cox. 'Turning up like that loaded down with breakfast.'

'I couldn't believe it,' Cox said. 'What possessed them?'

'Robert said that they both thought about it completely separately. Imagine that.'

Cox gave a wistful smile. 'It *was* lovely of them.'

'Did you see Commander Scully stealing a sandwich and stuffing his pockets with pastries?' Prince laughed out loud. 'He thought he was being so sly about it.'

'That's another two pounds added to his waistline.'

'It *was* lovely of them,' Prince agreed.

'We're so lucky.'

Prince nodded.

'But, back to business. I've got the rest of those texts to go through, and you're expected at the morning briefing.'

'I'm not sure that there will be much to brief us on. I heard that there's been no new sightings of Howell.'

'There's that one at Paddington.'

Prince shrugged. 'Nothing after that.'

'I heard someone phoned in a suspected car-jacking.'

'No evidence that it was Howell, but it's being followed up.'

'It wasn't far from Paddington.'

'I know, but no CCTV, no make and model, no identity of the driver. I fail to see how that can lead us anywhere.'

'You never know. Our luck has changed, so here's hoping.'

*

'Why are you dissing me?' Lorrie looked and sounded angry. 'I've explained my reasoning, and you seem hell-bent on lobbing a grenade at everything I've told you.'

Fredrickson pulled himself higher on his pillows and winced at the effort.

'I'm simply playing Devil's Advocate. Stop being so emotional.'

'Emotional? I'm not on my fucking period, so my emotions are pretty good, thank you very much. You've a bloody cheek accusing me of being emotional. You wouldn't say such an insulting thing to a man.'

'Yes, I would,' he said quietly.

'No, you fucking-well wouldn't.' She noticed a few pairs of eyes honing in on her outburst and lowered her voice to a hiss. 'You're showing your true colours. I never thought I'd hear you use my sex against me.'

'I haven't, but – now you come to mention it – you *are* acting like a deranged fishwife. Are you sure that you're not on your period?' He meant it as a joke, but it misfired phenomenally.

'You bastard.'

He sighed wearily. He really wasn't up to arguing with her. He'd made a few perfectly valid comments about Howell, and he'd not expected such an unjustified response.

'It's Howell,' she insisted. 'He did it. There's no one else.'

'What about Mackie? Have you forgotten all about him? We don't know why he cancelled the job offer in Birmingham.'

'He was running off to start a new life with Davidson. He was de-frocking himself and settling down.'

'Selfish, arrogant, sex-mad, Mackie?' He gave her a look of incredulity. 'The same Mackie who fucked a fifteen-year old child, who lied about his abduction, who screwed a woman who'd just given birth? That Mackie?'

'*That* Mackie wouldn't kill himself. No – it wasn't him.'

'Could Davidson be stringing you a tall tale?'

'Why would he?'

'To get you to drop your investigation of him.'

'The texts, the emails, the CCTV - they all support his story.'

'But, not that Howell did it. Davidson could still be the killer.'

She shook her head. 'I believe him.'

'Why?'

'Why...? Because I find him credible.'

'That's a sudden change of heart.'

He was quite right... it was a sudden change. 'I can't explain myself any better. I believe him. I don't, exactly, know why I believe him... I just do.'

'Okay.'

'Don't patronise me.'

'I'm not.'

'I wish that I hadn't come here.' She stood up to leave.

'Why, because you can't stand having your opinions challenged?'

'No... because you're a shit and – scrape through the surface – you're just the same as Scully.'

He watched her leave and his heart suddenly felt very heavy in his chest. He knew that he would never see her again. He said goodbye to her silently and began to plan.

DAY SEVEN: AFTERNOON

Howell woke with a start. The baby was screaming his lungs out and Lucy was trying to soothe him with words from her position tied to the chair.

'I think he's hungry,' she said. 'I can feed him, if you want.'

'No, you're all right... I'll do it.' He dragged himself to his feet and staggered through to the kitchen.

She watched him feed the baby and marvelled at the gentle way he held him. Considering he'd stuffed the infant into his rucksack, and very nearly suffocated him in the process, his soft hands and gentle crooning was bewildering. She came to the conclusion that he wasn't right in the head. That he was capable of the vilest crimes, she did not doubt, but, that he was capable of love? She doubted that most vehemently.

He'd told her that he'd loved the baby's mother. She could see he had convinced himself of that, but she didn't really believe him. He'd told her that he loved the child, and – again – she didn't believe him. She thought that, sometimes, his emotions ran the way of love, but those same emotions were too unstable, too volatile, to be sustained. That was why she didn't trust him to maintain the good feelings he had towards her. His trust in her could quite easily evaporate. He could get angry again, and he could hurt – even kill her. She was walking a fine line and it felt almost like walking a tightrope above a river full of crocodiles. One slip, and she'd be a goner.

*

'We think that we might know where he is,' Simon said to Lorrie. 'That car-jacking last night... shopping was left on the pavement and we found a credit card receipt in one of the bags.'

'What makes you think that Howell jacked the car?'

'It was close to his last known sighting. It's the sort of opportunity he would grab.'

'Whose car was it?'

'A woman's... a Lucy Matthews.'

'What do we know about her?'

'Well, we know that she didn't turn up for work this morning.'

'And, you know that, how?'

'There was an ID badge next to the receipt. It told us where she worked. We rang up and asked to speak to her... on the off chance that we could rule out an actual jacking, and rule out that she'd seen Howell. She wasn't there. She'd phoned in sick... Flu. The person who took the call said that she sounded all bunged up.'

'An injured nose would do that.'

He nodded. 'My thoughts, exactly.'

'Do we have eyes on her house?'

'Happening as we speak.'

'We'd better get over there.'

'We don't want to spook him.'

'Agreed. We'll stay out of sight and weigh everything up.'

*

'Can I ask you something?'

Howell placed the baby on the sofa and tucked cushions in his back. 'Sure,' he said. 'Ask away.'

'What happened in the church?' It was a dangerous question, and one that she didn't really want the answer to. She asked it on the spur of the moment, and immediately regretted it.

She saw him stiffen and expected a blow.

'My parents and my brother died at the church. *She* died at the church. I think they suffered.' He sat down next to the baby. 'I didn't like my parents very much, but my brother was okay.'

She swallowed and tried to keep her expression neutral. 'I'm sorry for your loss.'

He shrugged and seemed to mentally shake himself. 'What's done is done. No point complaining about it.'

'Who do you think did it?' she asked tentatively – dreading that he would admit to doing it himself.

'Who do I *think* did it?' He gave a bitter laugh. 'I know *exactly* who did it.'

*

Cox also knew who did it. It was all there in the texts – the whole sordid, evil plan. She had to tell the Guv' right away, but she was out on the road – heading for Lucy Matthew's home – and it took her several tries before she got her on the phone.

*

'I tried to stop it, but she blanked me. I told her that I'd forgiven her over Mackie, but she was having none of it. She'd made up her mind, you see? I think, having the baby, unhinged her... that was why she was so susceptible to Mackie. Then, the bastard did the dirty on her.'

'What do you mean?' Lucy thought that she knew, but it was too horrifying to contemplate.

'She had an affair with the priest... the one who'd been captured in Syria. It started before the baby was even two weeks old... when she was low and vulnerable. She told me all about it. She said that she was sorry, and all that, and I was so angry and so fucked-up that I threatened all sorts. I scared her...I know that I scared her.' He pondered for a moment. 'I scare myself sometimes, but I would never have hurt her. I even spoke to her husband... tried to get him to do something about Mackie, but he's such a fucking coward.'

'What are you saying? Are you saying that she did it?'

He nodded. 'She texted me that morning. She told me what she'd done to the wine. I didn't believe her... not at first. She was upset, you see? Mackie had found someone else... the bastard. She didn't know who it was, so was going to put belt and braces on it and take out the whole fucking lot of them. She was sure that she'd get the other woman in the mix.'

'Jesus.'

'I told her that I'd be happy to knife the bastard for her. I would've quite happily cut his balls off, but she didn't answer me. I texted her and texted her, and tried ringing her mobile and ringing the house and, then...'

Tears were coursing down his cheeks and Lucy almost felt sorry for him.

'I knew that she'd want me to take care of the baby. I couldn't leave him with that miserable coward, Davidson, or his deranged mother. She wouldn't give him to me. I told her that he was mine, but she lashed out at me and I had to stab her to get her off me. I...'

The telephone rang in the hall and cut him off in mid flow.

Lucy thought that the phone would unnerve him, and she prepared herself for the worst.

'You'd better get that,' he said, rising to free her. 'It's all over, now... I realise that.' He turned back to the sofa and picked up the child. 'I'm sorry, mate,' he said. 'You would've loved your mother.'

*

'It's ringing,' Lorrie said. 'Get everyone ready.'

'Hello?' It was a woman's voice.

'Hello. Is this Lucy Matthews?'

'Yes. Who is this?'

'It's the police, Lucy... Superintendent Sullivan... Are you all right?'

'I think so. My nose is broken, but I'm okay.'

'Is Anthony Howell with you?'

'Yes, and the baby.'

'Is the baby...?'

A few seconds passed and, then, 'He's fine.'

Lorrie didn't realise that she was holding her breath until in exploded from her mouth. 'Thank God.'

'I think Howell is ready to give himself up. He told me everything and I think he's realised it's the end of the road.'

'Okay. Can you ask him to give you the baby and ask him if he'll let you both come outside?'

'I can ask him. Hold on a minute.'

Lorrie heard a muffled conversation on the other end of the phone and found that she was holding her breath once more.

Lucy came back onto the phone. 'I have the baby,' she said. 'We're coming out.'

EPILOGUE

It took Lorrie two days to pluck up the courage to go back to the hospital to visit Fredrickson. She was ashamed of herself, and bitterly regretted her last meeting with him. She wondered if he would ever forgive her. She couldn't quite forgive herself and wouldn't blame him if he never spoke to her again.

She wanted to tell him, in her own words, the outcome of both the church case and the murder of Maxine Davidson. He deserved to hear it directly from her that she'd got it all wrong. Yes, Davidson was innocent – just as she'd said – but, nevertheless, she *was* wrong.

He wasn't in his usual bed. She thought that he'd been well enough to be transferred out of ICU, so went looking for someone who could tell her where he'd been moved to.

'Manchester,' the nurse said. 'He went yesterday.'

Lorrie felt her knees buckle. 'What? I don't understand.'

'He requested a transfer to a hospital in Manchester. We weren't happy about it, but he insisted.'

She left the hospital in a daze. He'd left her without so much as a word and she knew why. It was because she was such a bitch. It was because he had feelings for her and she'd trampled all over them. It was because she was damaged goods and would always be the cause of destroying those closest to her. It was because… It was because… It was because…

The Superintendent Lorrie Sullivan Series:

Book One: *Maelstrom of White*

Book Two: *A Murder of Clowns*

Made in the USA
Monee, IL
05 December 2021